GW01090783

Whispers in th

Book 2
Shadows of Corruption Series

By Morgan Steele

Published by Morgan Steele at Draft@Digital
11/2024

Whispers in the Shadows

Shadows of Corruption, Volume 2

Morgan Steele

Published by Morgan Steele, 2024.

This is a work of fiction. Similarities to real people, places, or events are entirely coincidental.

WHISPERS IN THE SHADOWS

First edition. November 1, 2024.

ISBN: 979-8227556578

Written by Morgan Steele.

Disclaimer

This book is a work of fiction only. Any resemblance of events, action, or persons alive or dead is purely coincidental.

2

Table of Content

Chapter 1

Chapter 2
Chapter 3
Chapter 4
Chapter 5
Chapter 6
Chapter 7
Chapter 8
Chapter 9
Chapter 10
Chapter 11
Chapter 12
Chapter 13
Chapter 14
Chapter 15
Chapter 16
Chapter17

Chapter 18

Chapter 19
Chapter 20
Chapter 21
Chapter 22
Chapter 23

Chapter 1

The night was unusually quiet in Washington, D.C. The city's usual buzz of late-night traffic and restless sirens was conspicuously absent as retired General James Donovan stood on the balcony of his Georgetown apartment. A cold breeze carried with it the distant hum of the Potomac River, the sound almost like a whisper, a reminder of the ever-flowing undercurrents of power and corruption that fueled the nation's capital. James had grown to detest those whispers, the subtle movements in the dark where men with too much money and too little conscience plotted the next steps in their long game of manipulation and control.

His eyes fell to the city skyline, the towering monuments of American democracy casting long shadows over the sleeping city. Three years had passed since he had helped dismantle one of the most dangerous cabals of elites, an underground syndicate led by billionaire Margaret Rothschild, who sought to destabilize the U.S. government for personal gain. It was a hard-fought victory, one that came with significant losses, but James had allowed himself to hope that it would be the last.

It wasn't.

His phone vibrated on the table behind him, breaking the silence that had settled like a shroud over the apartment. Without turning, he reached back to pick it up, half-expecting a late-night message from one of his contacts. His thumb swiped across the screen, and his eyes quickly scanned the incoming text.

"They're back."

Two words, but the weight of them settled like a stone in his chest.

The sender was Annika Valdez, one of his closest allies and former CIA operative who had worked with him to bring down the previous cabal. They had both gone their separate ways after the last mission, trying to carve out some semblance of a normal life. But normalcy was never meant for people like them.

James moved back inside the apartment, shutting the balcony doors behind him to block out the chill. He stared at the message again, feeling the tightness in his gut grow. It was the same feeling he'd had three years ago, the sense that something was brewing, something insidious, but this time it felt even more dangerous.

He immediately dialed Annika's number, pacing as he waited for her to pick up.

"James," her voice was steady, but he could hear the tension just beneath the surface.

"Tell me everything," he said without preamble, knowing there was no time for small talk.

"Not over the phone," she replied. "I'm sending you coordinates. Meet me there in two hours."

The line went dead before he could respond. James stood still for a moment, processing the sudden shift in his world. He had been out of the game for too long, trying to enjoy the peace that had come with their last victory. But peace, in his world, was always an illusion.

His phone pinged again with a set of GPS coordinates. They pointed to a location in rural Virginia, far from the prying eyes of anyone who might be listening. It was clear now, this wasn't just a warning. This was a call to arms. The game was starting again, and the stakes were higher than ever.

• • • •

The drive to Virginia was long, the highways dark and deserted as James sped down the interstate.

His mind raced as he pieced together what little information he had. "They're back." Who were they? Was it remnants of the Rothschild faction, or was it something entirely new? The old cabal had been powerful, sure, but it had also been fractured. With

Margaret Rothschild dead, the survivors had either gone underground or were being hunted by authorities. So, who was behind this new threat?

He didn't have time to dwell on it. The country road leading to the meeting spot was narrow, barely wide enough for two cars, and the trees on either side pressed in like dark sentinels. His headlights sliced through the gloom, casting long shadows that flickered in and out of view. A nondescript barn came into view just off the road, hidden behind a thicket of trees. This was the place.

He parked the car a few hundred yards away and approached on foot, his senses sharp, alert for any signs of movement. As he neared the barn, a figure stepped out from the shadows. Annika.

Her silhouette was familiar, the sharp lines of her face barely visible in the dim moonlight, but there was something different about her. She looked...tense, more so than he had ever seen her.

"Thanks for coming," she said as he reached her.

"I didn't really have a choice, did I?" he replied, trying to keep his tone light, though he could feel the weight of the situation bearing down on him.

"Follow me," she said, turning without further explanation.

They walked in silence into the barn, which smelled faintly of hay and oil. Annika led him to the far end, where an old wooden table sat under a dim hanging light. On it was a large manila folder, bulging with documents and photographs.

"This is everything I've gathered in the past six months," she said, flipping open the folder. "It started small, just rumors, whispers among the intelligence community. But it's grown into something bigger, something...darker."

James scanned the top photo. It was grainy, taken from a distance, but the subject was unmistakable: Governor Alexander Price of California, one of the most influential political figures in the country. He was shaking hands with a man James didn't recognize, but the name underneath the photo caught his attention.

"Klaus Reichter," James read aloud. "Who the hell is Klaus Reichter?"

Annika's expression hardened. "Reichter is a ghost. A German industrialist who immigrated to the U.S. after World War II. Officially, he's a philanthropist, a man who built a multi-billion-dollar empire in manufacturing and tech. But behind the scenes, he's something much worse. Reichter's real fortune comes from human trafficking, arms dealing, and money laundering, using American taxpayers' money."

"Wait, taxpayers' money? How does he pull that off?" James asked, his brow furrowing.

"Reichter's connections run deep," Annika explained, her voice tight with disgust. "He launders money through his many non-profits. They get government funding and then they turn around and uses a great deal of that money on certain political candidates campaigns, and let's not forget the government contracts, inflating costs on public projects, funneling the surplus into offshore accounts. He's using political allies to create shell companies that bid for those contracts, all while skimming taxpayer money in ways that are hard to trace. It's corruption on a scale we've never seen before, legal theft, sanctioned by the very people who should be stopping it."

James absorbed this new information, the anger rising in his chest. This wasn't just political corruption, this was systemic exploitation. Reichter was profiting from the very citizens who trusted their government to protect them.

"How has he managed to stay off the radar for so long?" James asked, still flipping through the documents.

"He's a master at covering his tracks," Annika replied. "And he's smart. He doesn't leave any loose ends. Everyone who's ever gotten close to exposing him has either disappeared or ended up dead. You know, single shot to the back of the head suicides."

James paused on a newspaper clipping detailing the sudden death of a prominent journalist. "Selena Grant, I remember when this happened. She was a great journalist and one hell of a patriot. I read they said she accidently drove her car off a cliff in a freak accident."

Annika nodded. "She was investigating Reichter when she died. That 'accident' was no accident."

A cold shiver ran down James's spine. Selena Grant had been one of them and a respected journalist, known for taking down corrupt politicians and exposing human trafficking rings. If Reichter had her killed, it meant he was more dangerous than James had imagined.

"Why now?" James asked. "Why make a move after all these years?"

"Power," Annika said simply. "Reichter's old. He's in his eighties now, and he wants to secure his legacy. He's backing key politicians, Governor Price from California, Senator Monroe from Minnesota, and Congressman Greene from Michigan. They're his new cabal, and they're positioning themselves to reshape the country. Reichter's funding their campaigns, pushing policies that benefit his businesses, and in return, they're giving him free reign."

James absorbed the information, feeling the weight of what Annika was saying. This wasn't just political corruption, this was a full-blown conspiracy. A new cabal, backed by one of the wealthiest, most dangerous men in the world, was slowly tightening its grip on American democracy.

"Where do we start?" James asked, already knowing there was no turning back.

Annika handed him a dossier on Governor Price. "We start in California. Price is hosting a fundraiser in two days. High-profile guests, lots of security. We need to get inside and find out how deep his connections to Reichter go."

James nodded, already planning the logistics in his head. "We'll need Kane."

Annika smiled for the first time that night. "Already contacted him. He's flying in tomorrow."

Oliver Kane, their Billionaire tech genius and former NSA hacker, had been instrumental in taking down the last cabal. If anyone could crack Reichter's digital fortress and get them the intel they needed, it was Kane.

"We're going back into the fire, aren't we?" James said with a sigh.

Annika's smile faded. "We never really left."

• • • •

The next day, James met with Kane at a private airstrip just outside D.C. The sight of Kane stepping off the jet, wearing his usual jeans and a hoodie, brought a strange sense of comfort. Despite the gravity of the situation, Kane's laid-back attitude always had a way of lightening the mood.

"Long time no see, Donovan," Kane greeted, tossing his duffel bag into the back of James's car.

"Too long," James replied, shaking his hand. Seems like we have some trouble on our hands.

"Yeah, well, trouble seems to follow you around," Kane quipped as they drove off.

As they made their way to the safe house where Annika was waiting, James filled Kane in on everything, Reichter, the new cabal, and their plan to infiltrate Klaus Reichter upcoming charity fundraiser.

"Sounds like we're going up against the usual psychos with too much money and not enough morals," Kane said. "But this Reichter guy... he's on a whole different level. I did some digging on him after Annika called me. Dude's got ties to every shady deal in the book, arms trading in the Middle East, human trafficking rings in Eastern Europe and the United States. And don't get me started on his money laundering business that the American tax payers are paying for. He has his hands in everything.

Chapter 2

The plane touched down at LAX as dawn's first light spread across the horizon. The tarmac buzzed with the usual airport activity, ground crew rushing about, service trucks weaving in and out of lanes, and passengers disembarking with sleepy expressions. But this wasn't a typical arrival. For General James Donovan, this marked the beginning of a war he thought he had left behind.

Standing at the private terminal exit, James adjusted his coat and glanced at his watch. It was 6:15 a.m., right on schedule. He had to be discreet, too much attention at this point could compromise everything. His eyes scanned the crowd for familiar faces, and then he saw him: Nathan Cross. Cross leaned against a black SUV, arms folded, his expression as unreadable as ever.

"Welcome to California," Nathan greeted, his voice carrying a hint of dry humor.

"Glad to be back," James replied, though there was no mistaking the tension in his posture.

They exchanged nods and climbed into the vehicle. The interior was as meticulously organized as Nathan's tactical mind, gear packed away in designated compartments, weapons stowed neatly in hidden panels. Nathan drove in silence, the streets of Los Angeles gradually giving way to the rolling hills and coastal vistas of Malibu.

"How secure is the safe house?" James asked, breaking the silence.

Nathan gave him a sidelong glance. "Secure enough. We have people watching the perimeter, surveillance feeds, and multiple escape routes. I've also disabled any public records linking the property to us."

"Good. We can't afford any mistakes."

Nathan's gaze hardened. "We won't make any."

It was a simple promise, but James knew it carried the weight of Nathan's past, his years in Special Forces, his loyalty to the team, and the personal vow he had made to bring down men like Klaus Reichter.

The SUV pulled into the driveway of a secluded property nestled in the hills. It looked like any other upscale beach house, its modern architecture blending into the surroundings. But appearances were deceiving. This was no vacation home.

As they entered, James was greeted by the hum of activity. Annika Valdez stood over a table scattered with blueprints and documents, her face illuminated by the soft glow of the monitors surrounding her. Next to her was Oliver Kane, typing furiously on a laptop, his fingers a blur on the keys. Two new faces looked up from where they were seated, a tall, broad-shouldered man with a military bearing and a petite woman with sharp eyes and an air of quiet intensity.

James nodded to the strangers. "New recruits?"

"Not exactly," Annika replied. "Meet David Sinclair, former Delta Force, and Sarah Chen, ex-FBI intelligence analyst. They've been working with us for a while now, tracking Reichter's movements."

David Sinclair extended a hand. "Honor to meet you, General."

"Likewise," James said, shaking it firmly. He turned to Sarah, who offered a brief but sincere smile.

"Kane's been keeping us in the loop," she said, her voice calm and measured. "We're ready to move when you are."

"And that makes five," James noted. "Where's the sixth?"

"He'll be here soon," Nathan said, his tone neutral. "Harper's just tying up some loose ends."

James arched an eyebrow. "Harper? The CIA's golden boy?"

"He's not so golden anymore," Annika said quietly. "After he went against Reichter's interests in a covert op three years ago, he became persona non grata. He's been off the grid since then, running solo missions. When I reached out, he didn't hesitate."

A flicker of admiration crossed James's face. "That's good to know. But it means we're dealing with someone who has a personal stake in this."

"Don't we all?" Nathan interjected.

James didn't argue. They all had their reasons for coming back. But Harper's involvement added a layer of complexity they'd have to navigate carefully.

"Alright," James said, turning his attention to the map spread out on the table. "What's the latest on Governor Price's fundraiser?"

Annika tapped a photo of a sprawling mansion in Beverly Hills. "The event is taking place tomorrow night. High-level security, a who's who of political donors and business moguls, and a media blackout. No press allowed, which means whatever they're discussing, it's not meant for public ears."

"Perfect," Nathan murmured. "What's our entry plan?"

"David and I will go in as catering staff," Sarah said. "I've got credentials that'll pass scrutiny, and David's role is to ensure nothing goes wrong inside. James, you and Nathan will monitor from the exterior and be our extraction team if things go south."

"And what about me?" Kane asked, still not looking up from his screen.

"You," Annika said with a smirk, "will be doing what you do best, hacking into their security system and disabling it long enough for us to move freely."

"Piece of cake," Kane muttered, but his focus remained intense. He didn't take threats to the team lightly, especially not when going up against someone with Klaus Reichter's resources.

James absorbed the information, nodding as each piece fell into place. It was a solid plan, but they were facing an enemy who could throw the unexpected at them without warning.

"Alright, we know our roles. Let's go over the details once more," he said, his voice carrying the authority that made him a natural leader.

They spent the next several hours refining the plan, discussing every possible scenario. By the time the sun dipped below the horizon, they were all running on caffeine and sheer willpower.

The door to the safe house creaked open, drawing everyone's attention. A tall figure stepped inside, his silhouette framed against the dying light. His sandy-blond hair and unshaven face made him look almost rugged, but his eyes, sharp and assessing, marked him as a man who had seen too much.

"Harper," James said, his tone neutral but welcoming.

"General," Harper replied, nodding in acknowledgment. He glanced around the room, his gaze lingering on Annika for a moment longer. There was history there, James noted, but he pushed the thought aside.

"You all know why we're here," James began, addressing the group. "Klaus Reichter is more than just a rich old man pulling strings behind the scenes. He's the linchpin holding together a network of corruption and terror that spans continents. Taking him down won't be easy. We'll have to dismantle his operations piece by piece and expose his political allies for what they are, traitors."

The room went silent as everyone absorbed the gravity of what they were about to undertake. It wasn't just about stopping a fundraiser or disrupting a few corrupt deals. It was about cutting off the head of a hydra that could bring the country to its knees.

"We start tomorrow," James said softly. "No mistakes. No hesitations. And no mercy."

His words hung in the air like a vow, binding them together. Each of them had been forged in the fires of their own battles, but now they were united against a common enemy.

Klaus Reichter may have thought he was untouchable, but he had underestimated one thing, the resolve of those willing to fight the corrupt that live in the shadows.

And this time, they weren't stopping until the job was done.

Chapter 3

The air in Beverly Hills felt thick with tension, the kind that clung to your skin and raised the hairs on the back of your neck. James Donovan sat in the back of a black, nondescript sedan parked a few blocks away from Governor Price's estate. Through the tinted windows, he could see the soft glow of chandeliers spilling out from behind tall, manicured hedges. The mansion loomed in the distance like a silent fortress, each window a glowing eye observing the powerful elite gathering within.

"Visuals are up," Kane's voice murmured through the earpiece, calm and confident. "I've tapped into the estate's exterior surveillance feeds. Looks like they've got at least twenty guards rotating shifts."

"Armed?" James asked, already knowing the answer.

"Of course," Kane replied. "And they're packing more than just pistols. I'm seeing submachine guns and tactical gear. Reichter's pulling out all the stops."

James stared out at the mansion, his mind working through scenarios and countermeasures. This wasn't just any political fundraiser. This was a meeting of the inner circle, the power brokers who moved money and influenced policy with a few whispered words over champagne.

But Reichter wouldn't be foolish enough to attend himself. No, Klaus Reichter was a master at staying in the shadows, using proxies and middlemen to do his dirty work. That meant someone else would be the point of contact tonight. The question was: who?

"Status on our inside team?" he asked.

"Annika, Sarah, and David are in," Nathan Cross's voice came through, a low murmur that held a note of approval. "They're blending with the catering staff. No red flags."

"Good. Let's keep it that way."

The team had spent weeks preparing for this, gathering intel and setting up cover identities. Every movement, every disguise, every line of conversation had been meticulously planned. But planning only got you so far. Once they were inside, it was a game of adaptation and instinct.

The line crackled slightly as Kane shifted. "Heads up. I've got eyes on Governor Price. He's in the east wing, surrounded by his usual entourage."

James's gaze sharpened. "What about Reichter's people?"

"Negative visual so far, but I'm scanning for facial matches on known associates."

James nodded to himself, the tension knotting in his chest. The waiting was always the worst part. It gave your mind time to wander, to conjure all the ways a mission could go sideways. But he pushed those thoughts away. This was their only chance to get close, to identify who was pulling Price's strings and to find a crack in Reichter's armor.

"Annika," he said softly into the mic, "what's your position?"

"Second-floor balcony," Annika whispered back. "I've got a clear view of the ballroom."

James knew that meant she had eyes on most of the VIP guests. Annika had a talent for reading rooms, assessing power dynamics with a glance. She'd know who was important and who was just there for show.

"Any sign of Weiss?" he asked.

There was a brief silence as Annika scanned the room. "Not yet. But there's a group of heavyweights gathering near the back. Oil tycoons, media moguls, some foreign diplomats. They're all watching the main entrance like they're expecting someone big."

"Keep your distance. We need to know who's calling the shots without tipping our hand."

"Understood."

James tapped his fingers lightly on the armrest. They were on the knife's edge, close enough to see their target but still waiting for the right moment to strike. One misstep and the whole operation could unravel.

Inside the mansion, Annika adjusted the tray of drinks she was carrying and moved through the throng of guests with practiced ease. The air was thick with perfume and expensive cologne, mingling with the faint scent of fresh flowers that adorned every table. Laughter and conversation floated around her, a web of meaningless pleasantries designed to disguise the true purpose of the evening.

As she moved, she caught sight of Sarah Chen, stationed near the far wall, her face a mask of serene detachment. They made brief eye contact, a silent confirmation that everything was on track. Then Annika shifted her focus back to the group she'd been watching.

The men clustered at the back of the room weren't just wealthy, they were powerful. She could see it in the way they stood, the slight tilt of their heads, the calculated smiles that never quite reached their eyes. These were men who made decisions that affected millions, and they were all gathered here for one reason: to secure their place in whatever twisted world Reichter was building.

Annika's pulse quickened as a figure entered the room, moving with the kind of casual arrogance that only came from holding the strings of power. He was tall, mid-forties, with a neatly trimmed beard and a tailored suit that screamed custom. He paused near the edge of the group, his presence drawing their attention like iron filings to a magnet.

"We've got movement," Annika whispered, her voice barely audible over the murmur of the crowd. "Alexander Weiss just entered the ballroom."

"Copy that," James replied. "Stick close, but don't engage. We need to know who he's here to meet."

Weiss exchanged brief pleasantries with the men around him, shaking hands, smiling, but his eyes were scanning the room. Annika felt her breath hitch as his gaze swept over her, lingering for just a fraction of a second before moving on. He didn't recognize her, he couldn't, not with her disguise. But there was something in his eyes, a predatory awareness that made her skin prickle.

"Careful," Sarah's voice whispered in her ear. "He's on edge."

Annika nodded subtly, keeping her movements fluid. She made her way to the bar, depositing the empty tray and picking up a fresh one. As she turned, she saw Weiss pull out a phone, his expression darkening as he read something on the screen. He glanced toward the east wing, toward Governor Price, and his jaw tightened.

"Something's wrong," Annika murmured. "Weiss just got a message, and it's not good news. He's heading for the east wing."

"Stay on him," James ordered. "David, what's your status?"

"Guard outside the study hasn't moved," David's voice came through, calm and steady. "But I think Price is starting to sweat. He's pacing."

Annika's pulse raced as she followed Weiss, weaving through the crowd with practiced ease. She kept her distance, never looking directly at him, but close enough to see him disappear down a side corridor. She glanced around, making sure no one was watching, then slipped into the hallway behind him.

"Weiss is on the move. I'm trailing him now."

"Copy," James said. "Sarah, get into position near the study. We need to know what's about to go down."

Inside the study, Governor Price was indeed sweating. He wiped his forehead with a trembling hand, his usually composed demeanor unraveling under the weight of whatever was hanging over his head. When the door swung open, he nearly jumped out of his skin.

Weiss stepped inside, his face a mask of cold fury.

"What the hell are you doing, Price?" he hissed, his voice low but dangerous. "I've got word that someone's asking questions about Reichter's operations. Someone close."

Price swallowed hard, his gaze darting to the closed door, as if expecting it to burst open at any moment.

"I... I don't know anything about it," he stammered. "I've been following orders, doing everything Reichter asked."

Weiss took a step closer, his presence looming over the smaller man. "Reichter doesn't tolerate loose ends. If there's a leak, it's your head on the block. So, you'd better start thinking very carefully about who might be sniffing around."

Price looked like he was about to collapse. "Please, I've done everything... "

"Shut up," Weiss snarled. He pulled out his phone, typed something, and then held it up to Price's face. "You see this? This is your last chance. Get your house in order, or Reichter will do it for you."

James's grip tightened on the armrest as he listened to the exchange, every instinct screaming that they were on the edge of something catastrophic.

"David, pull back," he ordered. "Annika, Sarah, fall back to extraction. We're not pushing our luck tonight."

"But we're so close," Annika protested softly.

"We'll get another shot. Right now, we're walking a razor's edge. We can't risk exposure."

There was a long pause, then Annika's resigned sigh. "Understood. We're pulling back."

One by one, the team disengaged, slipping out of the mansion and into the night. As the sedan pulled away from the curb, James couldn't shake the feeling that they were dancing on the edge of a knife. Klaus Reichter was a ghost, a shadow that moved unseen, but tonight they'd gotten a glimpse of the monster lurking beneath the surface.

"Weiss knows something's off," Nathan said quietly. "It's only a matter of time before he starts digging."

"Let him dig," James replied, his voice cold. "He won't find us."

They drove in silence, the tension thrumming in the air. They had what they came for, proof of Price's connections to Reichter's network. But it wasn't enough. Not yet. They needed more than just whispers and veiled threats.

They needed a smoking gun.

And James wasn't going to stop until he got what they needed.

Chapter 4

The team regrouped at a safe house nestled in the canyons outside Malibu, a secluded property shrouded by thick foliage and the eerie quiet of the surrounding wilderness. The house itself was unassuming, a two-story, Spanish-style villa with red-tiled roofs and aged stucco walls, but it was what lay beneath that mattered. Buried in the basement was a fully equipped command center: computers, surveillance monitors, and communication systems that Kane had painstakingly set up over the last forty-eight hours.

The air inside the command room buzzed with the hum of technology and the subdued tension of their latest mission. As the team assembled around the central table, James Donovan let his gaze move over each of them, assessing their reactions, their state of mind. They had pulled out just in time tonight, but the stakes had suddenly gotten much higher.

"Alright, let's go through it again," James began, his voice calm but authoritative. "What did we learn?"

Annika leaned forward, her fingers lightly tapping the edges of a stack of photographs she had laid out on the table. Each one captured a different moment from the fundraiser, showing key players in the room: Governor Price, Alexander Weiss, and several other men and women whose identities they had yet to confirm.

"Weiss's presence confirms what we suspected," she said. "Reichter's not just pulling Price's strings, he's micromanaging every move the Governor makes. Weiss isn't there to negotiate; he's there to ensure compliance. There's a difference."

"Compliance, intimidation, and threats," Nathan Cross added from his position against the wall. His arms were folded, the tension in his jaw visible. "Weiss might be dangerous, but he's a messenger. Reichter's using him to shield himself from direct exposure. Typical of someone who wants to avoid getting his hands dirty."

James nodded slowly, his mind sifting through the pieces of information they'd gathered, weighing each one against what they already knew. "We also know Weiss is getting nervous. That confrontation with Price wasn't just business. It was personal."

"Exactly," Annika continued. "Weiss doesn't like loose ends. He knows someone's looking into Reichter's operations. The question is: how much does he know, and what's he going to do about it?"

"Whatever it is, it won't be pretty," David Sinclair said grimly. The former Delta Force operative had been remarkably composed during the mission, his steady demeanor a testament to years spent in hostile territory. "Weiss is the kind of guy who sees problems and solves them with a bullet. If he thinks we're a threat, he'll start cleaning house."

"And when that happens, anyone connected to Reichter is in danger," Sarah Chen added, her voice low. "We're not just dealing with one man's paranoia. We're dealing with a network that's been operating in the shadows for decades. If Reichter decides to purge his contacts, it'll be nearly impossible to trace back to him."

A heavy silence settled over the room. They all knew what Sarah was implying, if they didn't move quickly, their opportunity to expose Reichter could vanish in a flurry of dead bodies and erased identities.

"Which is why we need more than just Weiss and Price," James said finally. "We need someone higher up. Someone who can't be erased so easily."

"But who?" Nathan asked, his brows knitting together. "Price is Reichter's main political ally in California. Who's left?"

Kane, who had been quietly monitoring his laptop from a corner of the room, finally looked up. His eyes were bloodshot from hours spent staring at screens, but there was a spark of excitement there, a hint of triumph.

"I think I've got something," he said, swiveling the laptop around to face the team.

On the screen was a grainy image pulled from what looked like a security camera feed. A group of men were seated around a conference table in a dimly lit room. The quality of the image was poor, but the man at the head of the table was unmistakable: Alexander Weiss.

"This footage was taken three weeks ago in Munich, Germany," Kane explained. "Weiss was meeting with several top executives from European banks and a representative from a shell corporation known as Rosetta Holdings. It's one of Reichter's fronts. They discussed a major transaction, one involving billions of dollars."

"Laundering?" Sarah asked, her interest piqued.

"Worse," Kane said grimly. "It's an acquisition. Reichter is trying to buy controlling shares in key tech companies, media outlets, and defense contractors, using taxpayer money siphoned from his non-profits."

"Damn," Nathan muttered, running a hand through his hair. "He's not just playing the political game. He's trying to control the entire narrative. Media, defense, tech, it's all about influence and power."

"That's the tip of the iceberg," Kane continued. "Weiss was there to negotiate, but there was someone else, someone who has the power to finalize these deals and make them legitimate."

James leaned forward, his gaze intent on Kane. "Who?"

Kane clicked a few keys, zooming in on the shadowed figure seated next to Weiss. The man's face was partially obscured, but the faint outline of his features was visible.

"Senator William Monroe of Minnesota," Kane said quietly.

There was a collective intake of breath around the table. Monroe wasn't just any senator. He was the chairman of the Senate Finance Committee and one of the most powerful lawmakers in Washington.

His influence over economic policy was unmatched, and his public persona was that of a champion for transparency and ethical governance.

"If Monroe is involved..." Annika began, her voice trailing off.

"Then Reichter has already infiltrated the highest levels of the U.S. government," James finished grimly. "This isn't just about Price or Weiss. It's about reshaping the country's power structure from the inside out."

"But why?" Sarah asked, her brow furrowed in confusion. "Reichter already has more money and influence than most heads of state. What does he gain by going after tech, media, and defense?"

"Control," Kane said simply. "Imagine if he owned the tech companies that manage our data, the media outlets that shape public opinion, and the defense contractors that build our weapons. He'd be untouchable. He'd control what people see, what they hear, and how the government responds."

James's jaw tightened as the implications sank in. They weren't just dealing with a shadowy conspiracy or a corrupt politician. They were facing a systematic takeover of the very institutions that defined the country's identity and security.

"Which means we need to cut him off at the source," he said softly. "Monroe is the linchpin. If we can get to him, expose his connections to Reichter, we can bring down the whole house of cards."

"But how do we do that?" Nathan asked, his voice laced with skepticism. "Monroe's one of the most well-protected figures in D.C. He's not going to just sit down for a chat and confess everything."

"We don't need him to confess," Annika said, her eyes narrowing thoughtfully. "We just need to find the right leverage."

"Leverage," Sarah repeated slowly. "Everyone has a weakness. Even a man like Monroe."

"What are you thinking?" James asked, turning to her.

Sarah hesitated, her gaze distant as she considered the possibilities. "We dig deeper. Find out who Monroe really is, his habits, his secrets, the things he doesn't want anyone to know. If we can expose something damaging, something that forces him into a corner, he might be willing to trade information to save his own skin."

"That's risky," Nathan warned. "If we push too hard, he could go to Reichter, and then we lose everything."

James nodded, understanding the stakes. But they were running out of options. They couldn't keep waiting for Reichter to make the next move.

"We'll take it slow," he said finally. "Gather everything we can on Monroe, financial records, personal connections, anything that might give us an edge. Then we plan our approach."

"And in the meantime?" David asked, his deep voice cutting through the silence.

"In the meantime, we keep monitoring Price and Weiss. If they start to shift assets or tighten security, we'll know they're onto us."

James glanced around the room, meeting each of their eyes in turn. He saw determination there, and resolve. But he also saw the shadows of doubt and fear. They were walking a tightrope, and one wrong step could send them plummeting into the abyss.

"This isn't going to be easy," he said quietly. "But we knew that going in. Reichter has played this game for a long time, but he made a mistake. He's underestimated us. And that's something we can use."

He straightened, his voice growing firmer. "We're not just here to expose him. We're here to bring him down. Piece by piece. No matter what it takes."

The silence that followed was heavy, but there was a current of electricity running through it. They were on the brink of something monumental, something that could change the course of the country's future.

They just had to take the next step carefully.

"Let's get to work," James said softly.

One by one, the team nodded and turned back to their stations, the hum of activity rising as they began to dig deeper into the web of secrets surrounding Senator Monroe and Klaus Reichter.

And in the quiet moments that followed, James allowed himself a small, grim smile.

Reichter thought he was untouchable.

But the Patriots were just getting started.

Chapter 5

The sun dipped low over the Malibu hills, casting long shadows across the winding roads that led to the Patriots' safe house. Inside the command center, the team worked quietly, their faces illuminated by the dim blue glow of computer screens and the soft overhead lights. It was a familiar rhythm, the steady flow of data, the hushed voices trading bits of information, the constant sense of urgency simmering beneath the surface.

But tonight felt different. Heavier.

James Donovan watched them from where he stood at the edge of the room, his arms crossed over his chest. He had been in enough war rooms to know that tension like this didn't dissipate easily. It built, layer by layer, until it either broke you or forced you to act. And right now, his team was teetering on that edge.

He let his gaze linger on each of them, studying the way they moved, the way they interacted. He knew them all so well, their strengths, their weaknesses, the invisible scars they carried. But there was always something more to learn, another layer to peel back. And in this game, against an enemy like Klaus Reichter, every detail mattered.

Annika Valdez, her dark hair pulled back into a tight ponytail, was hunched over a map spread across the table, tracing lines with her fingertips. A former CIA operative, Annika had spent years mastering the art of covert operations, learning to navigate the murky waters of espionage and subterfuge. But there was more to her than just skill and experience. There was a deep-seated drive, almost a hunger, to expose the darkness she had once been a part of. She glanced up as James approached, her brown eyes sharp and focused.

"We've identified several properties linked to Monroe," she said, her voice low but steady. "Mostly in D.C. and New York. A few offshore accounts too, but they're buried under layers of shell companies. It'll take time to untangle."

"Time we might not have," James replied softly. He reached out, tapping the corner of one of the photos. It showed a sleek, modern high-rise overlooking Central Park. "What about this one?"

Annika frowned. "Corporate apartment. Owned by a subsidiary of Rosetta Holdings. Monroe's been seen entering a few times, but only late at night, and never for long. My guess is it's more of a rendezvous point than a residence."

"Rendezvous for who?" James asked.

"Could be anyone," Annika murmured, her gaze distant as she considered the possibilities. "But given how careful Monroe is, I'd bet on someone he trusts. Someone connected to Reichter's operations."

James nodded thoughtfully. "Keep digging. We need to know who he's meeting there."

Annika nodded, turning back to the map with renewed intensity. As she did, James's attention shifted to the far corner of the room, where Nathan Cross stood with his back against the wall, arms folded, his expression inscrutable. Nathan had always been the team's anchor, a man who could face down impossible odds without flinching. His background in Special Forces had honed his instincts and turned him into a force of nature in the field.

But it was what came after that had defined him, what he'd lost, what he'd seen. Nathan never talked about it, but the shadows in his eyes spoke volumes. He caught James looking and raised an eyebrow.

"Something on your mind, General?" he asked, his tone casual.

"Just wondering if you've slept at all since last night," James replied.

Nathan's lips quirked into a faint smile. "I'll sleep when we've got Reichter behind bars. Besides, I'm used to running on fumes. You should know that."

James nodded, a faint smile of his own tugging at his lips. Nathan's resilience was one of the reasons he had recruited him in the first place. The man could go days without rest if the situation demanded it, and right now, it looked like it might.

"What's your take on Monroe?" James asked quietly, leaning against the table next to Nathan.

Nathan's gaze turned hard. "He's dangerous. More so than Price. Monroe's a career politician. He's built his empire on secrets and alliances. If he's in Reichter's pocket, it means he's sold out everything he once stood for. And that makes him unpredictable."

"Which means we need to be even more careful," James said.

"Yeah," Nathan agreed, his voice low. "And we need to be ready to move the moment we see an opening. He's not going to let us get close without a fight."

James's gaze shifted across the room to where David Sinclair sat, his broad shoulders hunched as he stared at a screen filled with lines of financial data. The former Delta Force operator had always been a man of action, but tonight, he looked almost... contemplative.

"You alright, David?" James asked, his voice cutting through the silence.

David glanced up, his piercing blue eyes meeting James's. "Yeah. Just... thinking."

"About?"

David hesitated, his gaze dropping back to the screen. "About how deep this goes. About how many people Reichter's got in his pocket. It's not just Monroe. I'm seeing connections to defense contractors, pharmaceutical companies, even some in the intelligence community. It's like an infection that's spread everywhere."

"It's how men like Reichter operate," James said softly. "They create webs of influence so vast and complex that cutting one thread barely makes a difference. That's why we have to find the heart of it."

David nodded slowly. "I know. But it's hard not to think about all the people he's corrupted. All the lives he's ruined."

James placed a hand on David's shoulder, squeezing gently. "That's why we're here. To put an end to it. To give people a chance to take back what's been stolen from them."

David looked up, a flicker of determination in his eyes. "Yeah. And we will."

Across the room, Sarah Chen sat in front of a laptop, her fingers flying over the keyboard as she sifted through data with the kind of focus that came from years spent in the FBI's cyber division. Sarah was their intel specialist, capable of uncovering secrets that most people didn't even know existed. But she wasn't just a tech whiz. She had a way of seeing patterns where others saw chaos, of connecting dots that seemed entirely unrelated.

James walked over, watching the rapid stream of code and text on her screen. "What've you got, Sarah?"

She didn't look up, her gaze glued to the screen. "I'm cross-referencing Monroe's known associates with his voting record and financial contributions. Trying to identify any irregularities that could indicate a deeper connection to Reichter's network."

"And?"

Sarah sighed, pushing a loose strand of hair behind her ear. "It's like looking for a needle in a haystack, but I've found a few discrepancies. There's one name that keeps popping up, someone who's made significant contributions to Monroe's campaigns but has almost no public profile."

"Who?" Nathan asked, moving closer.

Sarah clicked a few keys, pulling up a profile. "His name's Jack Dalton. No social media presence, no business listings. Just a series of donations through shell corporations. But get this—Dalton was a key advisor to Monroe back when he was first elected to the Senate.

Then, about ten years ago, he vanished. No records, no appearances, nothing."

"Sounds like the kind of guy who knows how to stay hidden," Nathan muttered.

"Or someone who was made to disappear," James added quietly. "Can you find out more?"

Sarah nodded. "I'll dig deeper. If Dalton's still in the picture, he might be the leverage we need."

"Good," James said, his voice firm. "But be careful. If Monroe and Reichter know we're looking into him, they'll bury him even deeper."

Sarah's eyes flashed with determination. "They can try."

James felt a surge of pride as he looked around the room. Each of them had their own reasons for being here, their own demons to face. But they had come together, forged by a shared purpose, a common enemy. They weren't just a team. They were a family. A family that had been through hell and back, and was willing to go through it again if it meant stopping men like Klaus Reichter.

James's gaze shifted to the only empty chair in the room. Oliver Kane had disappeared upstairs hours ago, muttering something about needing more caffeine. The tech genius had always been a bit of an enigma, brilliant, eccentric, and fiercely loyal. He could break into the most secure systems in the world, but he had a tendency to lose himself in his work, shutting out everything and everyone around him.

"I'll check on Kane," James said, pushing away from the table.

He found Kane in the kitchen, staring intently at his laptop, a half-empty cup of coffee in one hand. His hair was tousled, his shirt wrinkled, but his eyes were clear and alert.

"Anything new?" James asked, leaning against the counter.

Kane looked up, blinking as if coming out of a trance. "Oh, hey. Didn't hear you come in. Yeah, I've been digging through Monroe's digital footprint. It's... strange."

"Strange how?"

Kane hesitated, frowning at the screen. "There are gaps. Places where there should be data, but it's been scrubbed. Not just deleted, erased. Like someone went in and removed entire chunks of his history. Conversations, transactions, even emails. "Like someone's been keeping Monroe's slate clean," Kane finished, shaking his head in disbelief. "I've seen cover-ups before, but this is on another level. Whoever did this had access to top-tier clearance. Government level, maybe even above that."

James's expression tightened. "Reichter's reach must be deeper than we thought. He's not just using his wealth and influence, he's got allies on the inside. People who can pull strings and rewrite history."

"That's exactly it," Kane agreed, his fingers dancing over the keyboard again. "Every time I think I'm close to finding a connection, it disappears. There's something, no, someone, shielding Monroe. And I'm guessing it's not just Weiss or Reichter."

James frowned, considering the implications. "So, there's another player in the game. Someone working behind the scenes to keep Monroe untouchable."

"Yeah," Kane said softly, his gaze fixed on the screen. "But here's the thing: I found traces of one data stream that wasn't completely erased. It's encrypted, but there are fragments left behind. Enough to give me a clue. Whatever it was, it originated from a secure server inside a federal building. Not just any building, though the Department of Homeland Security."

A heavy silence fell between them. James felt the weight of the revelation settle in his chest like a lead ball. Homeland Security was supposed to be a bastion of national security, a shield against threats both foreign and domestic. If someone there was helping Reichter, it meant they were playing a dangerous double game, one that could compromise the entire country.

"Can you pinpoint who's behind it?" James asked, his voice tight.

"Not yet," Kane admitted reluctantly. "But I'm working on it. Whoever this is, they're good. It's going to take time."

James nodded slowly. "Alright. Keep at it. This might be the break we've been looking for. If we can identify this third party, we might be able to expose Monroe and Reichter in one move."

Kane's lips twitched into a brief smile. "You got it, General."

James nodded, then turned back toward the command room. His mind was racing, the pieces of the puzzle shifting and rearranging themselves in new and unexpected ways. They were dealing with more than just a corrupt politician and a shadowy billionaire. This was a conspiracy that reached into the heart of the government itself.

He stepped back into the command room, where the rest of the team had regrouped around the central table. Annika glanced up, her eyes questioning. James took a deep breath, then relayed what Kane had just told him.

The reaction was immediate.

"Homeland Security?" Nathan muttered, his voice laced with disbelief. "Jesus, that's not just playing dirty, that's playing with fire. If Reichter's got someone in DHS, we're talking about a level of infiltration that could cripple national security."

"It makes sense, though," Sarah said quietly, her brow furrowed in thought. "Reichter's been using his charities and front companies to funnel money into political campaigns and terrorist groups for years. But to operate on this scale? To avoid detection? He'd need someone inside who could control the flow of information, manipulate records, and bury evidence. Homeland Security would be the perfect place to do that."

"So what's the play?" David asked, his tone grim. "If we go after someone in DHS without proof, we'll be stepping on a landmine."

"We don't go after them," James said firmly. "Not yet. We use this information to our advantage. If Reichter and Monroe are relying on this third party to cover their tracks, then that means there's a digital trail somewhere. Kane's going to keep digging, and when he finds the link, we'll use it to rip their whole operation open."

"And what about Monroe?" Annika asked. "If we push too hard, we risk alerting him that we're onto him."

James considered this, weighing the options. "We keep the pressure low. Continue gathering intel, but no direct moves. We focus on tracing the money, identifying the key players. When we're ready, we'll hit them all at once."

There were nods of agreement around the table, but the tension was still thick in the air. They all knew what they were up against, a network of corruption that could reach anywhere, touch anyone. And if they weren't careful, it could crush them before they even made it to the first punch.

"Alright," James said quietly. "Let's talk about Monroe's schedule. Any upcoming appearances?"

Sarah nodded, tapping a few keys on her laptop. "He's scheduled to speak at a charity gala in New York next week. The event is closed to the press, just high-profile donors and political allies. Security will be tight, but it's the perfect place to observe without drawing attention."

"We'll send in a small team," James decided. "Annika, Nathan, you're our eyes on the ground. Get a read on Monroe, see who he's meeting with, and if there's a way to plant any surveillance devices, take it."

"And the rest of us?" David asked.

"You, Sarah, and Kane stay here," James said. "Work on identifying the DHS contact and mapping out Monroe's network.

I want to know who else he's in bed with and where they're vulnerable."

David nodded, his jaw set with determination. "Got it."

James looked around at his team, his gaze steady. "We're walking a fine line here, but we've got an advantage, Reichter doesn't know how much we know. Let's use that to stay one step ahead."

They all nodded, the air of resolve settling over the room. One by one, they turned back to their stations, their focus shifting back to the screens and files in front of them.

But before they could get too absorbed, the sound of a cell phone buzzing broke the silence. James glanced down at his own phone, but it wasn't his. The buzzing continued, growing louder.

"It's mine," Annika said, pulling out her phone and glancing at the caller ID. Her eyes widened slightly, and she quickly answered. "Annika Valdez."

She listened for a few moments, her expression tightening. "What? When?"

Everyone watched as her face went pale. She glanced up at James, her voice a strained whisper.

"Reichter's moving money," she said, her voice taut with urgency. "A lot of it. They just transferred nearly fifty million dollars from one of his charity accounts into an offshore bank in the Cayman Islands."

"Fifty million?" Kane's voice was incredulous. "That's not a bribe that's a war chest."

"Which means he's preparing for something big," James said, his mind racing. "We need to find out what that money's for and who it's going to."

Annika nodded, already tapping at her laptop to pull up the transaction details. "It's going to take time to trace it, but, wait."

She froze, staring at her screen, and then looked up, her face a mask of shock.

"It's not just one transfer," she whispered. "There are multiple withdrawals, all to different accounts, all within the last twenty-four hours. We're talking hundreds of millions of dollars moving around like pieces on a chessboard."

James felt a chill run down his spine. "He's not just protecting Monroe. He's buying something. Setting up a new operation."

"But what?" Sarah asked, her voice laced with dread.

"I don't know," James said softly. "But whatever it is, we have to stop it. Fast."

They all looked at each other, the gravity of the situation settling in like a shroud. This wasn't just a power play. This was something bigger, something that could tip the balance of everything they'd been fighting for.

James took a deep breath, his gaze hardening. "We need to move. Now. Annika, focus on those transfers. Find out where that money's going. Nathan, prepare the team for the New York mission. David, Sarah, get me everything on Monroe's past dealings. And Kane, stay on the DHS angle. I want to know who's helping Reichter cover his tracks."

They all nodded, their faces set with determination. The Patriots were back in the fight, and this time, they were going to hit Reichter where it hurt.

But as they turned back to their work, a single thought lingered in James's mind, a thought that sent a shiver of unease down his spine.

Reichter was making his move. And whatever it was, it was going to be big enough to change everything.

Chapter 6

The morning sun had barely risen over the Malibu hills, casting long shadows across the dew-covered grass, when James Donovan stood on the porch of the safe house, staring out at the thick blanket of fog that rolled in from the coast. The ocean beyond was hidden, shrouded in a gray mist that felt almost oppressive. It suited his mood.

Last night's revelations still weighed heavily on him. Reichter's sudden movement of hundreds of millions of dollars meant only one thing: something big was coming. Something that would shift the balance of power and threaten everything they were trying to protect.

He rubbed his hand over the back of his neck, trying to ease the tension that had built up there. He wasn't the kind of man to get rattled easily, but this... this was different. They were facing an enemy with limitless resources, deeply embedded allies, and a plan that was moving faster than they'd anticipated.

"Not sleeping well again?"

James turned to see Nathan Cross leaning against the doorframe, a cup of black coffee in his hand. There was no judgment in Nathan's voice, just a quiet understanding that came from years of working side by side. He knew James as well as anyone could, better, even, given the hell they'd been through together.

"Not much," James admitted with a tight smile. "But I don't think any of us have been getting much sleep."

Nathan nodded slowly, his gaze following James's out to the foggy horizon. "Yeah. Feels like we're running on fumes. But we'll push through. We always do."

James let out a slow breath, the tension easing just slightly. Nathan's presence was a comfort, a steadying force that had anchored the team more times than he could count. He thought back to when they'd first met, Afghanistan, nearly a decade ago. Nathan had been leading a Special Forces unit, a hard-eyed soldier with a knack for finding trouble and an uncanny ability to get his men out of it alive. They'd been thrown together on a joint operation, an extraction gone wrong. That night, when everything had fallen apart and the bullets had been flying, Nathan hadn't hesitated. He'd stayed behind, covering their retreat, even when it meant putting himself in the crosshairs.

That loyalty, that refusal to back down, was what had drawn James to him. He'd known then that Nathan was someone he could trust, someone who would stand by his side no matter what. It was a bond forged in fire, and it hadn't broken since.

"Speaking of pushing through," Nathan said, breaking into James's thoughts, "I heard Kane got another break on the DHS contact."

"Yeah," James said, his expression darkening. "It's not confirmed yet, but he thinks he's narrowed it down to three suspects. High-level officials with access to the kind of data scrubbing we've been seeing. We're going to need more intel before we can make a move."

Nathan grunted in agreement, then glanced back over his shoulder into the safe house. "What's the plan for the day?"

"Annika and I are going to dig deeper into Monroe's financial ties. Sarah's following up on those transfers Annika traced last night. I want to know where that money's going and who's on the receiving end. Meanwhile, you and David prep for the New York mission. We need to make sure we're ready for anything."

"Got it," Nathan said. He hesitated for a moment, then added, "And you?"

"I'm going to keep an eye on everyone," James said, his voice soft but firm. "We're getting close, Nathan. Closer than we've ever been. But that means Reichter's going to get desperate. We can't afford any mistakes."

Nathan nodded, his gaze searching James's for a long moment before he turned away, heading back inside. James watched him go, then took a deep breath and squared his shoulders. There was no time for doubt or hesitation. They were in this now, and they had to see it through.

When James reentered the command room, he found Annika already hunched over a laptop, her fingers flying over the keys as she sifted through a dizzying array of financial documents. He could see the strain in her posture, the tightness in her jaw, but there was also a fire in her eyes, a relentless drive that refused to be extinguished.

"How's it going?" he asked, pulling up a chair beside her.

Annika didn't look up. "Monroe's finances are a mess. He's got money moving through at least six different accounts in five different countries, and that's just what I can see on the surface. Half of it is disguised as investments, the other half as charitable donations. But they're all connected to Reichter's shell companies."

"Anything that stands out?" James asked, leaning in closer to look at the screen.

"There's one account," Annika said slowly, her fingers hovering over the keyboard. "It's in a small private bank in Zurich. Almost no activity for years, then suddenly, last month, a deposit of twenty million dollars."

James frowned. "Where did the money come from?"

"That's the thing," Annika said, a note of frustration creeping into her voice. "The trail's cold. But if I had to guess, I'd say it came from one of Reichter's fronts. The timing's too perfect. That deposit coincides with Monroe introducing a new bill in the Senate, one that just so happens to favor a defense contractor with ties to Reichter."

James's eyes narrowed. "You think it's a payoff?"

"I know it is," Annika said fiercely. "But proving it's another story. We need more than just a few suspicious transactions to make this stick. We need direct evidence that Reichter and Monroe are working together."

"Then let's get it," James said softly. He paused, studying her for a moment. "How are you holding up?"

Annika blinked, surprised by the question. "I'm fine," she said quickly. Too quickly.

"Are you?" James pressed gently. "You've been pushing yourself hard, even for you. I know how personal this is for you, Annika. But don't let it consume you."

For a moment, something flickered in her eyes, something raw and painful, but she quickly masked it. "I'm not letting it consume me," she said quietly. "But I'm not going to let it go, either. Not after what Reichter did to my family."

James felt a pang of sympathy, but he knew better than to press. Annika's family had been caught in the crossfire of a covert operation gone wrong years ago. An operation funded and orchestrated by one of Reichter's shell companies. She had never forgiven herself for not seeing the connection sooner, for not being able to protect them.

"We'll get him," James said softly. "We'll make sure he pays for everything he's done."

Annika nodded, her jaw tight with determination. "I know. And I'm going to make sure of it."

James left her to her work and moved across the room to where Sarah was hunched over her own computer, the screen filled with complex data patterns and lines of code. Her brow was furrowed in concentration, her lips moving silently as she deciphered the web of transactions Annika had uncovered.

"Sarah," he said softly, and she looked up, blinking as if coming out of a trance.

"Sorry," she murmured, rubbing her eyes. "Got lost in the data for a second. There's just... so much of it. It's like trying to untangle a spider's web. Every time I pull on one thread, three more appear."

"That's Reichter's specialty," James said, leaning against the desk. "He hides in complexity. But you're one of the best analysts I've ever met. If anyone can find the connection, it's you."

Sarah offered a small, tired smile. "Thanks. But I'm not sure even I'm good enough to untangle this mess."

"You are," James said firmly. "And you're not alone. We'll figure it out together."

Sarah nodded, her eyes softening. "I know. And I'm not giving up. But there's something you should see."

She turned the laptop toward him, showing a series of transactions linked to one of the offshore accounts Annika had flagged. "This account, one of Reichter's, is making regular payments to a consulting firm in D.C. The firm's small, barely on the radar, but guess who's on their payroll?"

"Who?" James asked, leaning closer.

"Jack Dalton," Sarah said softly. "The same Jack Dalton who disappeared from Monroe's advisory team a decade ago."

James's eyes widened. "He's still in the picture?"

"Looks like it," Sarah said. "But there's more. Dalton isn't just some ghost. He's been acting as a liaison between Monroe and Reichter. I've found records of him making calls to Monroe's office every few weeks, always from the same burner phone. Whatever they're planning, Dalton is the go-between."

James's mind raced. "Which means if we can find Dalton... "

"We can get to Monroe," Sarah finished. "And maybe even Reichter."

"Good work, Sarah," James said, a note of excitement creeping into his voice. "Keep tracking those calls. If Dalton's still in D.C., we'll find him."

He turned away, his thoughts spinning. They were getting closer, piece by piece, to unraveling Reichter's operation. But the stakes were rising, and every step forward brought new dangers.

James glanced back at his team, the people he trusted more than anyone else in the world, and felt a surge of determination.

They had faced insurmountable odds before, but this time, something felt different. It was more than just Reichter's wealth and influence, it was the sheer scale of the conspiracy they were unraveling. But the Patriots had always thrived in the shadows, and they'd taken down enemies who seemed untouchable before.

He shifted his gaze to David Sinclair, who was pouring over a set of blueprints spread out across a side table. David's background in Delta Force had made him invaluable in tactical planning, and James knew he was already thinking three steps ahead. But as he watched David's expression tighten, James couldn't help but wonder what was going through his friend's mind.

"Got something?" James asked, moving over to join him.

David glanced up, his jaw clenched. "Maybe. I've been looking at the blueprints of the hotel where Monroe's gala is being held next week. Security's tight, private contractors with federal licenses. This isn't just the usual political event. It's more like a fortified bunker."

"Reichter's influence again," James muttered.

"Exactly. They're using state-of-the-art surveillance, motion sensors, biometric scanners, encrypted communication lines. We'll have to disable most of it remotely, but I need to figure out the physical layout, too. There are only a few blind spots we can exploit, and I'm thinking we should have a couple of contingencies in place."

James nodded, then leaned in closer, his voice low. "David, I've seen you work through more complex tactical challenges without breaking a sweat. What's really bothering you?"

David's shoulders stiffened slightly, and for a moment, it seemed like he wasn't going to answer. But then he let out a slow breath, his gaze turning inward.

"It's just... this is reminding me of Cairo," he said quietly.

James froze. Cairo. The word alone carried a weight of memories and emotions that few could understand. It had been a black ops mission gone horribly wrong, one of the few times David's team hadn't been able to pull everyone out. It wasn't just the physical losses; it was the betrayal, the realization that someone inside their own government had sold them out. David had never talked about it, but James knew it haunted him.

"You're thinking there's another setup coming?" James asked softly.

David nodded slowly. "It's a gut feeling, but yeah. Reichter's too good to let us get this close without making a counter move. If he knows we're going to that gala, he might be setting up a trap. Monroe's the bait, and we're the fish."

James placed a hand on David's shoulder, squeezing gently. "Then we'll be ready. You said it yourself, we know how to handle fortified bunkers. And if it's a trap, we'll spring it on them."

David's lips curved into a faint smile, though it didn't reach his eyes. "Yeah. We'll see. Just... let's be careful, alright? No unnecessary risks."

"We'll play it smart," James promised. "You know me."

"That's what I'm worried about," David muttered, but there was a hint of warmth in his voice.

James moved on, letting David return to his work. He could feel the unspoken worry threading through the room, each of them grappling with their own doubts and fears. But there was no room for hesitation now. Not when they were so close.

He glanced at his watch. It was time to brief the team on the next steps. Clearing his throat, he moved to the center of the room, drawing everyone's attention.

"Alright, everyone, listen up," he began, his voice steady and commanding. "We're making progress, but Reichter's not going to sit back and let us pick his operation apart. We've got new leads on Monroe's financial dealings and a possible link to Homeland Security, but we're going to need more before we can make a move."

Annika straightened, her eyes narrowing. "What's the plan?"

James glanced at Kane, who was still hunched over his laptop in the corner, looking more like a mad scientist than a tech specialist. His hair was disheveled, his eyes bloodshot, but his fingers never stopped moving across the keys.

"Kane, you want to fill them in?"

Kane didn't look up, but his voice carried across the room with surprising clarity. "I've got a list of suspected DHS contacts down to three people. Two of them are mid-level administrators, easy to eliminate based on their backgrounds. But the third is a problem."

"Who is it?" Nathan asked, pushing off from the wall to join the group.

"Robert Lansing," Kane said, finally turning to face them. "Senior advisor in the Office of Intelligence and Analysis. He's been with DHS for over twenty years, has top-level clearance, and, get this, he's been the one reviewing the financial activity flagged by internal audits. Every suspicious transaction linked to Monroe's shell companies? Lansing's name is on the approval sheets, buried in the paperwork."

Sarah's brow furrowed. "So he's the one scrubbing the records."

"Exactly," Kane said, his voice tense. "But there's more. Lansing isn't just covering up for Monroe. He's connected to at least a dozen other politicians and corporations, most of which have direct ties to Reichter's network. He's not just a cog in the machine. He's one of the key players."

"Which means we need to find a way to get to him," Annika said, her voice cold. "If we can turn Lansing, we can blow this whole thing wide open."

James shook his head. "It's too risky. If Lansing even suspects we're onto him, he'll go dark and take all that intel with him. No, we need to handle this differently."

"Like how?" Nathan asked.

"Like making him think we're not after him," James said quietly. "We leak false intel, make it look like we're focusing on another target, someone lower down the chain. We keep him comfortable, keep him thinking he's safe, and then, when the time is right, we make our move."

The team exchanged glances, weighing the plan. It was dangerous, but it was the best shot they had.

"Alright," Annika said finally. "What's the next step?"

"We split up," James said. "Annika, you keep working on Monroe's financials. Track every cent until we find the smoking gun. Nathan, David, prep for the New York mission. If there's any sign of a trap, I want eyes on it before we walk into it. Sarah, Kane, you stay on Lansing. Monitor his communications, his movements. Anything out of the ordinary, and you let me know immediately."

"What about you?" David asked.

"I'm going to reach out to an old contact in D.C.," James said. "Someone who might be able to help us get more background on Lansing without raising suspicion."

Nathan's gaze sharpened. "Who?"

James hesitated for just a moment. "Charlotte Grayson. She's still with the Bureau."

Nathan's eyes widened slightly, and a murmur of surprise rippled through the group. Charlotte Grayson wasn't just any contact. She was one of the top agents at the FBI, brilliant, ruthless, and utterly uncompromising. But she and James had history. Complicated history.

"Are you sure that's a good idea?" Nathan asked carefully.

"It's the best one we've got," James said firmly. "She's the only person I trust to dig into someone like Lansing without tipping him off."

The others exchanged glances, then nodded reluctantly. They trusted James, even if they didn't like the idea of bringing in an outsider, especially someone as volatile as Charlotte.

"Alright," Nathan said finally. "But be careful. Last thing we need is the Bureau breathing down our necks."

James managed a faint smile. "Don't worry. Charlotte and I have an understanding."

"Yeah, I'm sure you do," Nathan muttered, but he didn't push it further.

James glanced around the room, taking in the determined faces of his team. They were about to step into uncharted territory, but they'd done it before. They could do it again.

"Let's get to work," he said softly.

And with that, the Patriots dispersed, each heading to their station, each preparing for the storm that was about to break.

James took a deep breath, steeling himself for what lay ahead. They were on the brink of something monumental, something that could shatter the very foundation of Reichter's empire.

But as he picked up his phone and scrolled to Charlotte Grayson's number, he couldn't shake the feeling that this time, they were the ones being hunted.

With a steady hand, he dialed the number and waited, listening to the soft ring on the other end. When her voice finally answered, low and edged with curiosity, James felt a rush of emotions he hadn't expected.

"James Donovan," Charlotte said, a hint of amusement in her tone. "To what do I owe the pleasure?"

"We need to talk," James said softly.

There was a brief pause, then a quiet sigh. "It's been a long time. Is this business or personal?"

"Both," James admitted.

"Interesting," she murmured. "Meet me at the old place in an hour. And James?"

"Yeah?"

"Don't keep me waiting."

The line went dead, and James lowered the phone slowly. He stared at it for a moment, then slipped it into his pocket. The past was creeping back in, and he wasn't sure if that was a blessing or a curse.

Either way, there was no turning back now.

James slid his phone into his pocket and straightened. He could feel the weight of the mission pressing down on him, the stakes, the risks, the lives hanging in the balance. He'd been down this road before, but there was something different about this one. It wasn't just about taking down Reichter; it was about everything Reichter represented, the corruption, the manipulation, the unchecked power. This time, failure wasn't an option.

Steeling himself, he turned to his team, each of them already engrossed in their respective tasks. He knew he had to keep his own emotions in check, especially with Charlotte involved. Their history was complicated, to say the least, and it had ended on a note that was neither clean nor resolved. She had her own reasons for not trusting him, just as he had his for needing her help. But he also knew that if there was anyone who could get him the intel he needed on Lansing, it was Charlotte Grayson.

With one last look at his team, James slipped quietly out of the command room and made his way to the garage. The safe house was equipped with an array of vehicles, all chosen for their anonymity. He picked a dark gray sedan, simple, nondescript, and perfect for blending in.

The drive into the city was quiet, the coastal roads winding and treacherous, flanked by towering cliffs on one side and the endless expanse of the Pacific Ocean on the other. The early morning fog still lingered, wrapping everything in a veil of mist that made the world feel small and contained. It was almost comforting, in a way. Like stepping into another realm, where the rules of reality were suspended.

As he approached the outskirts of Los Angeles, the fog began to lift, revealing the familiar sprawl of the city below. Skyscrapers rose against the horizon, a testament to human ambition and greed. Somewhere in that maze of concrete and steel, Klaus Reichter's influence seeped through the cracks, like a cancer spreading through the body of the city.

James turned onto a side street, heading toward a quiet neighborhood lined with old craftsman homes. The meeting place Charlotte had chosen was one they'd used before, a small, unassuming coffee shop tucked away on a tree-lined street. It was the kind of place where people came to escape the noise and chaos of the city, a place where time seemed to slow down.

He parked a block away and walked the rest of the distance, his senses on high alert. Every shadow, every passerby, every glint of light reflecting off a window caught his attention. But it was all habit, all ingrained instinct. No one followed him. No one paid him any mind. He was just another face in the crowd.

When he stepped inside the café, the smell of freshly brewed coffee enveloped him, mingling with the scent of pastries and the faint murmur of conversation. It was a cozy place, filled with mismatched furniture and shelves lined with well-worn books. But there, in the far corner, sitting with her back to the wall and a cup of coffee in her hand, was Charlotte Grayson.

She looked almost exactly as he remembered, tall and lean, her auburn hair pulled back in a loose knot at the nape of her neck, her sharp green eyes scanning the room with the detached efficiency of a predator assessing its territory. But there was something softer about her now, a hint of weariness in the lines around her eyes. It made her look more human, less like the force of nature he'd known back then.

"James," she said softly, as he slid into the chair across from her. "It's been a long time."

"Too long," James agreed, his voice low. He kept his gaze steady, taking in every detail of her face, searching for any sign of what might lie beneath the calm exterior.

Charlotte raised an eyebrow, a faint smile tugging at her lips. "You look good. For a man who's supposed to be keeping a low profile."

"You know me," he said with a shrug. "Trouble always finds me."

Her smile faded, replaced by something more serious. "And now it's brought you back to me. What's going on, James?"

He leaned forward, lowering his voice so that only she could hear. "I need information on someone in Homeland Security. Robert Lansing."

Her eyes narrowed. "Lansing? He's a heavy hitter. Senior advisor. He's got his fingers in everything from counterterrorism to financial oversight. Why do you want him?"

"Because he's connected to Reichter," James said softly. "He's been covering up transactions, scrubbing records, making sure Reichter's network stays invisible. I need to know everything there is to know about him, where he goes, who he talks to, what he's hiding."

Charlotte's gaze turned speculative, and she took a slow sip of her coffee, watching him over the rim of her cup. "This isn't just business for you, is it? You're personally invested."

"Reichter's trying to take over the country from the inside out," James said quietly. "I'm not going to let that happen. Not while I'm still breathing."

For a moment, she was silent, her gaze never leaving his. Then she nodded slowly, as if coming to a decision. "Alright. I'll help you. But you know this is going to cost you."

James met her gaze steadily. "Name your price."

"Truth," she said simply. "No more half-answers, no more evasions. You tell me why you're really doing this, why you're so willing to go up against someone as powerful as Reichter. And I mean all of it."

He hesitated, then nodded slowly. "Alright. I'll give you the truth."

She seemed satisfied with that, and reached into her bag, pulling out a slim folder. "I've already started looking into Lansing. He's slippery, but there's one weak point—his son, Ethan."

"Ethan Lansing?" James repeated, frowning. "I thought he was in Europe."

"He was," Charlotte said. "But he's back in D.C. now. Moved back a few months ago, just around the time Lansing started cleaning up Reichter's messes. From what I've gathered, Ethan's not exactly on good terms with his father. They've been estranged for years. But he might be our way in."

"You think Ethan could help us?" James asked, his mind already spinning with possibilities.

"Maybe," Charlotte said cautiously. "Or maybe he's just a loose end Lansing's trying to tie up. Either way, if we can get to Ethan, we might be able to leverage him against Lansing. Force him to make a mistake."

James nodded thoughtfully. "Alright. I'll look into Ethan. See if I can make contact."

"You'll need to be careful," Charlotte warned. "If Lansing suspects anything, he'll shut us down before we even get close."

"Careful's my middle name," James said with a wry smile.

Charlotte snorted softly. "Sure it is. Just don't get yourself killed, okay? I'd hate to have to explain to your team why you went and did something stupid."

James sobered, his gaze softening. "I'll be careful. I promise."

For a moment, something unspoken passed between them, an acknowledgment of shared history, of things left unsaid. Then Charlotte looked away, breaking the connection.

"Good," she murmured. "Because if you're going after Reichter, you're going to need all the help you can get."

She reached across the table, sliding the folder toward him. "This is everything I have on Lansing so far. Use it wisely."

"Thanks, Charlotte," he said quietly, taking the folder. "I owe you one."

She smiled faintly. "You owe me more than one, James. But we'll settle that later."

With that, she stood, her gaze lingering on his for just a moment longer before she turned and walked away, the soft chime of the café door marking her departure.

James sat there for a long time, staring at the folder in his hands. He knew that reaching out to Charlotte had been a risk. But it was a risk he had to take. With a deep breath, he opened the folder and began to read.

It was time to put the next piece of the puzzle into place.

He only hoped it didn't blow up in their faces.

Chapter 7

The low hum of activity filled the command center as the Patriots reconvened in the safe house later that evening. Outside, the Malibu night was still and quiet, a deceptive calm that belied the turmoil churning within the room. Monitors glowed softly, casting sharp lines of blue and white light over focused faces. Maps, printouts, and dossiers cluttered every surface, the physical manifestation of their relentless hunt for Klaus Reichter's network of corruption.

James Donovan stepped into the room, the weight of his meeting with Charlotte Grayson still pressing down on his shoulders. He hadn't expected her to bring up Ethan Lansing, but it made sense. The son of a powerful man like Robert Lansing would have insights that no amount of surveillance or hacking could uncover. The only question now was whether Ethan would be a willing ally, or another obstacle.

"Everyone, listen up," he said, drawing the team's attention as he set the slim folder Charlotte had given him on the table. "We've got a new angle. Robert Lansing, the senior advisor at Homeland Security, has a son. Ethan Lansing. He's back in D.C. after being off the grid in Europe for a few years. Charlotte thinks he might be our way in."

"His son?" Nathan asked, leaning forward. "That's... unexpected. What's his story?"

James glanced at the folder, flipping it open to the sparse profile inside. There wasn't much, Ethan had done a good job of keeping a low profile. But what little there was, painted a complicated picture. "Ethan was a political prodigy in his twenties, worked as an analyst for the State Department, advised on several high-profile international negotiations. But then he dropped off the radar. No one knows exactly why. The official story is he took a 'sabbatical,' but we know that's code for something deeper."

"Maybe he got burned out," David suggested from where he stood near the back of the room, arms crossed over his chest. "Politics can chew you up and spit you out. If he's anything like his father, he'd have had a lot of people gunning for him."

"Or he's hiding something," Annika countered, her tone skeptical. "People like Ethan don't just disappear. There's always a reason."

"Either way," James said, cutting off the speculation, "he's back now, and he's a potential vulnerability for Lansing. If we can get to Ethan, we might be able to leverage him. Find out what Lansing's been up to, what Reichter's next move is."

"Assuming Ethan's willing to talk," Sarah added quietly. "If he's been estranged from his father, he might not want anything to do with us, or he could be hostile."

"We're not going in blind," James assured her. "We're going to gather more intel, get a sense of who Ethan is now. Kane, you're up."

Oliver Kane looked up from his workstation, where he'd been hunched over a series of complex code strings and encryption programs. His eyes were bloodshot, and his hair stuck up in wild tufts, but his expression was sharp.

"I've been working on it since you called," he said, his voice edged with weariness. "Tracked Ethan's movements over the last few months, he's staying at a condo in Georgetown. Security's tight, private detail, unlisted address, but I managed to get access to some of the building's cameras. He's been laying low. Doesn't go out much, and when he does, it's to private clubs, mostly in the company of a woman named Rachel Klein. She's an old family friend, used to work in the same circles as him."

"Family friend or something more?" Annika asked, her tone probing.

Kane shrugged. "Hard to say. Could be either. They don't show any overt signs of being romantically involved, but they're definitely close."

"We'll need to know more about her too," James said. "If she's still in contact with Ethan after all these years, she might be able to help us get close."

Nathan frowned thoughtfully, his gaze fixed on the folder in front of him. "What's our approach going to be? We can't just walk up to him and start asking questions about his father."

"Agreed," James said. "We need a way to get Ethan's attention without spooking him. Something that'll make him curious enough to reach out to us."

"Maybe we don't go to him directly," Sarah suggested, her voice soft but steady. "If we approach Rachel Klein instead, she might be more receptive. We can use her to gauge Ethan's state of mind before we make a move."

"Good thinking," James said with a nod. "Kane, dig up everything you can on Rachel Klein, contacts, affiliations, current employment. The more we know, the better prepared we'll be."

"Already on it," Kane said, turning back to his computer.

James glanced at the others, noting the focused expressions and the set determination in their eyes. They were all exhausted, he could see it in the way they held themselves, the slight droop in their shoulders, but none of them would back down. Not now.

Nathan Cross was the first to break the silence. "If we're going after Ethan, we should keep an eye on his father too. Lansing might get wind of this and try to shut us down before we get close."

"I've already put him under surveillance," Annika said, her tone crisp and efficient. "There's no sign that he suspects anything yet, but if he does, he'll probably start tightening his security protocols. We need to be prepared to move fast if things start heating up."

James nodded, his gaze shifting to David. "And you? How's the prep for the New York mission?"

David straightened, his expression intent. "Everything's set. We've got blueprints of the hotel, and I've identified a few potential entry points that we can use if we need to infiltrate. But I'm still concerned about security. There's too much at stake for them not to have a backup plan in place. If Monroe's in Reichter's pocket, he'll be expecting trouble."

"We'll deal with that when we get there," James said quietly. "For now, focus on contingency plans. I want to be ready for anything."

David nodded, but there was a hint of tension in his gaze, the same tension James had seen earlier. He made a mental note to check in with David later. They couldn't afford any distractions, not when they were this close.

"Alright, let's split up," James said, bringing the meeting to a close. "Annika, Nathan, and I will start working on the approach for Rachel Klein. David, keep refining the tactical plans for New York. Kane and Sarah, stay on surveillance and intel gathering. We'll regroup in a few hours."

The team dispersed, each moving with the focused efficiency of seasoned operatives. James lingered for a moment, watching them go. They were all pushing themselves to the limit, each for their own reasons.

Nathan had been a steadying force in James's life for years, but there were cracks starting to show. The long hours, the constant pressure, it was taking a toll. James had seen the way Nathan's hands sometimes shook when he thought no one was looking, the flash of something dark in his eyes whenever the past was mentioned. Cairo had scarred them both, but for Nathan, it had been more than just a failed mission. It had been a personal betrayal, one that had cost him more than just men. It had cost him his faith in the very people they were sworn to protect.

David, on the other hand, had always been a rock, unshakable, unflinching. But something about this mission had him on edge. James had known David since their days in Delta Force, had seen him take on impossible odds without breaking a sweat. But lately, there was a tightness in his voice, a hesitancy that hadn't been there before. James suspected it was the parallels to Cairo, the way the situation seemed to mirror that doomed mission. He needed to keep an eye on David, make sure he didn't get lost in the ghosts of the past.

And then there was Annika. Of all of them, she was the one James worried about most. Her thirst for justice, no, vengeance, had always been a driving force. It made her relentless, pushed her to go above and beyond. But it also made her reckless. She blamed herself for what had happened to her family, for the way Reichter's machinations had destroyed their lives. He could see it in her eyes every time his name was mentioned, the burning need to make Reichter pay. It was a fire that could either fuel her resolve or consume her completely.

Kane was the wildcard. Brilliant, eccentric, and always teetering on the edge of obsession. He'd been with them since the beginning, using his skills to crack codes and systems that no one else could touch. But there was a darkness in him too, a restlessness that sometimes made James wonder how long Kane would last in this fight. His loyalty was unquestionable, but his methods, his willingness to blur ethical lines, made him a liability as much as an asset.

And then there was Sarah. Quiet, meticulous, and often overlooked. She was their analytical backbone, the one who could see patterns in chaos. But Sarah was driven by more than just a sense of duty. There was something else there, something that made her push herself harder than anyone else. James didn't know what it was—she'd never talked about her past, never shared what had brought her to them. But he respected her privacy. They were all running from something, haunted by ghosts that lingered in the shadows of their minds. As long as Sarah continued to channel that energy into unraveling Reichter's schemes, James wouldn't push. When the time was right, she'd share what drove her, or she wouldn't. And he'd accept that.

James glanced at the clock on the wall. Time was slipping away, and with each passing minute, Reichter's grip tightened. He turned back to the central table and began sketching out a basic outline for their approach on Ethan Lansing. They needed to establish contact soon, and if possible, before Lansing Sr. caught wind of what they were up to.

"Let's do a deep dive on Ethan's last few months," James called out. "Everything, his contacts, his routine, his spending habits. If there's a pattern, we need to find it."

The team fell into a rhythm. Annika and Nathan combed through the physical records they'd compiled, while Kane and Sarah dissected the digital footprint Ethan had left behind. David joined them at the main table, his expression intent as he studied the maps and blueprints, his mind already running through tactical scenarios.

Hours passed in silence, interrupted only by the occasional murmur of conversation or the soft clatter of keyboards. Outside, the fog had lifted, revealing a clear, crisp night. But inside the command center, the air was heavy with the unspoken anticipation of what lay ahead.

"Found something," Kane said suddenly, breaking the quiet. He leaned back in his chair, rubbing a hand over his tired eyes. "It's not much, but it's something."

James moved closer, along with the others. "What do you have?"

"Ethan's been making regular visits to a bookstore in Georgetown," Kane explained, pulling up a series of grainy surveillance stills. They showed Ethan entering a small, nondescript storefront, his expression guarded. "It's a hole-in-the-wall place, no obvious connection to any of his known associates. But get this, he always goes alone, and he always stays for at least an hour."

"Reading habits don't usually scream 'covert meetings,'" Nathan said dryly.

"No, but here's the thing," Kane continued, his gaze sharpening. "The bookstore isn't just any bookstore. It's a front. The owner, Daniel Grant, is a former NSA analyst. He retired about ten years ago, set up shop in D.C., and has been quietly running the store ever since. But his customer list reads like a who's who of former intelligence operatives. It's a place for people in the know."

"So Ethan's going there to meet someone," Annika said, a hint of excitement in her voice. "Maybe getting advice, or making contact with old allies."

"Or," Sarah interjected, "he's hiding something there. Something he doesn't want anyone else to find."

James nodded thoughtfully. "Either way, it's our first real lead. We need to get inside, see what he's up to."

"Surveillance?" Nathan asked.

"Yes, but subtle," James said firmly. "We can't afford to spook him. If we move too fast, he'll bolt, and we'll lose our only chance at getting close."

"I'll handle it," Annika offered. "I can get in and out without drawing attention."

James hesitated, then nodded slowly. "Alright. But you're not going in alone. Nathan, you'll back her up from outside. Keep an eye on the bookstore and be ready to extract if things go sideways."

Nathan glanced at Annika, then nodded. "Got it."

"Good. We'll plan the surveillance for tomorrow night. Let's go over the details and make sure we're ready."

As the team gathered around the table, James watched them with a mixture of pride and concern. They were the best at what they did, but this mission was stretching all of them to their limits. And they were about to push even further.

The Next Evening , Georgetown, Washington, D.C.

The streets of Georgetown were quiet, the evening crowd thinning as the night deepened. A light breeze stirred the leaves of the old trees lining the narrow sidewalks, carrying with it the faint scent of damp earth and distant rain. Annika Valdez moved silently through the shadows, her footsteps barely making a sound against the cobblestones.

She wore a simple black jacket and jeans, her hair pulled back into a loose bun that softened her normally sharp features. To anyone watching, she looked like just another passerby, a local resident taking a late-night stroll. But every movement was calculated, every glance deliberate.

Nathan Cross followed at a distance, his posture relaxed but his eyes constantly scanning the surroundings. He looked completely at ease, but Annika knew better. Beneath that calm exterior, he was like a coiled spring, ready to snap into action at the first sign of trouble.

"Positioned outside the bookstore," Nathan murmured softly into his comms. "No sign of Ethan yet."

"Copy that," Annika replied, her voice low and steady. "I'm heading inside. Stay alert."

"Always," Nathan said with a hint of a smile in his voice.

Annika approached the small bookstore, her gaze flicking over the faded sign and the darkened windows. There was something almost quaint about the place, with its weathered wood exterior and rows of dusty books displayed in the front. But she knew better than to trust appearances.

Taking a deep breath, she pushed the door open and stepped inside. A small bell chimed softly overhead, announcing her presence. The interior of the bookstore was dimly lit, the air filled with the scent of old paper and leather bindings. Shelves lined the walls, crammed with books of every genre and age, creating a maze-like effect.

At the back of the store, behind a cluttered counter, a man in his early sixties looked up. His hair was gray, his face lined with the faint traces of old scars. He wore wire-rimmed glasses and a worn flannel shirt, his expression one of casual disinterest.

"Evening," he said in a gravelly voice. "Can I help you find something?"

Annika offered a polite smile, stepping closer. "Just browsing, thanks. But I heard you might have some rare editions. I'm looking for something... unique."

The man's gaze sharpened slightly, his eyes narrowing as he studied her. "That so? Any particular genre?"

"Something related to international relations. Maybe something on covert diplomacy," Annika said softly, letting a hint of meaning slip into her tone.

The man's eyes flickered, a brief flash of recognition. He leaned back, his expression turning wary. "Not many people ask for that kind of thing."

"I'm not most people," Annika said quietly, holding his gaze.

There was a long silence, the tension between them crackling like static electricity. Then the man sighed, his shoulders relaxing just a fraction.

"You're looking for answers," he murmured. "But I'm not sure I'm the one who can give them to you."

"Maybe not," Annika said softly. "But someone who comes here regularly might be."

The man's eyes darkened, and he glanced around the empty store before lowering his voice. "You shouldn't be here. You don't know what you're getting into."

Annika leaned in, her voice barely more than a whisper. "Then tell me. Help me understand."

The man hesitated, then shook his head slowly. "You're playing a dangerous game, lady. If I were you, I'd walk out that door and never come back."

"Can't do that," Annika said, her voice firm. "Not until I know what Ethan Lansing is hiding."

The man stiffened, his expression turning wary. "Who are you?"

"Just someone looking for the truth," Annika replied evenly. "And someone who can help you if you let me."

For a moment, she thought he was going to shut her down, tell her to leave. But then he sighed, a long, weary exhale that seemed to deflate him.

"Ethan's a good kid," he murmured, almost to himself. "But he's in over his head. He's trying to fix something that can't be fixed. And if you're here to drag him into whatever mess you're part of, you'd better think twice."

"I don't want to hurt him," Annika said softly. "I want to help. But I need to know what's going on."

The man looked at her for a long moment, then nodded slowly. "Fine. But not here. Meet me tomorrow night, after the store closes. There's a park a few blocks east. I'll tell you what I can."

Annika nodded, her heart pounding in her chest. "Thank you."

"Don't thank me yet," the man said grimly. "If Ethan finds out I talked to you, we'll both be in more trouble than you can imagine."

With that, he turned away, busying himself with a stack of books on the counter, effectively dismissing her.

Annika lingered for a moment, then turned and walked out of the store, the bell chiming softly behind her. She stepped onto the sidewalk, the cool night air brushing against her face.

"Everything okay?" Nathan's voice came through her earpiece, low and tense.

"Yeah," Annika murmured, her gaze sweeping the street for any sign of trouble. "We've got a lead. But we're going to have to play this one very carefully."

"Roger that," Nathan said softly. "Heading to exfil now."

Annika nodded, her mind racing as she started down the street. Every instinct screamed at her to look over her shoulder, to scan every shadow and listen for footsteps behind her. But she forced herself to move casually, her pace unhurried. This was the most crucial part, getting out clean, without tipping anyone off.

"Watch your six," Nathan murmured softly through the comms. "Someone's been keeping tabs on the bookstore. Black SUV parked three blocks down."

Annika's pulse quickened. "Are they following me?"

"Not yet. But don't take any chances."

"Understood." She turned the corner, slipping into the glow of a streetlamp. "I'm heading back to the vehicle. Keep eyes on them."

"Copy that," Nathan said. "If they make a move, I'll let you know."

Annika quickened her pace slightly, keeping her breathing steady as she made her way to the extraction point. The night felt colder now, each breath misting in the air. She could hear the faint hum of traffic in the distance, the murmur of conversations drifting out from nearby bars and cafes. But her focus was on the task at hand, reaching the vehicle without drawing attention.

When she rounded the last corner, she spotted the dark sedan they'd parked earlier. Nathan was already leaning against it, his posture relaxed but his eyes scanning the street behind her.

"Get in," he said quietly, opening the door for her.

Annika slid into the passenger seat, and Nathan closed the door behind her before moving around to the driver's side. He glanced in the rearview mirror as he started the engine.

"Black SUV's still there," he murmured. "No movement."

"Let's not wait for them to get curious," Annika said softly. "Drive casually, don't draw them in."

Nathan nodded and pulled out onto the street, keeping his speed just under the limit. Annika resisted the urge to look back, instead focusing on the soft glow of the dashboard lights.

"Did you get what you needed?" Nathan asked after a few moments of silence.

"Not everything," Annika admitted, her gaze distant. "But the bookstore owner is willing to talk. He knows Ethan, maybe even cares about him. He's agreed to meet tomorrow night. He'll tell us what he knows then."

"Tomorrow night?" Nathan repeated, his brow furrowing. "And you trust him?"

"Not completely," she said, shaking her head. "But he's afraid, for Ethan and for himself. That makes him valuable. And he mentioned something about Ethan trying to fix something that can't be fixed. Whatever it is, it's tearing him apart."

Nathan nodded slowly, his expression thoughtful. "Sounds like Ethan's carrying a hell of a lot of baggage. Could be the leverage we need."

"Could be," Annika agreed, but there was something in her voice, an uncertainty that Nathan hadn't heard before.

"What is it?" he asked softly.

Annika hesitated, then sighed, rubbing a hand over her face. "I don't know. It's just... he reminds me of me. That desperation, that need to make things right, no matter what it costs. I've seen that look in the mirror too many times. If we push him too hard, he might break."

"We'll handle him carefully," Nathan assured her. "We're not here to break anyone, we're here to get the truth."

"I know," Annika murmured, her gaze drifting out the window. "But people like Ethan don't just bend. They snap."

Nathan didn't respond immediately, his thoughts drifting back to a younger version of Annika, the fiery, determined agent who'd joined them after her family had been caught in the crossfire of one of Reichter's covert operations. She'd been so full of anger, so desperate for answers and revenge. And in some ways, that fire had never gone out. It had just been tempered by time and experience.

"We'll get through to him," Nathan said finally, his voice firm. "You'll get through to him."

Annika looked at him, her eyes softening slightly. "Thanks, Nathan."

"Don't mention it," he said with a faint smile. "Now let's get back to the safe house and brief the others. We've got a long day ahead of us."

Back at the Safe House

The drive back to the safe house was uneventful, and when they arrived, the rest of the team was already gathered in the command room. James looked up as they entered, his gaze sharp and assessing.

"How'd it go?" he asked, his voice calm.

Annika glanced at Nathan, then stepped forward. "We've got a meeting set up with the bookstore owner. He's agreed to talk, but it's going to have to be on his terms. Tomorrow night, after the store closes. He's worried about Ethan, thinks he's in over his head."

James nodded slowly, his gaze thoughtful. "That's good. It means he's got a personal stake in this. What's your read on him?"

"He's cautious, but I don't think he's trying to mislead us," Annika said quietly. "He knows more than he's saying, but he's scared. If we can convince him that we're not here to hurt Ethan, he might open up."

"Alright," James said softly. "We'll keep the pressure low. No sudden moves. We're playing the long game here."

Nathan nodded in agreement. "And if Lansing or Reichter get wind of this?"

"Then we adapt," James said firmly. "We're not going to let them dictate the terms. We make the rules."

He looked around at the others, noting the exhaustion etched on their faces, the weight of the mission pulling at them. But there was also determination there, resolve that wouldn't be easily shaken.

"Kane, Sarah," James continued, turning his attention to the tech duo. "Any progress on the digital front?"

Kane's fingers flew over his keyboard as he pulled up a series of screens on the main monitor. "Yeah, we've been tracing Lansing's communications, both personal and professional. He's been more active lately, calls to Reichter's known associates, meetings scheduled at unlisted locations. It's almost like he's preparing for something. Or someone."

"Us," Sarah finished quietly. "He knows something's coming, but he doesn't know what. He's tightening his circle, cutting off loose ends."

"Which means he's vulnerable," James said, his gaze narrowing. "If he's cleaning house, he's going to leave gaps. We just need to be ready to exploit them."

David, who had been quietly observing the conversation, spoke up then. "And Ethan? If he's really trying to 'fix' something, that means he's aware of what's happening. He might even have access to information that could turn the tide in our favor."

"That's what we're counting on," James agreed. "But we can't push him too hard, or he'll clam up. Annika and Nathan will handle the meeting tomorrow night. The rest of us will stay back and keep an eye on Lansing. If he makes a move, we'll be ready."

He glanced around the room, his gaze lingering on each of them in turn. "We've come too far to back down now. Reichter's network is starting to crack, but we need to be patient. Every piece of information, every ally we gain, that's another nail in his coffin."

The others nodded, the tension easing slightly as they fell back into the familiar rhythm of planning and preparation.

"Alright," James said softly. "Get some rest if you can. Tomorrow's going to be a long day."

One by one, the team dispersed, heading to their respective stations or slipping off to catch a few hours of sleep. But James remained where he was, staring at the map of D.C. spread out across the table, his mind already spinning with possibilities and contingencies.

They were close, closer than they'd ever been. But close wasn't good enough. They needed to be precise, to strike at the heart of Reichter's operation with the full force of everything they had.

And they would. Because this time, there would be no retreat.

No surrender. Just the Patriots, standing against the shadows, and the enemy they were sworn to destroy.

Chapter 8

The early morning light filtered through the windows of the safe house, casting a soft, golden glow over the command center. It was a stark contrast to the somber mood that permeated the room. The Patriots had gathered again, faces tight with resolve. There was no idle chatter, no wasted movements, only the quiet focus of a team that had spent too long staring into the abyss of conspiracy and corruption.

James Donovan stood at the head of the central table, watching his team as they sifted through files, scrolled through surveillance feeds, and murmured updates to each other. The silence was comforting in its familiarity, the calm before the storm. They'd been here before, in one way or another, standing on the brink, preparing to dive headfirst into the unknown. But this time, the stakes felt higher, the tension sharper.

"Alright, everyone," James began, his voice cutting through the murmur of activity. "Let's go over where we stand."

He gestured to the map of Washington, D.C., spread out before them, with red and blue markers indicating key locations. "Our objective is clear: get to Ethan Lansing and find out what he knows. Tonight's meeting with the bookstore owner is our first real opportunity to gather actionable intel. Annika and Nathan will be handling that."

Annika and Nathan exchanged a brief glance. There was a subtle shift in the air between them, an unspoken understanding that came from years of working together. They'd been partners on countless missions, each watching the other's back, each trusting the other to be there when it mattered most.

"I'll be in and out before they even know I'm there," Annika said confidently, her voice low and sure.

Nathan nodded, a faint smile tugging at his lips. "I'll be on overwatch. You won't be alone for a second."

"Good," James said with a nod. "While they're handling that, I want the rest of you focused on two things: surveillance and contingency planning. Kane, Sarah, I want you tracking Robert Lansing's movements. He's our linchpin. If he makes any sudden moves, I want to know about it immediately."

"Got it," Kane said, his gaze flicking up from his laptop. "I've been monitoring his encrypted communications. He's been quiet so far, but I'm seeing signs of increased activity around his office. Might be nothing, but it could be prep for a counter-move."

"Keep digging," James said. "The quieter he gets, the more I want to know what he's hiding."

"On it," Kane murmured, his fingers already flying over the keys.

"David," James continued, turning to the broad-shouldered man standing beside the table, "you're our tactical lead. I want a full breakdown of the bookstore's surroundings. Identify choke points, escape routes, potential blind spots. If things go sideways, I want to know exactly how we're getting Annika and Nathan out of there."

David nodded, his expression focused. "I've already scouted the area. There's an alley two blocks east that's perfect for extraction. Narrow, low visibility. I'll have a secondary vehicle waiting there just in case. But I need to do a few more checks before I can finalize the plan."

"Good," James said, his tone approving. "Do what you need to. And keep the vehicle nondescript. If we have to make a quick exit, we don't want to draw attention."

David inclined his head, his eyes scanning the map as he mentally ran through various scenarios. It was a role he was born for, assessing risk, planning for contingencies, ensuring everyone got out alive. And he did it with a calmness that belied the storm brewing beneath the surface.

James knew that beneath David's stoic exterior was a man who'd lost too many friends, seen too much blood spilled. It was why he was so thorough, why he never left anything to chance. Failure wasn't just a word to David, it was a specter that haunted his every decision, a reminder of all the times he hadn't been able to save the people who'd trusted him with their lives.

"Anything else we need to consider?" Sarah asked, breaking the silence. She sat with her hands clasped in front of her, her gaze thoughtful. "If Ethan is really in over his head, he might have his own safeguards in place. We should be prepared for the possibility that he knows more than he's letting on."

"That's a good point," James said, nodding. "Annika, Nathan, if there's even a hint that Ethan suspects something, pull back. We're not here to burn our only lead."

"Understood," Annika said softly. "But we need to be ready to capitalize if he does open up. I'm not expecting him to spill everything right away, but if we can show him that we're not his enemies, we might get somewhere."

James nodded, his gaze steady. "It's a delicate balance. We don't want to spook him, but we need answers. Trust your instincts. You've got a good read on people, Annika. Use that."

She met his gaze, a flicker of something unspoken passing between them. Gratitude, perhaps, or a shared recognition of what was at stake. Then she looked away, her expression hardening.

"Alright, then," James said, straightening. "Everyone knows their roles. We execute tonight, no mistakes."

The team dispersed, each falling into their familiar rhythms. David moved to the tactical display, checking and rechecking the building layout, while Sarah and Kane delved deeper into Robert Lansing's communications. Annika and Nathan exchanged a few quiet words before slipping out of the room to run through their own pre-mission prep.

James watched them go, his mind already spinning with possibilities and contingencies. He couldn't shake the nagging feeling that they were missing something, some small detail that could unravel the entire mission. But he pushed the thought aside. They'd come too far to let doubt get in the way now.

Later that afternoon, with most of the team occupied, James found himself alone in the kitchen, nursing a cup of coffee. The rich aroma filled the small space, mingling with the faint scent of cleaning supplies and the low hum of the refrigerator. He stared into the dark liquid, his thoughts drifting back to when this team had first come together.

It had been after the Rothschild takedown, one of the most dangerous and chaotic operations they'd ever pulled off. They'd taken down a cabal of elites who had been manipulating global markets, destabilizing governments for their own gain. The victory had come at a high cost, and the aftermath had left them fractured and raw.

But they'd made it through. Each of them had their reasons for staying in the fight, for joining the Patriots. Annika, with her fierce need to avenge her family's deaths and prevent others from suffering the same fate. Nathan, who'd lost men under his command due to bureaucratic incompetence and wanted to ensure no one else had to face that kind of betrayal. David, haunted by the ghosts of failed missions, determined to make every life he saved count. Kane, who'd grown disillusioned with a system that rewarded greed and punished integrity, choosing instead to fight for a cause he believed in. And Sarah, whose past remained a mystery even to him, but who had shown unwavering dedication and resolve since the day she'd joined them.

They were more than just colleagues or friends. They were family, each flawed, each broken in their own way, but stronger together than apart. It was what made them dangerous, what gave them the edge over Reichter's network of mercenaries and corrupt officials.

"Penny for your thoughts?" Nathan's voice broke through the silence, pulling James from his reverie.

James looked up to see Nathan leaning against the doorway, a knowing smile playing on his lips. He was dressed in tactical gear, his stance casual but ready.

"Just thinking about how far we've come," James said, setting his cup down. "How much we've been through."

Nathan nodded slowly, his gaze thoughtful. "We've been to hell and back, that's for sure. But we're still standing. And we're going to see this through, no matter what it takes."

"Yeah," James murmured. "We are."

There was a pause, then Nathan pushed off the doorframe and moved closer, his expression turning serious. "You think Annika's ready for this? I mean, I know she's capable, but..."

"But this feels personal," James finished for him.

Nathan nodded. "Yeah. I've seen that look in her eyes before. I don't want her to do something reckless because she's too close to this."

"She'll be fine," James said softly, but there was a hint of uncertainty in his voice. "She knows what's at stake."

Nathan studied him for a moment, then sighed. "I hope you're right."

He turned and headed back toward the command center, leaving James alone with his thoughts once more.

As the sun dipped below the horizon, casting long shadows over the historic streets of Georgetown, the Patriots made their final preparations. Annika and Nathan were dressed in casual attire, their weapons concealed beneath light jackets. Their expressions were calm, their movements controlled.

They slipped out of the safe house and into a nondescript sedan, the engine humming softly as Nathan pulled away from the curb. The drive to the bookstore was quiet, the tension between them palpable but unspoken.

"You good?" Nathan asked quietly as they turned onto the bookstore's street.

Annika glanced at him, then nodded. "Yeah. Just... focused."

"Good," Nathan said softly, his gaze flickering between her and the road ahead. "Just remember, we're in and out. We don't push him unless we have to."

"Right," Annika murmured, but there was a shadow of something in her voice, something dark and unresolved. She knew the stakes, knew that Ethan Lansing could be the key to bringing down his father and, ultimately, Reichter's entire operation. But what if he was just another pawn? What if this was all just another dead end?

Nathan reached out, his hand hovering over her shoulder for a moment before he finally let it rest there, his touch warm and steady. "We've got this, Annika. Whatever happens, we'll handle it. Together."

She managed a faint smile, the tension in her chest easing slightly. "Yeah, we will."

The bookstore loomed up ahead, its windows darkened, the neon "Closed" sign glowing faintly in the window. Nathan pulled into a narrow alley a block away, cutting the engine and letting the car settle into silence.

"Radio check," Nathan murmured, his voice barely more than a whisper.

"Loud and clear," David's voice crackled through their earpieces. "I've got eyes on the entrance. No sign of movement."

"Copy that," Kane added, his tone calm. "We're monitoring the digital feeds. No unusual activity on Lansing's comms or surveillance networks."

"Let's do this," Annika said softly, unbuckling her seatbelt and slipping out of the car.

Nathan followed, his gaze sweeping the darkened street as they made their way toward the bookstore. The air was cool, carrying the scent of rain on the wind. Everything felt sharper, more vivid, as if the world itself was holding its breath.

They reached the bookstore door, and Annika rapped lightly on the glass. For a moment, there was nothing, just the faint hum of distant traffic and the whisper of leaves rustling in the breeze. Then, the sound of a lock clicking, and the door swung open.

Daniel Grant, the grizzled bookstore owner, stood in the doorway, his expression guarded. He glanced past them, his eyes narrowing as if searching for signs of anyone else.

"You came alone?" he asked, his voice a low growl.

"Just us," Annika said quietly. "Like I promised."

Grant hesitated, then stepped aside, motioning for them to enter. "Alright. Come in."

They slipped inside, and Grant closed the door behind them, turning the lock with a soft click. The interior of the bookstore was dimly lit, the shelves casting long shadows across the floor. The faint scent of dust and old books filled the air, a comforting, nostalgic smell that contrasted sharply with the tension thrumming beneath the surface.

"Follow me," Grant muttered, leading them toward the back of the store.

They wound their way through narrow aisles until they reached a small office tucked behind a row of shelves. The space was cramped and cluttered, papers and books piled haphazardly on every available surface. Grant gestured for them to sit, then leaned against the edge of the desk, his arms crossed over his chest.

"So," he said, his voice flat, "you wanted to talk about Ethan."

"Yes," Annika said softly. "We know he's been visiting you. We know he's been trying to 'fix' something. But we don't know what. We need you to help us understand what he's dealing with."

Grant's eyes flickered, and for a moment, he looked almost pained. "Ethan's... he's not like his father. He's a good kid. Always has been. But he's caught up in something way over his head."

"Caught up how?" Nathan asked, his tone gentle but insistent. "What's he trying to do?"

Grant shook his head slowly, his gaze distant. "He's been trying to find something, some piece of information that can take down his father's entire network. He thinks if he can get his hands on it, he can expose everything. But it's dangerous. He's being watched."

"By his father?" Annika pressed.

"And others," Grant muttered. "People who don't want those secrets getting out. I told him to let it go, to leave before he gets himself killed, but he won't listen. He thinks he can make things right."

Annika felt a pang of sympathy. She knew what that kind of desperation felt like, the need to right wrongs, to undo the damage caused by people who had no regard for anyone but themselves.

"Do you know what he's looking for?" she asked quietly. "What this information is?"

Grant hesitated, his jaw tightening. "I don't know exactly. But I've heard him mention something called the Veritas Files. He thinks they're some kind of master record, proof of every illegal deal, every bribe, every backroom agreement his father's been involved in."

"The Veritas Files," Nathan murmured, exchanging a glance with Annika. "Do you know where he's looking for them?"

Grant shook his head. "No. He's keeping that part to himself. But I know he's been meeting with someone, an old contact of his from his State Department days. A man named Carl Thompson. If anyone knows where Ethan's going next, it's Thompson."

"Thompson," Annika repeated, committing the name to memory. "Where can we find him?"

"He works as a consultant now," Grant said. "Mostly in Europe. But he's back in D.C. for a few days. He and Ethan have been meeting at a private club downtown. The Astoria."

Nathan frowned. "That's a high-profile place. Too many eyes. If we approach them there, we could blow Ethan's cover."

"Exactly," Grant said, his expression tight. "If Lansing or Reichter find out Ethan's looking for the Veritas Files, they'll eliminate him without a second thought."

"Then we won't let that happen," Annika said firmly. "We'll get to him before they do."

Grant's eyes narrowed. "And what happens then? You use him to get what you want and toss him aside? Like every other agency that's tried to take down men like his father?"

Annika felt the sting of the accusation, but she met his gaze steadily. "We're not here to use him, Grant. We're here to help him. But we need his cooperation. If he's willing to talk to us, we can protect him."

"Protect him," Grant repeated bitterly. "No one can protect him if this goes wrong."

"Then we won't let it go wrong," Nathan said quietly. "We're not leaving him out to dry."

Grant studied them for a long moment, his gaze hard and searching. Then, finally, he sighed, the fight seeming to drain out of him.

"Fine," he muttered. "But if anything happens to him, if you get him killed, I swear to God, I'll... "

"It won't come to that," Annika said softly. "We're not going to let him get hurt."

Grant looked away, his shoulders slumping. "You'd better not."

Silence fell, heavy and oppressive. Annika glanced at Nathan, then back at Grant.

"Thank you for trusting us," she said quietly. "We'll take it from here."

Grant nodded stiffly, his gaze distant. "Just... be careful. Ethan's not as strong as he thinks he is."

"We will," Annika promised.

With that, they turned and made their way back through the darkened bookstore, the tension thrumming between them like a live wire. When they stepped outside, the cool night air hit them like a slap, washing away some of the oppressive weight of the conversation.

"David, status?" Nathan murmured into his comm.

"Clear," David replied. "No sign of movement."

"Let's move out," Nathan said.

They slipped back into the sedan, and Nathan started the engine, pulling away from the bookstore with practiced ease. The streetlights cast long shadows across the road, the city around them quiet and still.

Annika stared out the window, her mind racing. The Veritas Files. If Ethan really had a lead on them, it could be the key to everything. But it also meant he was in even more danger than they'd thought.

"He's a liability," Nathan murmured, his voice low and tense. "If he's this deep, we need to pull him out before it's too late."

"We will," Annika said softly, her gaze never leaving the passing cityscape. "But we have to be smart about it."

Nathan glanced at her, his expression tight. "You're worried."

"Yeah," Annika admitted. "But not just about him. About what happens if we do find those files. This isn't just going to take down Lansing. It's going to burn a lot of people."

"Then let it burn," Nathan said grimly.

Annika nodded slowly, but the unease in her chest didn't ease. "Yeah. Let it burn."

They drove on in silence, the weight of the mission pressing down on them both. But beneath it all, there was a flicker of something else, hope. If they could find Ethan, if they could get their hands on the Veritas Files, they could finally bring Reichter's empire crashing down.

And this time, there would be no escape.

Chapter 9

The morning sun barely peeked over the horizon as the Patriots regrouped in the safe house's command room. It had been another long night with few hours of sleep, but none of them showed signs of slowing down. They were used to running on adrenaline and willpower alone, pushing themselves beyond the limits that would have broken most people. There was something in the air that morning, a sense of urgency and anticipation. They were on the cusp of something big, and every one of them felt it.

James Donovan stood at the head of the room, his gaze sweeping over his team. They'd been through hell together, each of them carrying their own scars, their own burdens. But they were still here, still standing.

"Let's get started," he said quietly, and the murmur of conversation ceased as all eyes turned to him. "We're moving in two directions now. Annika and Nathan, you're going to focus on getting close to Ethan Lansing. That means following up on the lead Grant gave us, this Carl Thompson guy. I want you to make contact, find out what he knows about the Veritas Files."

Annika nodded, her expression resolute. "We'll head to the club tonight. If Thompson's there, we'll get him to talk."

"Carefully," James emphasized. "We don't want to spook him. If Ethan's in as deep as we think, Thompson will be on high alert. Approach him slowly, see what he's willing to share."

"Understood," Nathan said, leaning back in his chair. He glanced at Annika, his gaze steady. "We'll play it cool."

"Good." James turned to the rest of the team. "David, Sarah, and Kane, your focus is Robert Lansing. We need to know what he's doing and who he's meeting with. If we can establish a pattern, we might be able to predict his next move."

"I've already pulled his recent call logs," Kane said, his fingers moving deftly over the keyboard. "Most of it's standard government communications, meetings with other Homeland Security officials, briefings, that sort of thing. But there's one number that's been popping up more frequently than usual. It's a burner, and the calls have been short, less than a minute each time. I'm working on tracing it."

"That could be our connection to Reichter," David said, leaning over Kane's shoulder to study the screen. "If we can identify who's on the other end of that call, we might be able to get a clearer picture of how deep this goes."

"Exactly," James said. "Sarah, I want you to work with Kane on that. See if you can cross-reference the timing of those calls with Lansing's schedule. If we can figure out where and when he's making those calls, we might be able to intercept."

"On it," Sarah said quietly, already pulling up a new set of files on her laptop.

David straightened, his gaze intent. "And in the meantime?"

"In the meantime, we keep an eye on Lansing's movements. If he heads somewhere unexpected or deviates from his routine, we need to be ready to move."

There was a murmur of agreement, the tension in the room palpable. They all knew what was at stake. One wrong move, and Lansing could disappear—taking all of Reichter's secrets with him.

"Alright," James said softly. "Let's get to work."

A Quiet Moment

As the team broke off into smaller groups, James moved to the back of the room, his gaze lingering on the maps and charts spread across the walls. He felt a presence beside him and turned to see David standing there, his expression thoughtful.

"Something on your mind?" James asked quietly.

David shrugged, his gaze drifting to the map of Washington, D.C. pinned to the wall. "Just thinking about how far we've come. And how much further we have to go."

James nodded slowly. "It's been a long road."

"Yeah," David murmured. He glanced at James, a flicker of concern in his eyes. "You holding up okay?"

James managed a faint smile. "I should be asking you that."

David snorted softly, shaking his head. "I'm fine. Just... you know how it is. One step forward, two steps back. But this thing with Ethan, it feels different. Like we're finally getting somewhere."

"We are," James said firmly. "We've got momentum now. We just need to keep pushing."

"Right," David murmured. He hesitated, then added, "But don't push yourself too hard, okay? We need you in this fight, James. All of you."

The sincerity in David's voice caught James off guard, and for a moment, the weight of everything, the sleepless nights, the endless tension, seemed to settle more heavily on his shoulders.

"I'm not going anywhere," he said softly. "We're going to see this through, David. No matter what."

David nodded, his expression easing slightly. "Good. Because I've got a feeling the next few days are going to get rough."

"They always do," James said wryly. "But we're used to rough, aren't we?"

David chuckled, a low, rumbling sound that held more warmth than amusement. "Yeah. I guess we are."

With that, David clapped James on the shoulder and moved off to rejoin Sarah and Kane. James watched him go, a sense of gratitude settling in his chest. They'd been through so much together, lost people, fought battles they hadn't always won. But they were still here, still standing side by side.

And as long as they had each other, they could face whatever came next.

Tracking the Enemy

The hours passed in a blur of data and quiet conversation. The command room hummed with activity, the low murmur of voices mixing with the faint clatter of keyboards and the rustle of papers. Kane and Sarah worked in tandem, dissecting Robert Lansing's communications, while Annika and Nathan reviewed their strategy for approaching Carl Thompson.

It was during one of these quiet lulls that Kane suddenly straightened, his eyes widening as a new string of data appeared on his screen.

"Guys," he said, his voice cutting through the silence. "I think I've got something."

The others immediately converged on his workstation, their expressions alert.

"What is it?" James asked, leaning over Kane's shoulder.

"Lansing just made a call to that burner number," Kane said, his gaze fixed on the screen. "It was only ten seconds, but look at the location ping."

He tapped a few keys, and a small red dot appeared on the map of D.C., marking a point just outside the city center.

"That's near the Arlington Memorial Bridge," Sarah murmured, frowning. "What's there?"

"Nothing obvious," Kane said. "But the location is odd. It's not a business district or a residential area. The call could have been routed through a tower there, or... wait."

He zoomed in on the map, his eyes narrowing. "There's an old federal building nearby. It's mostly abandoned, but I did some digging, it used to be a storage facility for Homeland Security records."

"Abandoned?" James asked, his gaze sharpening.

"Yeah," Kane confirmed. "Officially, it's been shut down for years. But if Lansing's meeting someone there, it could mean there's something left behind. Files, equipment, something he doesn't want traced back to him."

"Or something he's trying to get rid of," Annika added quietly. "If Lansing's cleaning house, this could be where he's disposing of evidence."

James nodded slowly. "It's worth checking out. David, Annika, I want you to head over there. See what you can find. But keep it quiet, no alarms, no backup. If Lansing's using that location, it means he's got eyes on it."

David nodded. "We'll be ghosts."

"Good." James glanced at Sarah and Kane. "You two keep monitoring his communications. If Lansing makes another move, I want to know about it immediately."

"We're on it," Sarah said, her expression intent.

"Alright," James said softly. "Let's move."

Reconnaissance at the Memorial Bridge

The drive to the Arlington Memorial Bridge was quiet, the tension in the car thick and palpable. Annika sat in the passenger seat, her gaze focused on the road ahead. David drove with his usual calm precision, his eyes flicking to the rearview mirror every few seconds.

"You ready for this?" David asked quietly as they approached the bridge.

"Always," Annika murmured, but there was a note of uncertainty in her voice.

David glanced at her, his brow furrowing. "What's on your mind?"

Annika hesitated, then sighed softly. "It's just... if the Veritas Files really exist, this could be bigger than anything we've ever dealt with.

It won't just take down Reichter and Lansing, it could expose entire networks of corruption. People we didn't even know were involved."

"Then we do what we always do," David said firmly. "We adapt. We dig deep, find the truth, and expose it."

"But at what cost?" Annika whispered, her gaze distant. "How many lives are we going to destroy to get to it?"

David was silent for a moment, then reached out, his hand brushing hers briefly. "We're not the ones destroying lives, Annika. They are. We're just pulling back the curtain. Whatever happens after that... it's on them."

Annika nodded slowly, but the unease in her chest didn't ease. "Yeah. I just hope we're ready for what we find."

"We will be," David said quietly, his gaze steady on the road. "We always are."

The car rolled to a stop a few blocks away from the federal building. They had chosen a secluded spot on a side street, out of view of any potential surveillance cameras or passing vehicles. David killed the engine, and the two of them sat in silence for a moment, each mentally preparing for what came next.

David reached into the glove compartment and pulled out a small black case. He opened it to reveal two sets of earpieces, a compact camera, and a pair of suppressors. He handed one earpiece and a suppressor to Annika, who took them with a nod of thanks.

"Let's do this clean and quiet," David murmured as they fitted the equipment.

"Like ghosts," Annika agreed, echoing his earlier words.

With a final nod, they slipped out of the car and moved down the deserted street, sticking to the shadows. The old federal building loomed up ahead, an imposing structure of concrete and steel, its windows dark and empty. It looked as though it had been abandoned for decades, but something about the way the security gate was half-open, the faint glow of light from one of the upper windows, suggested otherwise.

"Building looks empty from the outside," Annika whispered into her comm. "But I'm seeing signs of recent activity, footprints in the dust by the door, a couple of fresh cigarette butts near the entrance. Someone's been here recently."

"Copy that," Nathan's voice crackled softly through the earpiece. "I'm tracking you from the car. No movement outside. Proceed with caution."

Annika and David exchanged a glance, then moved toward the side of the building, keeping low and silent. They reached a small, rusted door that looked like it hadn't been opened in years. But when David pressed against it, the door swung inward with a soft creak, revealing a narrow corridor lined with peeling paint and flickering fluorescent lights.

"Clear," David murmured, stepping inside and holding the door for Annika.

They moved through the building with practiced efficiency, their footsteps muffled against the cracked linoleum floor. Each room they passed was empty, filled with only the remnants of old office furniture and forgotten file cabinets. But the further they went, the more the hairs on the back of Annika's neck stood up.

"This place feels... wrong," she whispered as they rounded a corner, pausing at the edge of a stairwell that led down into the basement. The air was thick and stale, carrying the faint scent of mildew and something acrid, like chemicals.

"I know what you mean," David replied quietly. "But if Lansing's been using this place, it's for a reason. Let's see what he's hiding."

They descended the stairs, their breaths slow and controlled. The basement was even darker, the only light coming from the weak glow of a single emergency bulb near the end of the hallway. David pulled out a small flashlight and clicked it on, casting a narrow beam of light that cut through the gloom.

The hallway stretched out before them, lined with heavy metal doors, each one marked with a number. Most of them were ajar, revealing nothing but empty rooms filled with dust and debris. But as they approached the last door on the left, they both froze.

This door was different. It was shut tight, the metal gleaming as if it had been recently polished. A thick padlock hung from the handle, and a faint hum of electricity vibrated through the air.

David glanced at Annika, raising an eyebrow. "Think this is it?"

"Only one way to find out," she murmured, reaching into her pocket and pulling out a set of slim lockpicks.

David watched her work, his gaze sharp and focused. Annika's fingers moved deftly, her touch light and precise as she manipulated the tumblers within the lock. After a few tense moments, there was a soft click, and the padlock fell away.

"Nice work," David whispered.

Annika flashed him a quick smile, then pushed the door open slowly, peering inside.

The room beyond was small, no more than ten feet by ten feet, but it was filled with an array of equipment, computers, file cabinets, and stacks of documents. A single laptop sat on a metal table in the center of the room, its screen glowing softly in the darkness.

"Bingo," Annika breathed, stepping inside.

David followed, his gaze sweeping the room. "Looks like this is where Lansing's been doing his dirty work. Let's see what we've got."

Annika moved to the laptop and began scrolling through its contents, her eyes narrowing as lines of text and numbers flashed across the screen.

"This is it," she whispered, her heart pounding. "Financial records, communication logs... it's all here. He's been funneling money through multiple shell companies, using them to bribe officials, fund covert operations, even support extremist groups overseas. And look, there's a file labeled '*Veritas.'"

David moved closer, his breath catching. "Open it."

Annika hesitated, then clicked on the file. The screen went dark for a moment, then a series of images and documents appeared. Each one was more damning than the last, photographs of secret meetings, transcripts of conversations between high-ranking officials, details of covert deals that had changed the course of entire nations.

"Jesus," David whispered, his voice tight. "This... this is everything. This is enough to take down half the government."

"Which means it's exactly what Reichter and Lansing don't want us to have," Annika murmured. "We need to get this back to the team. But we need to be careful."

"Agreed." David pulled out a portable hard drive and handed it to her. "Copy everything. I'll keep watch."

Annika nodded, inserting the drive into the laptop and beginning the transfer. The minutes stretched on in tense silence, every small sound, every creak of the building, every hum of the laptop's processor, amplified in the stillness.

Finally, the transfer completed, and Annika removed the hard drive, slipping it into her pocket. "Got it. Let's move."

They turned to leave, but as they stepped into the hallway, they both froze.

Footsteps echoed from the stairwell above, slow and deliberate.

"Shit," David hissed, his hand going to the gun holstered at his side. "We've got company."

Annika's heart pounded in her chest, adrenaline surging through her veins. "It's gotta be Lansing's people. They must've known someone was here."

"Or they've been monitoring the laptop," David whispered. "Doesn't matter. We need to get out, now."

They moved quickly and silently down the hallway, sticking to the shadows. But as they reached the base of the stairs, the footsteps grew louder, closer. Annika exchanged a glance with David, and he nodded once, his jaw set.

"Follow me," he murmured, taking a step back and scanning the hallway for any alternative exits.

There, a narrow vent near the floor, just big enough to crawl through. It was covered by a rusty grate, but David wrenched it off with a sharp tug, then motioned for Annika to go first.

"Hurry," he whispered, his gaze flicking nervously toward the stairwell.

Annika dropped to her knees and squeezed into the vent, wincing as the metal scraped against her arms and shoulders. The air inside was thick and musty, but she forced herself to keep moving, inching forward until she reached the end of the vent.

"Clear," she whispered back.

David followed, his larger frame making the tight space even more difficult to navigate. But he made it through, the grate clanging softly as he pulled it back into place behind them.

They crouched in the darkness for a moment, their breaths harsh and ragged. Then, slowly, they moved forward, navigating the vent system with painstaking care.

Finally, they reached another grate, this one opening out onto an alley behind the building. Annika pushed it open and slipped out, breathing in the cool night air like a lifeline.

David emerged behind her, his expression grim. "We need to get back to the car. Now."

They moved quickly but quietly, sticking to the shadows until they reached the car. Nathan's voice crackled through their earpieces.

"What's your status?"

"We've got the data," Annika whispered, her heart still racing. "But we've also got trouble. Lansing's people showed up while we were inside."

"Get out of there," Nathan ordered. "We'll figure out our next move back at the safe house."

"Copy that," David murmured as he started the engine, pulling away from the curb.

They drove in tense silence, every turn of the wheel, every passing car sending a jolt of adrenaline through Annika's system. But no one followed them, and as they left the old federal building behind, she felt a small spark of hope flicker in her chest.

They had the Veritas Files. They had the proof they needed.

But as they approached the safe house, she couldn't shake the feeling that they'd only just begun to uncover the true depths of Reichter's conspiracy.

And that the real fight was only just beginning.

Chapter 10

The safe house was steeped in a tense silence as dawn broke over Washington, D.C. The Patriots moved through the hallways quietly, each of them carrying the weight of what was to come. The morning felt fragile, as if a single word could shatter the calm and send everything spiraling into chaos.

James Donovan stood alone in the command center, his eyes scanning the digital map displayed on the main screen. The layout of the server farm outside Baltimore flickered with red and green indicators, showing the locations of cameras, patrols, and access points. It was a fortress, a testament to Lansing's paranoia and obsession with control. But it was also their target.

"Everything set?" Nathan Cross's voice broke through James's concentration.

James turned to see Nathan standing in the doorway, his expression serious but steady. He gave a brief nod. "We're as ready as we'll ever be."

Nathan moved to stand beside him, his gaze sweeping over the map. "You've got that look again."

"What look?" James asked, raising an eyebrow.

"The one that says you're carrying the weight of the world on your shoulders," Nathan replied quietly. "We're in this together, you know. All of us."

James exhaled slowly, a faint smile tugging at his lips. "Yeah. I know."

Nathan clapped him on the shoulder, his touch firm and reassuring. "We've got your back, James. Whatever happens tonight, we'll get through it."

James nodded, his gaze softening. Nathan's unwavering loyalty had been a cornerstone of their team, a steadying force that had kept them grounded through the most turbulent of times. He reached up, covering Nathan's hand with his own in a brief, silent acknowledgment.

"Thanks, Nate."

"Don't mention it," Nathan said with a faint smile. "Now let's get everyone together. We've got a mission to run."

The Patriots gathered in the command room, their expressions solemn but determined. Annika, dressed in her usual tactical gear, sat beside David, her gaze fixed on the digital display. Sarah and Kane were huddled together by the far wall, whispering softly as they made final adjustments to the comms system. James stood at the head of the table, his presence a calming anchor amidst the storm of nerves and anticipation.

"Alright, everyone," James began, his voice firm and steady. "We've been through the plan a dozen times, but let's go over it one more time. Our primary objective is to neutralize Lansing's failsafe at the server farm. Once we've shut it down, we'll be able to move on Lansing and Reichter without the threat of a mass data release hanging over our heads."

David leaned forward, his fingers tracing the lines on the map. "We'll breach from the west side of the facility, here, using the blind spot in their camera coverage. From there, we'll split into two teams. Annika and I will handle the security grid, taking out any remaining cameras and disabling their backup power system."

"Meanwhile, Nathan and I will move to the main server room," James continued. "Kane will guide us through the digital security protocols, and Sarah will monitor Lansing's communications. If there's even a hint that he's onto us, we pull out immediately."

Kane nodded, his expression focused. "I'll keep an eye on all incoming and outgoing data streams. If Lansing tries to send a signal or activate any of his backup systems, I'll shut it down."

"And once we're inside?" Sarah asked, her voice soft but clear.

"We locate the primary server," James said. "It'll be isolated, likely in a secured room with limited access. That's where Lansing will have stored the master files. We extract the data, wipe the servers, and get out."

"Quick and clean," Nathan murmured. "No unnecessary risks."

"Right," James said firmly. "We've got a narrow window of opportunity here. We move fast, stay focused, and get out before they know we're there."

There was a murmur of agreement around the table, the tension in the room building like a coiled spring.

"Alright," James said softly, looking at each of them in turn. "We've all faced worse than this. We know what's at stake. But we've also got each other's backs. Remember that. We're not alone in this fight."

He paused, letting his gaze linger on each of them, Annika, with her fierce determination; Nathan, steady and unflinching; David, focused and precise; Sarah, quiet but unyielding; and Kane, brilliant and relentless.

"We're a team," James continued, his voice low and steady. "We've always been a team. No matter what happens tonight, we do this together."

There was a moment of silence, a shared understanding passing between them. Then Nathan stepped forward, a faint smile curving his lips.

"Let's bring these bastards down," he said quietly.

Night fell swiftly, casting the server farm in a shroud of darkness. The facility was a sprawling complex of concrete and steel, surrounded by high fences and patrolled by armed guards. The Patriots moved through the shadows like ghosts, their movements precise and silent.

David led the way, his senses attuned to every sound, every flicker of movement. Annika moved beside him, her gaze sweeping the perimeter as they approached the western entrance.

"Cameras are down," Kane's voice crackled softly through their earpieces. "You're clear to proceed."

"Copy that," David murmured, reaching out to disable the electronic lock on the gate.

Annika slipped through first, her gun at the ready. The courtyard beyond was empty, the only sound the faint hum of electricity from the nearby power lines. She glanced back at David, who nodded, then gestured for the others to follow.

"Stay low and keep to the shadows," James whispered, his voice barely audible. "We don't want to engage unless we have to."

They moved as a single unit, navigating the maze of security barriers and checkpoints with practiced ease. Every step was deliberate, every breath measured. Annika's heart pounded in her chest, the anticipation thrumming through her veins like a live wire.

"Approaching main entry point," David reported softly. "Annika, take the lead."

Annika nodded and stepped forward, her eyes locked on the keypad beside the reinforced steel door. She pulled out a small device from her pack and attached it to the keypad. The device hummed softly, a series of numbers flashing across its screen.

"Override initiated," she murmured, her fingers flying over the controls. "Ten seconds."

The seconds ticked by with agonizing slowness. Then, with a soft beep, the keypad turned green, and the door slid open.

"Good work," James said quietly. "Let's move."

They slipped inside, the door sliding shut behind them with a quiet hiss. The interior of the building was dimly lit, the walls lined with rows of server racks and tangled cables. The air was cool and sterile, the faint hum of machinery filling the silence.

"David, Annika, handle the security grid," James murmured. "Nathan, you're with me."

David and Annika broke off, moving toward the secondary control room. The door was locked, but Annika made quick work of it, her lockpicks glinting briefly in the low light.

"Grid control's just ahead," David whispered as they entered the small, cluttered room. "I'll take out the main feed. You handle the backups."

"Copy," Annika replied, her hands moving deftly over the control panel.

"Disabling main feed... now," David muttered, his gaze fixed on the readouts. "All cameras and motion sensors are down."

"Switching off backups," Annika confirmed. She hesitated for a moment, then looked up at David, her expression serious. "This is it."

David nodded slowly. "We're committed now. No turning back."

"Right," Annika murmured, taking a deep breath. "Let's get this done."

Meanwhile, James and Nathan moved deeper into the facility, following the schematic layout Kane had provided. They reached a large, reinforced door marked "Primary Server Access." A digital lock glowed faintly beside it, its security level far beyond anything they'd encountered so far.

"This is it," James whispered, glancing at Nathan. "We're going in."

Nathan nodded, stepping forward to examine the lock. "This is military-grade. We'll need Kane to bypass it."

"Kane," James murmured into his comm. "We need a remote bypass on the main access lock. Can you do it?"

"Give me a minute," Kane replied, his voice tense. "Sending a code injection now... Okay, try it."

Nathan keyed in the code, and the lock flashed green. The door slid open with a low hum, revealing a large, sterile room filled with towering server racks.

"Primary server's at the far end," Nathan said, his gaze sweeping the room. "Let's move."

They made their way through the maze of equipment, the air thick with the hum of machinery and the faint scent of ozone. Every step felt heavier, every breath laced with anticipation.

"Got it," James whispered as they reached the main server terminal. He pulled out a portable drive and inserted it into the terminal's port. "Kane, we're in. Starting the download now."

"Copy that," Kane replied. "I'm monitoring the data stream. You've got about five minutes before the system starts flagging the activity."

"Five minutes," James murmured. "Let's make it count."

The download bar inched forward with agonizing slowness, the small green line crawling across the screen. James kept his gaze locked on it, his muscles tensed for any sign of trouble. Nathan stood beside him, his eyes scanning the room, every sense on high alert.

"Kane, status?" James murmured, his voice barely more than a whisper.

"You're at thirty percent," Kane replied, his voice tense. "No alarms yet, but I'm seeing some unusual activity on the network. It's like the system is sensing something's off but can't quite pinpoint it yet. We need to hurry."

"Understood," James said softly, his heart pounding in his chest. "Keep monitoring."

The seconds ticked by, each one stretching into an eternity. James watched the download progress, his breath shallow. Fifty percent. Sixty percent. The hum of the servers filled the room, a low, steady pulse that seemed to match the beat of his racing heart.

"Eighty percent," Kane reported. "Come on, come on..."

Suddenly, a soft chime echoed through the room, and the terminal's screen flickered.

"Uh, guys?" Kane's voice crackled through the comms, laced with urgency. "The system's picking up on the intrusion. You've got about two minutes before it locks you out, and sends an alert straight to Lansing."

James exchanged a quick glance with Nathan, his jaw tightening. "How much longer?"

"Ninety percent," Kane said, his voice rising slightly. "Just a little more..."

James clenched his fists, willing the download bar to move faster. "Come on..."

The green line inched forward, and then, finally, with a soft beep, the screen flashed.

"Download complete," Kane said, relief flooding his voice. "You've got it all."

James didn't waste a second. He yanked the portable drive from the terminal and slipped it into his pocket, his gaze already shifting to the door. "We're moving out."

Nathan nodded, his expression tense. "Let's go."

They turned and made their way back through the server room, their movements quick and efficient. But as they reached the door, a shrill alarm suddenly blared to life, echoing through the facility.

"Shit," Nathan hissed, his gaze snapping to the ceiling-mounted cameras. "We're made."

"Kane, what's happening?" James demanded, his voice tight.

"The system flagged the data transfer," Kane said, his voice filled with urgency. "It's broadcasting an alert across all channels. Every guard in that place is about to converge on your location."

"Annika, David," James barked into his comm. "We're compromised. Get to the extraction point, now!"

"On our way," Annika's voice crackled through the earpiece. "David and I are moving. We'll meet you at the west exit."

James and Nathan bolted from the server room, sprinting down the narrow hallways. The lights overhead flashed red, casting eerie shadows along the walls. Footsteps echoed from somewhere nearby, and the unmistakable clatter of boots on concrete sent a jolt of adrenaline through James's veins.

"Left," Nathan murmured, his voice calm despite the chaos. "Take the next left."

They rounded the corner just as a group of guards appeared at the far end of the hall, their guns raised. James didn't hesitate. He dove to the side, his weapon drawn, and fired off a quick burst. The guards scattered, ducking behind cover as bullets ricocheted off the walls.

"Go, go!" Nathan shouted, covering James's flank as they sprinted down the hallway.

They burst through a set of double doors and into a sprawling storage area filled with towering metal shelves and crates. The sound of gunfire echoed behind them, growing louder with each passing second.

"West exit's two floors up," Nathan said, his breath coming in short, controlled gasps. "Elevator's out, have to take the stairs."

James nodded, his gaze scanning the room. He spotted the stairwell door at the far end and motioned to Nathan. "This way!"

They raced across the room, the pounding of their footsteps drowned out by the blaring alarm. Just as they reached the stairwell, the door burst open, and Annika and David appeared, their faces set in grim determination.

"You two always know how to make an entrance," David muttered, his gun raised as he scanned the hallway behind them.

"We like to keep things exciting," Nathan shot back, his eyes glinting with a hint of humor despite the danger.

"Let's move!" Annika said sharply, gesturing to the stairs. "Guards are converging from all sides. We don't have much time."

They bolted up the stairs, their movements quick and precise. The stairwell echoed with the sounds of boots thundering up the steps, but they kept moving, each step bringing them closer to the exit.

"Second floor," James murmured. "We're almost there."

They burst through the door onto the second floor, their weapons at the ready. The hallway beyond was empty, but they could hear the distant shouts of guards and the clatter of weapons being loaded.

"West exit's through here," Annika said, leading the way.

They sprinted down the hallway, their breaths harsh and ragged. The west exit loomed up ahead, a heavy steel door marked with a red "Emergency Exit" sign. David reached it first, his fingers flying over the keypad as he keyed in the override code.

"Come on, come on..." he muttered, his eyes narrowing as the door beeped and the lock disengaged.

The door swung open, and they spilled out into the cool night air. The courtyard beyond was dark and deserted, the faint glow of the moon casting long shadows across the pavement.

"Extraction point's a hundred yards west," David murmured, glancing around. "We need to move."

They bolted across the courtyard, keeping low and sticking to the shadows. The sound of sirens wailed in the distance, growing louder with each passing second.

"Move faster!" Kane's voice crackled through their earpieces. "I'm seeing activity on the perimeter. Guards are closing in from the north and east!"

"Copy that," James murmured. "We're almost at the extraction point."

They rounded a corner, and the dark shape of an SUV came into view, its engine idling quietly. Nathan reached the vehicle first, yanking the door open and motioning for the others to get inside.

"Go, go, go!" he shouted as they piled into the vehicle.

James slid into the passenger seat, his heart racing as David floored the accelerator, the tires screeching against the pavement. They shot forward, the SUV weaving through the narrow access roads that crisscrossed the facility's grounds.

"Perimeter's about to be locked down," Kane warned. "You've got maybe thirty seconds before they seal the gates."

"Noted," David muttered, his knuckles white on the steering wheel.

They sped toward the perimeter fence, the looming metal barrier a stark silhouette against the night sky. A gate up ahead began to close, the heavy steel panels sliding together with a low groan.

"We're not gonna make it," Nathan hissed, his gaze locked on the closing gate.

"Yes, we are," David growled, his foot pressing down on the accelerator.

The SUV roared forward, the engine straining as they hurtled toward the narrowing gap. James gritted his teeth, bracing himself as the vehicle shot through the gate, the metal panels slamming shut inches behind them.

"Damn," Nathan breathed, his eyes wide. "That was close."

"Too close," Annika muttered, her gaze flickering to the rearview mirror.

They sped away from the facility, the sound of sirens fading into the distance. The SUV's interior was filled with the harsh rasp of their breathing, the adrenaline still coursing through their veins.

"Status?" James asked, his voice low and steady.

"All clear," Kane replied, relief flooding his tone. "You're out. No pursuit."

"Good," James murmured, leaning back in his seat. "Good work, everyone."

There was a moment of silence, then Annika let out a shaky breath, a faint smile tugging at her lips. "We did it."

"Yeah," Nathan murmured, his gaze distant. "But the hard part's just beginning."

"Agreed," James said softly. He reached into his pocket, pulling out the portable drive they'd risked everything to obtain. "We've got the data. Now it's time to bring the fight to Lansing."

• • • •

The mood in the safe house was a strange mix of relief and tension when they returned. They'd made it out alive, but the mission was far from over.

Kane immediately set to work, plugging the drive into his secure terminal and bringing up the files. The rest of the team gathered around, their expressions grim as they watched the data unfold on the screen.

"It's all here," Kane said softly, his eyes widening as he scrolled through the files. "Every transaction, every communication... It's enough to take down Lansing and everyone connected to him."

"But it's not just Lansing, Reichter's name is all over this. He's been using Lansing as a front, laundering money through his operations and using it to finance covert projects."

"And here..." Kane pulled up a series of encrypted messages. "There's correspondence between Reichter and a half-dozen other operatives, discussing contingency plans. They're preparing for something big."

James's gaze hardened as he leaned closer to the screen. "What kind of contingency plans?"

Kane's fingers moved rapidly over the keys, decrypting the files and scanning through pages of data. His brow furrowed as he pulled up a series of detailed blueprints and schedules.

"It looks like they've got multiple safe houses and fallback locations scattered across the U.S.," Kane said, his voice grim. "There's one in Virginia, another in Texas, and several overseas. But that's not all, these documents detail personnel movements and plans for a rapid evacuation. They're preparing to disappear if we get too close."

"Which means they know someone's coming," Nathan muttered, his jaw tightening. "This isn't just a contingency plan, it's an exit strategy. Reichter's trying to get ahead of us."

"They're ready to cut and run," Annika added, her eyes narrowed as she scanned the files. "If Lansing thinks he's exposed, he'll disappear. We need to move fast, before they have a chance to vanish."

"Agreed," James said softly, his mind racing as he absorbed the information. "We've got to strike now, before they can activate these plans. If we let Lansing slip through our fingers, we might not get another chance."

"But we can't just go in blind," Sarah interjected, her voice calm and measured. "We need a plan, a way to hit them where it hurts, to disrupt their escape routes and cut off their resources."

"Right," James murmured, nodding thoughtfully. He glanced at Kane. "Can you map out their communications and financial transactions? I want to know who they're working with, who's financing them, and where their money's moving."

"Already on it," Kane said, his fingers flying over the keyboard. "Give me a few minutes."

James turned to Annika and Nathan, his gaze steady. "We're going to need boots on the ground. If we can disrupt their movements, we can force them into the open."

Nathan nodded, his expression fierce. "We'll take point. Just give us the locations, and we'll make sure they don't go anywhere."

"And I'll coordinate the intel," Sarah said. "If we can identify key personnel, people who are critical to their escape plans, we can target them directly. Make it impossible for Reichter and Lansing to move without us knowing."

"Good," James said softly, his gaze shifting to David. "I want you to handle the tactical side. Map out the best approach for each location, plan the entries and exits. We need to be in and out before they even know what hit them."

David nodded sharply. "I'll set up a series of tactical briefs for each team. We'll be ready."

There was a quiet determination in the air as the team fell into their roles, each of them focusing on their tasks with laser-like precision. This was what they were good at, taking down powerful enemies piece by piece, dismantling their operations until there was nothing left but the truth.

James watched them for a moment, a sense of pride and resolve swelling in his chest. They'd been through so much together, faced so many impossible odds. But they were still here, still standing. And now, they were closer than ever to bringing down the men who'd been hiding in the shadows for so long.

"Let's break this down," James said, his voice steady. "We're hitting three primary locations: the server farm's sister sites in Virginia and Texas, and the primary fallback location Reichter's set up in New York. We'll coordinate simultaneous strikes. Nathan and Annika, you'll take Virginia. David and I will handle Texas. Sarah, you'll run command and control from here with Kane's support."

"What about New York?" Nathan asked, his gaze narrowing. "That's a lot to cover with just two teams."

"We'll bring in support for New York," James said. "I've got a few contacts who owe me favors, former operatives who can help lock down the perimeter and keep Reichter pinned. We won't let him slip through our fingers."

There was a murmur of agreement around the room, the tension easing slightly as the plan took shape.

"Kane, how's the data looking?" James asked, turning back to the tech genius.

"Still parsing through it," Kane muttered, his eye, people who've been coordinating these movements. I'm seeing connections to a few familiar faces. Looks like Reichter's using a lot of the same operatives who were part of the Rothschild operation."

"Loyalty, or leverage?" Annika murmured, her gaze thoughtful.

"Probably both," James said. "But that means we've got the advantage. We know their playbook. We've seen it before."

"Which means we can predict their moves," Nathan said quietly. "Force them into positions where they're vulnerable."

"Exactly," James murmured. "We're going to hit them hard and fast. No mercy."

There was a moment of silence, the gravity of what lay ahead settling over them like a heavy weight. Then Annika straightened, her gaze fierce and unyielding.

"We've come this far," she said softly. "We're not backing down now."

"No," James agreed, his voice low and steady. "We're not."

The hours stretched into the early evening as they continued to refine the plan, each of them pushing themselves to the limit. By the time they broke for a brief rest, the safe house was filled with the quiet buzz of anticipation.

Annika found herself alone in the small kitchen, nursing a cup of black coffee. She stared down at the dark liquid, her mind racing with everything they'd uncovered. They were so close, closer than they'd ever been. But the stakes had never been higher.

"Hey."

She looked up to see Nathan standing in the doorway, his expression softening as he met her gaze. He moved to stand beside her, leaning against the counter.

"You okay?" he asked quietly.

Annika managed a faint smile. "Yeah. Just... thinking."

"About what?"

"About what happens next," she murmured, her gaze distant. "If we take down Lansing and Reichter... what's left? What do we do then?"

Nathan shrugged lightly, finding the people who need to be stopped, and stopping them."

Annika nodded slowly, her fingers tightening around the cup. "It's just... this is big, Nathan. Bigger than anything we've faced. What if... "

"Hey," Nathan interrupted gently, reaching out to cover her hand with his own. "We've got this, Annika. We've faced worse, and we've made it through. We'll make it through this too."

Annika looked up at him, her heart swelling with gratitude. Nathan's steady presence, his unwavering confidence, it had been her anchor through so many storms. She reached out, squeezing his hand briefly before letting go.

"Thanks, Nate," she murmured.

"Anytime," he said softly. "You know that."

There was a moment of silence, a shared understanding passing between them. Then Nathan smiled, a faint twinkle of mischief in his eyes.

"Now, come on. Kane's probably about to blow a fuse if we don't get back in there and keep him in check."

Annika laughed softly, the tension easing slightly. "Yeah, you're probably right."

They made their way back to the command room, where the rest of the team was gathered. Kane was hunched over his workstation, his fingers flying over the keyboard, while Sarah and David pored over the maps and blueprints spread across the table.

"Alright, everyone," James said as they rejoined the group. "This is it. We're moving out in an hour. Get your gear, check your comms, and be ready."

There was a murmur of agreement, the air crackling with anticipation.

"Remember," James continued, his gaze sweeping over each of them. "We're going in fast and hard. We take out the servers, neutralize the failsafe, and force Lansing and Reichter into the open. No mistakes. No second chances."

He paused, his gaze lingering on each of them. "We've been through hell together. We've fought battles most people can't even imagine. But we're still here. We're still fighting. And we're going to finish this, together."

The silence that followed was filled with unspoken words, the bond between them stronger than ever. Then, one by one, they nodded, resolve etched into every line of their faces.

"Let's bring these bastards down," Nathan murmured, his voice low and fierce.

They moved as one, gathering their gear and making final preparations. The calm before the storm settled over them, a strange, almost surreal sense of stillness that belied the chaos that was about to erupt.

James stood by the door, watching his team with a sense of pride and determination.

"This is it," he whispered softly. "The beginning of the end."

And as the Patriots stepped out into the night, ready to bring down the shadows that had haunted them for so long, there was no doubt in his mind that they would succeed.

Because they were more than a team. They were family. And together, they were unstoppable.

Chapter 11

The SUV's tires crunched over gravel as the Patriots pulled into a secluded lot deep in the Maryland woods. Moonlight filtered through the dense canopy above, casting long shadows that flickered across the ground like ghostly sentinels. It was a place that seemed designed to swallow sound and light, leaving only a hushed stillness in its wake. They'd chosen this location for the final briefing before splitting into their respective teams, a place far from prying eyes and ears.

James Donovan stepped out of the vehicle first, his eyes scanning the treeline with the sharpness of a hawk. The air was cool and crisp, carrying with it the faint scent of pine and damp earth. He took a deep breath, letting the tension seep into his bones. The weight of what lay ahead settled heavily on his shoulders, but it was a familiar burden, one he'd carried countless times before.

The rest of the team gathered around the SUV, their faces etched with determination. Annika Valdez stood at James's left, her expression a mask of focus and resolve. Nathan Cross hovered near the rear of the vehicle, checking his gear one last time, while David Ellis unfolded a large tactical map on the hood, his fingers tracing routes and entry points with practiced ease.

Oliver Kane and Sarah Chen were the last to join them, the faint glow of their laptops casting a soft light over their features as they pulled up the latest satellite imagery and security feeds.

"Alright, everyone," James began, his voice low but firm. "This is it. Tonight, we hit three key locations: the server farm in Virginia, the communications hub in If we pull this off, we'll cripple Lansing's network and force Reichter into the open."

David nodded, his gaze locked on the map. "Nathan and Annika will take Virginia. I'll handle Texas with you, James. And we've got reinforcements ready for New York. We're covering all our bases."

"Good," James said softly. He glanced at Sarah and Kane. "You two will be running command and control from here. I want every piece of intel coming through you. If anything changes on the ground, I want to know about it immediately."

"Understood," Sarah said, her voice steady. "I'll monitor all communications and coordinate our movements. Kane's set up secure channels and remote access to their surveillance systems."

Kane nodded, his fingers tapping lightly against the screen of his laptop. "I've got eyes on all three locations. The moment we make our move, they'll know something's up, but we'll have the advantage. We're hitting them where they least expect it."

"Good," James repeated. He looked around at each of them, his gaze lingering on their faces. They'd been through so much together, fought battles that had pushed them to their limits. But through it all, they'd never faltered, never broken. And now, as they stood on the brink of their most dangerous mission yet, that bond felt stronger than ever.

"Whatever happens tonight," James said quietly, "we stick together. We watch each other's backs. No one gets left behind. Understood?"

There was a murmur of agreement, each voice carrying a thread of resolve and solidarity.

"Alright," James murmured, nodding. "Let's break this down one last time."

David pointed to the map, his expression intent. "Nathan and Annika will breach the server farm here, on the western perimeter. There's a gap in their camera coverage that should give you just enough time to get inside without being detected. Once you're in, you'll need to disable the security grid and access the primary server. Kane will guide you through the system and monitor for any signs of resistance."

"Got it," Annika said, her gaze flickering to Nathan. "We'll handle it."

"Once you've secured the data," James continued, "move to the secondary server room. There's a secondary control hub there that Lansing uses as a failsafe. Disable it, and you'll cut off his access to the entire network."

Nathan nodded sharply. "We'll take care of it."

"Good," James said, his gaze shifting to David. "You and I will be hitting the communications hub in Texas. It's heavily guarded, but if we can shut down their ability to communicate, we'll have a window to move on New York without them being able to coordinate a response."

David's jaw tightened, his eyes darkening. "We'll get in, take out their relay stations, and disrupt their comms. They won't even know what hit them."

"And New York?" Sarah asked, her brow furrowed.

"We'll coordinate with our backup team on the ground," James said. "They'll secure the perimeter and make sure no one leaves the safe house. Once we've neutralized Virginia and Texas, we'll converge on New York and take out the primary safe house. With Lansing's network crippled, Reichter will have nowhere left to run."

"Sounds like a plan," Kane murmured, his gaze still locked on his laptop. "I'm setting up backdoors into their systems now. Should be able to keep you one step ahead of their security protocols."

"Good," James said softly. He glanced around the group, his gaze steady. "We've got a lot of moving parts here, but we've prepared for this. We know what we're up against, and we know how to beat them. Let's stay focused, stay sharp, and get the job done."

There was a moment of silence, then Nathan stepped forward, his eyes glinting with determination.

"Let's show them what we're made of."

An hour later, Annika and Nathan moved silently through the dense forest that bordered the Virginia server farm. The moon hung high above, casting a faint silver glow over the landscape. The air was thick with tension, every rustle of leaves and snap of a twig amplified in the stillness.

"Approaching the perimeter," Annika murmured into her comm. "Kane, what's our status?"

"Cameras are blind," Kane replied, his voice a calm anchor in her ear. "You're clear to proceed."

Annika glanced at Nathan, who nodded once. They moved forward, their movements precise and controlled. The chain-link fence loomed up ahead, its razor wire glinting faintly in the moonlight. Nathan reached into his pack and pulled out a pair of wire cutters, snipping a small section of the fence with careful, deliberate movements.

"Entry point secured," Nathan whispered. "Let's move."

They slipped through the opening and made their way across the open courtyard, keeping low and sticking to the shadows. The server farm's main building rose up before them, a hulking structure of concrete and steel. Faint lights glowed from within, casting eerie shadows across the ground.

"Main entry's on the left," Nathan murmured. "I'll cover you."

Annika nodded and moved to the keypad beside the reinforced door. She pulled out a small device from her belt and attached it to the panel. The device hummed softly, a series of numbers flashing across its screen.

"Override initiated," she whispered, her fingers flying over the controls. "Almost there..."

The seconds stretched into an eternity. Then, with a soft beep, the keypad turned green, and the door slid open.

"Good work," Nathan murmured. "Let's go."

They slipped inside, the door sliding shut behind them with a quiet hiss. The interior of the building was dimly lit, the walls lined with rows of server racks and tangled cables. The air was cool and sterile, the faint hum of machinery filling the silence.

"Kane, we're inside," Annika whispered. "Where's the main server?"

"Two floors up," Kane replied. "Take the stairwell on your left. It'll lead you straight to the server room. I'm disabling the security protocols now, but you'll need to move fast. They've got a two-minute lag before the system resets."

"Copy that," Nathan murmured. "Moving now."

They ascended the stairs quickly, their footsteps barely making a sound against the metal steps. The stairwell was narrow, the air heavy with the scent of metal and concrete. Annika's heart pounded in her chest, the anticipation building with each step.

"Server room's just ahead," Kane said softly. "I'm seeing minimal activity, just one guard on patrol."

"We'll handle it," Nathan murmured.

They reached the top of the stairs and peered around the corner. The server room's door was slightly ajar, a faint glow spilling out into the hallway. A lone guard stood just inside, his back to the door as he stared at a series of monitors.

Annika moved first, slipping through the doorway and approaching the guard with silent, predatory grace. She was on him in an instant, one hand clamping over his mouth while the other jabbed a syringe into his neck. The guard stiffened, then slumped forward, unconscious.

"Clear," she whispered, lowering the guard gently to the floor.

Nathan moved past her, his gaze scanning the rows of servers. "There," he murmured, pointing to a large, central terminal. "That's the one."

Annika moved to the terminal and plugged in a small drive. The screen flashed briefly, then a series of files began to upload.

"Data's transferring," she whispered. "We're almost there."

"Copy that," Kane murmured. "I'm seeing increased activity on the network. They know something's up. Get what you need and get out."

"Roger," Annika said, her gaze locked on the progress bar. The bar inched forward slowly, each tick of percentage points feeling like an eternity. Annika could feel the tension coiling in her muscles, every nerve on edge as she kept her gaze fixed on the terminal's screen. Beside her, Nathan shifted slightly, his eyes flicking between the entrance and the unconscious guard slumped on the floor.

"Almost there..." Annika murmured under her breath, willing the bar to move faster.

The soft hum of the servers seemed to amplify in the silence, and the faint buzz of the overhead lights thrummed in sync with her racing pulse. They were so close, but each passing second increased the risk of discovery.

"Come on, come on," Nathan muttered, his fingers flexing restlessly on the grip of his weapon.

Finally, with a soft chime, the screen flashed green, and a message appeared:

TRANSFER COMPLETE.

"Got it," Annika whispered, yanking the drive from the terminal. "Kane, we have the data. Heading to the secondary control room now."

"Copy that," Kane replied, his voice tense. "Security protocols are still down, but they're starting to ping the system. Move fast."

Annika nodded and motioned to Nathan. They slipped out of the server room, their movements quick and silent. The hallway beyond was empty, but Annika could feel the building's pulse shifting, the faint tremors of increased activity as the security system began to recalibrate.

"Secondary control room is down this way," Nathan murmured, his voice low. "We take out the backup grid, and Lansing's entire network goes dark."

"Let's finish this," Annika said softly, her gaze hardening.

They moved through the labyrinthine corridors, their steps light and purposeful. The secondary control room was a smaller, more secure area located in the heart of the building. It was where Lansing's technicians managed the redundant systems, ensuring that even if the main servers were compromised, critical data would be preserved.

As they approached the door, Annika paused, glancing back at Nathan.

"Ready?" she asked, her voice a soft murmur.

"Always," Nathan replied, his gaze steady.

Annika nodded and keyed in the access code Kane had provided. The door slid open with a soft hiss, revealing a compact room filled with rows of blinking monitors and control panels. Two technicians sat at the consoles, their backs to the door, oblivious to the danger creeping up behind them.

Annika and Nathan moved simultaneously, each taking a target. Annika's blade glinted briefly in the dim light before it pressed against the first technician's throat. He froze, a strangled gasp escaping his lips as his eyes went wide with fear.

"Don't make a sound," Annika whispered, her voice cold and precise.

Nathan had the other technician pinned against his chair, one hand clamped over his mouth while the other pressed a small tranquilizer syringe into his neck. The man's eyes fluttered closed, and he slumped forward, unconscious.

"Easy," Nathan murmured, lowering the man gently to the ground. He glanced at Annika. "What's next?"

Annika moved to the nearest console and began typing rapidly, her fingers a blur over the keys. "I'm setting up a loop in the security feed. It'll look like everything's normal from the outside, but it'll buy us time to disable the backup systems."

"Make it quick," Nathan said, his gaze sweeping the room. "We won't be alone for long."

Annika's eyes narrowed in concentration as she accessed the system's core commands. Lines of code scrolled across the screen, each keystroke a calculated step toward severing Lansing's grip on his network.

"Almost there," she murmured, her heart pounding.

A faint beep echoed through the room, followed by a series of green lights flashing across the control panel.

"Done," Annika said, a hint of satisfaction in her voice. "Backup systems are offline. The entire network's vulnerable."

"Great work," Nathan said softly, a small smile tugging at his lips. "Now let's get out of here."

They turned and moved back toward the door, but just as they reached the threshold, a soft click echoed behind them. Annika froze, her breath catching in her throat.

The unconscious guard they had left in the server room now stood in the doorway, a pistol trained on them, his eyes cold and calculating.

"Drop your weapons," he growled, his voice a low, dangerous rumble.

Annika's mind raced, her gaze darting to Nathan. He gave the barest of nods, his eyes flicking briefly to the guard's stance, the slight shake of his hand, the tension in his shoulders. He wasn't as steady as he looked.

"We're not here to hurt anyone," Annika said softly, her tone calm and measured. She slowly lowered her weapon, placing it on the floor. "We just need to get out of here."

The guard's grip tightened on the pistol, his knuckles white. "You're not going anywhere," he snarled. "I don't know who you are, but... "

Nathan moved like lightning. He dropped to the ground, sweeping the guard's legs out from under him in one fluid motion. The man hit the floor with a grunt, his pistol skittering across the tiles. Annika was on him in an instant, one knee pressing into his chest as she jabbed a tranquilizer into his neck.

The guard's struggles weakened, his eyes fluttering closed as the sedative took effect.

"Nice timing," Annika muttered, her breath coming in short bursts.

"Didn't think we'd have company so soon," Nathan murmured, hauling the unconscious guard to the side. "But we're still on schedule. Let's move."

They slipped back into the hallway, making their way toward the exit. The building seemed to vibrate with a low hum of activity, the faint tremors of Lansing's network unraveling from within. Annika could almost feel the tension in the air, the sense of impending collapse as the systems that had supported his empire began to crumble.

"Kane, we're clear," Annika whispered into her comm. "Backup systems are offline. The network's exposed."

"Copy that," Kane replied, his voice crackling softly through the earpiece. "Get to the extraction point. I'm already seeing signs of the system destabilizing. We've got about five minutes before they realize what's happened."

"Roger," Annika murmured. She glanced at Nathan, who nodded, his gaze sharp and focused.

"Let's go."

Meanwhile, James and David moved through the dense brush surrounding the communications hub in Texas, their bodies low and movements precise. The air was heavy with the scent of rain, the ground slick and uneven beneath their boots.

"Perimeter's tight," David murmured, his gaze sweeping over the chain-link fence topped with razor wire. "They're running full security protocols. Must know something's up."

"They're expecting trouble," James said quietly. "Good thing we came prepared."

They crouched beside the fence, their eyes scanning the guard towers and surveillance cameras that dotted the compound. David pulled out a small device from his pack and attached it to the base of the fence. A faint click echoed through the stillness, followed by a soft hum as the device emitted a low-frequency signal.

"Signal's jamming the sensors," David murmured. "We've got a ten-second window to get through."

"Go," James whispered.

They slipped through the narrow opening, their movements smooth and practiced. The courtyard beyond was bathed in the soft glow of floodlights, casting long shadows across the concrete.

"Main relay station's straight ahead," David murmured, pointing to a low, squat building in the center of the compound. "That's where they're controlling all outgoing and incoming communications."

"Let's make it quick," James said, his gaze sharp. "We don't have much time."

They moved across the courtyard, keeping low and sticking to the shadows. The relay station loomed up ahead, its reinforced doors and security cameras a silent testament to Lansing's paranoia.

David reached the door first, his fingers flying over the keypad as he keyed in the access code Kane had provided. The door slid open, and they slipped inside, their weapons raised and ready.

The interior of the building was dimly lit, the walls lined with rows of monitors and control panels. A single technician sat at a console, his back to them as he stared intently at the screens.

James moved forward silently, his steps measured and precise. He was on the technician in an instant, one hand clamping over the man's mouth while the other jabbed a tranquilizer syringe into his neck. The technician slumped forward, unconscious.

"Clear," James whispered.

David moved to the nearest console, his gaze scanning the readouts. "Main relay's here. I'll disable the outgoing signals. Kane, I'm going to need you to reroute the internal communications to our system."

"On it," Kane replied. "Give me a few seconds..."

The seconds stretched on, every small sound amplified in the stillness. James's gaze swept the room, his muscles coiled with anticipation.

"Alright," Kane murmured finally. "You're good to go. Internal comms are linked to our network. They won't be able to send or receive anything without us knowing."

"Nice work," David said softly. He glanced at James, his expression grim. "Let's finish this."

They moved to the main control terminal, disabling the backup relays and rerouting the power. The screens around them flickered, then went dark, the faint hum of the machinery fading into silence.

"It's done," James murmured, his voice barely a whisper in the sudden, oppressive silence. The dim glow of emergency lighting cast eerie shadows over the now-darkened relay station. "Communications are down. Lansing's network is officially cut off."

David nodded, his gaze lingering on the dark screens. "They won't be able to coordinate their response or alert anyone outside. We've got the upper hand now."

"Let's not waste it," James said firmly. "We need to secure the facility and extract before they realize what's going on. Keep it quiet, keep it clean."

David nodded, his jaw tight. They moved silently through the relay station, checking each room for any signs of resistance. It was deserted, the technicians and guards likely stationed elsewhere throughout the compound.

"We're clear," David murmured as they reached the final corridor. He glanced at James, his expression serious. "Now what?"

"We hold position here for another three minutes," James said, glancing at his watch. "That gives Nathan and Annika time to finish up in Virginia. Once we're sure their backup systems are offline, we extract."

David nodded, his gaze shifting to the darkened relay consoles. "Let's hope this buys us enough time to hit the New York site before they can regroup."

"It will," James said softly. "We've come too far to back down now."

They stood in silence, the weight of the moment pressing down on them. Every muscle in James's body was coiled with tension, his senses sharp and alert. He could feel the pulse of the mission around him, the delicate balance they were teetering on. One misstep, and everything could come crashing down.

"Kane, status on Virginia?" James asked quietly into his comm.

"Annika and Nathan are clear," Kane replied, his voice steady. "They've disabled the backup systems and are en route to the extraction point."

"Good," James murmured. "What about New York?"

"I've got eyes on the perimeter," Sarah's voice came through, calm and controlled. "No signs of movement yet, but I'm seeing increased activity on Lansing's private channels. He knows something's wrong, but he hasn't connected the dots yet."

"Then let's keep it that way," James said softly. "We move to New York as soon as everyone's out. David and I will rendezvous with the extraction team in Texas and head straight there."

"Copy that," Sarah said. "I'll coordinate the strike on New York once you're in position."

"Roger," James murmured, his gaze shifting to David. "You ready?"

David nodded, his expression fierce. "Let's go."

They moved quickly but carefully, retracing their steps through the darkened hallways. The relay station was a fortress of concrete and steel, designed to withstand physical and digital assaults. But now, it lay vulnerable and exposed, its heart ripped out by the Patriots' strike.

As they reached the outer perimeter, the faint sound of footsteps echoed through the stillness. James froze, his hand raised in a silent signal for David to halt. The footsteps grew louder, accompanied by the low murmur of voices.

"Patrol," David whispered, his voice barely audible.

"Get down," James murmured, dropping to a crouch behind a low wall. David followed suit, his movements smooth and silent.

A group of guards appeared around the corner, their weapons slung casually over their shoulders. They moved with a lazy, almost bored gait, their expressions indifferent. James watched them intently, his body tensed like a coiled spring.

"They haven't noticed the comms are down yet," David whispered. "They're still on routine patrol."

"Good," James murmured. "Let's keep it that way."

They waited, barely daring to breathe, as the guards passed by. The faint scent of cigarette smoke lingered in the air, carried on the breeze as one of the men took a long drag and exhaled slowly. James's gaze flicked to David, who gave a slight nod.

Slowly, carefully, they edged away from the patrol, their movements precise and controlled. The guards continued down the path, oblivious to the danger lurking just a few feet away.

As soon as they were out of earshot, James and David slipped through the gate and into the dense brush surrounding the compound. The SUV they'd used for insertion was parked a few hundred yards away, hidden under a canopy of branches and leaves.

"Extraction point in sight," David murmured, his breath coming in short, controlled bursts. "Kane, we're clear."

"Copy that," Kane replied. "Annika and Nathan are already at their extraction point. They'll be in the air in less than five minutes."

"Good," James said softly. He glanced at David, a faint smile tugging at his lips. "Let's get out of here."

They reached the SUV and slipped inside, the engine purring to life as David turned the key. The vehicle eased forward, headlights off as they navigated the narrow, winding path through the woods. The tension in the air seemed to ease slightly, the sense of impending danger fading as they put distance between themselves and the relay station.

"Nice work in there," James murmured, his gaze shifting to David. "Clean and efficient. Just like old times."

David chuckled softly, the sound low and rumbling. "Yeah. Felt good to be back in the field."

"You never really left," James said quietly, his voice filled with a note of fondness. "None of us did."

There was a moment of silence, a shared understanding passing between them. Then David nodded, his gaze steady on the road ahead.

"We're almost there," he murmured. "Let's link up with the team and finish this."

Two hours later, the Patriots reconvened at a secluded airfield outside New York City. The mood was electric, the sense of urgency palpable as they made final preparations for the assault on Lansing's primary fallback location.

Annika and Nathan stood by the open ramp of a sleek, black helicopter, their expressions tense but determined. David and James approached from the other side of the hangar, their gear slung over their shoulders.

"Glad you made it out in one piece," Nathan called out, a faint grin tugging at his lips.

"Likewise," James replied, his gaze sweeping over the team. "Everyone's accounted for?"

"All present and accounted for," Annika said softly. "Kane's already linked up with the New York support team. They're positioning around the safe house perimeter now."

"Good," James murmured. "We hit them hard and fast. No hesitation."

David moved to stand beside him, his gaze sharp. "What's the plan for the safe house itself? It's likely to be heavily fortified."

"It is," Sarah's voice came through the comms, clear and crisp. "But we've identified several weak points in the perimeter. The safe house is a converted brownstone, with multiple access points through the adjacent buildings. If you enter from the south side, you'll be able to bypass the main defenses and reach the inner courtyard without drawing attention."

"Once we're inside, we split into two teams," James said. "Annika and Nathan, you take the ground floor and secure the central command room. David and I will move to the second floor and neutralize Lansing's security detail."

"And Reichter?" Nathan asked, his gaze narrowing.

"Reichter won't be there," James said softly. "But his top lieutenants will be. If we take them out, we cut off the head of his operation in the States. That'll force Reichter to go to ground, and when he does, we'll be waiting."

There was a murmur of agreement, each voice carrying a thread of resolve and determination.

"This is it," James said quietly, his gaze sweeping over the team. "We've got one shot at this. We take down Lansing, dismantle his network, and force Reichter into the open. No second chances."

"Understood," Annika said softly, her gaze fierce.

Nathan nodded, his expression hard. "We're with you, James. All the way."

"Good," James murmured. "Let's finish what we started."

The helicopter hovered silently over the darkened streets of Manhattan, its rotors a barely perceptible hum against the night sky. Below, the city stretched out in a maze of lights and shadows, a living, breathing entity that seemed to pulse with anticipation.

The Patriots moved with practiced efficiency as they rappelled down from the helicopter, landing lightly on the rooftop of the adjacent building. The wind whipped around them, carrying the faint scent of rain and exhaust. James glanced at Annika, who nodded, her gaze focused.

"We're in position," James whispered into his comm. "Kane, status?"

"Perimeter's clear," Kane replied. "I'm seeing minimal activity inside the safe house. Looks like they're not expecting trouble."

"Good," James murmured. He turned to the others, his voice low but firm. "We move in three... two... one. Go."

They slipped over the edge of the rooftop, descending silently into the narrow alley below. The brick walls loomed on either side, casting long shadows that seemed to swallow them whole.

Annika took point, her movements smooth and deliberate as she approached the south entrance. She reached out, her fingers brushing the door's lock. With a soft click, the door swung open.

"Entry point secured," she whispered.

They moved inside, the narrow hallway beyond dark and empty. The air was heavy with the scent of old wood and dust, the faint creak of floorboards underfoot echoing softly in the silence. James motioned for the team to spread out, his gaze sweeping over the dimly lit hallway. The house's age was evident in every crevice, every cracked tile. But the subtle, modern upgrades, the reinforced steel doorframes, the faint hum of hidden electronics, spoke of a place that had been meticulously fortified.

"Remember," James murmured, his voice barely a whisper. "Stay focused. Stay quiet. We want to be in and out before they know what hit them."

Annika nodded, her eyes narrowing as she peered around a corner. Nathan was right behind her, his body poised and ready, every muscle coiled like a tightly wound spring. David moved with the same predatory grace, his weapon held steady as he scanned the corridor ahead.

"Ground floor is clear so far," Nathan whispered. "No sign of movement."

"Roger that," James replied. "Move to the central command room. Disable any security systems you find along the way."

Annika led the way, her footsteps soundless on the polished wooden floors. They moved through the house like shadows, each turn of a corner bringing them deeper into the belly of the beast. Every instinct in Annika's body screamed at her to be ready, to anticipate the ambush that could come at any moment.

They reached a set of heavy double doors at the end of the corridor, faint light spilling out from the crack beneath them. Annika glanced back at Nathan, who nodded once, his gaze sharp.

"Ready?" she mouthed.

Nathan gave a curt nod, his fingers flexing on the grip of his weapon. David moved to the opposite side of the door, his eyes locking with Annika's. He raised three fingers, counting down silently.

Three... two... one.

Annika shoved the door open, and they burst into the room, weapons raised. The command room was a hive of activity, rows of monitors lining the walls, each one displaying security feeds and data readouts. A half-dozen technicians turned at the sudden intrusion, their eyes widening in shock.

"Hands up!" Annika barked, her voice a cold, commanding snap.

The technicians froze, their hands going up slowly, fear etched into their faces.

"Down on the ground," Nathan growled, his gaze sweeping the room. "Now."

They dropped to the floor, their bodies trembling as Annika and Nathan moved among them, checking for weapons or hidden devices. Annika's gaze locked onto a control panel on the far wall, its screen flashing with lines of code.

"Kane, we're in the command room," she whispered into her comm. "I'm seeing active security protocols on the primary server. Looks like they're trying to reroute power to a backup generator."

"Copy that," Kane replied. "I'm overriding their commands now. Hold tight... there. Security protocols are down. You're clear to disable the network."

"Roger," Annika murmured. She moved to the control panel and keyed in a series of commands, her fingers flying over the keys. The screens flickered, then went dark, the hum of electronics fading into silence.

"Security grid's down," Annika reported softly. "Lansing's blind."

"Nice work," James's voice crackled through the comm. "David and I are moving to the second floor. Hold position and secure the room."

"Copy that," Annika murmured. She glanced at Nathan, who was standing over the cowering technicians, his expression cold and unyielding.

"What now?" Nathan asked quietly.

"We hold position," Annika said softly, her gaze shifting to the darkened screens. "And wait for the others."

Second Floor: Securing the Lieutenants

James and David moved swiftly and silently up the winding staircase, their eyes scanning every shadow, every corner. The second floor was dark and eerily quiet, the only sound the soft creak of the old house settling around them.

"Perimeter's clear," David whispered, his voice barely audible. "No sign of guards."

"They'll be in the inner rooms," James murmured. "Stay close."

They reached the top of the stairs and paused, their eyes locking onto a door at the end of the hallway. Faint light glowed from beneath the door, the low murmur of voices drifting through the silence.

"That's them," David muttered, his gaze narrowing. "Lansing's lieutenants."

"Let's not give them a chance to run," James said quietly.

They moved forward, weapons raised. The door was ajar, and James pushed it open with a slow, deliberate motion. Inside, four men sat around a large wooden table, their faces drawn and tense. The room was filled with the scent of cigar smoke and expensive liquor, and a half-dozen monitors lined the walls, each one displaying feeds from various locations.

The men looked up as the door swung open, their eyes widening in surprise.

"Who the hell... "

"Hands where I can see them," James snapped, his voice a low, dangerous growl.

The lieutenants froze, their gazes darting between James and David. One of the men, tall and broad-shouldered, with a thin scar running down the side of his face, slowly raised his hands, his eyes narrowing.

"You've got some nerve," he sneered. "Do you know who we are?"

"I know exactly who you are," James replied coldly. "And I know exactly what you've done."

The man's lip curled in a snarl. "You think you can just walk in here and... "

David moved like a striking viper, slamming the butt of his rifle into the man's temple. The lieutenant crumpled to the floor, unconscious before he hit the ground.

"Anyone else want to try?" David growled, his gaze sweeping over the remaining men.

There was a tense silence, then one of the lieutenants, a thin, nervous-looking man with glasses, raised his hands higher, his face pale.

"We don't want any trouble," he stammered. "We'll cooperate."

"Good," James murmured, his gaze cold and hard. "Because you're going to tell us everything you know about Lansing's operation. Every safe house, every fallback plan, every contact."

The man swallowed hard, sweat beading on his forehead. "You'll never get to Lansing. He... he's already planning to..."

"To disappear?" James interrupted, his voice a low, dangerous rumble. "We know. But that's not going to happen. Not this time."

He stepped forward, his gaze boring into the man's. "You're going to tell us where he's hiding. You're going to give us the access codes to his secure network. And you're going to help us take him down."

The lieutenant hesitated, fear and defiance warring in his eyes. Then, slowly, he nodded, his shoulders sagging in defeat.

"Alright," he whispered. "Alright. I'll talk."

"Good choice," David muttered. He glanced at James, his expression fierce. "Let's wrap this up."

James nodded and reached for his comm. "Annika, Nathan, we've secured the second floor. You're clear to move up."

"Copy that," Annika's voice came through, steady and calm. "On our way."

The minutes that followed were a blur of activity as the team swept through the rest of the house, neutralizing the remaining personnel and securing the perimeter. By the time they gathered back in the command room, the house was silent, the tension in the air replaced by a sense of grim satisfaction.

"We've got the data and Lansing's lieutenants," James said softly, his gaze sweeping over the team. "But this isn't over yet. Lansing's still out there. And he's going to know we're coming."

"Then let him know," Nathan growled, his eyes glinting with a fierce light. "We're not hiding anymore."

"No," James agreed, a cold smile curving his lips. "We're not."

Back at the safe house's command center, the Patriots regrouped, their expressions set and determined as they pored over the data they'd recovered. Kane's fingers flew over the keyboard, decrypting files and cross-referencing coordinates with known safe house locations.

"Got it," Kane murmured, his eyes widening. "Lansing's primary location, his real safe house, it's in Washington, D.C. He's been hiding in plain sight."

"Of course he has," Annika muttered, her gaze hardening. "It's the last place anyone would look."

"And the perfect place for him to make his final stand," James said softly. "We're going to hit him where it hurts. We take out Lansing, and the entire network collapses."

"And Reichter?" Sarah asked quietly.

James's eyes darkened, a fierce light burning in their depths. "He'll come to D.C. He won't be able to resist. And when he does, we'll be there to welcome him."

There was a murmur of agreement, the air crackling with anticipation.

"This is it," James said, his voice low but steady. "We're bringing the fight to Lansing. And when Reichter shows up, we finish this once and for all."

There was a long, heavy silence as the gravity of his words settled over them. Then Nathan stepped forward, his expression fierce and unyielding.

"Let's take these bastards down," he growled.

And with that, the Patriots moved out, united, determined, and ready to bring an end Klaus Corrupt network.

The atmosphere in the safe house's command center was electric as the Patriots regrouped, their faces etched with determination and a shared sense of purpose. Kane's fingers flew over the keyboard, decrypting files and pulling up every last bit of data they'd extracted from Lansing's safe house in New York. The room hummed with a quiet, intense energy, the energy of a team that knew they were closing in on their prey.

"Alright, I've cross-referenced everything," Kane said, his voice a low murmur as he pointed to a map of Washington, D.C. projected on the wall. "Lansing's been using multiple shell companies and false fronts to hide his movements, but this... " he highlighted a small cluster of buildings in the Capitol Hill district, "... this is his main operations hub."

"It's right under our noses," Nathan growled, shaking his head in disbelief. "All this time, and he's been hiding in D.C.?"

"Brilliant move, if you think about it," Annika muttered, leaning over Kane's shoulder to study the map. "Who would think to look for him here? Everyone would assume he'd run to the other side of the world the moment we started digging."

"Except he didn't," James said softly, his voice laced with admiration and anger. "He's been right here, probably watching every move we made, thinking we'd never get close."

"Overconfident," David added, his eyes narrowing. "Arrogant. He thought his failsafe in New York would keep us at bay."

"But now we've got him," Sarah murmured, a rare, fierce smile curving her lips. "We're going to turn that confidence into his downfall."

"Exactly," James agreed, his gaze sweeping over the team. "But we're not just going to storm in and start shooting. We're smarter than that. Lansing's got eyes and ears everywhere. We need to approach this carefully, methodically."

"Agreed," Annika said. She looked around at the others, her gaze steady. "So what's the plan, James?"

James took a deep breath, gathering his thoughts. "We're going to split into three teams, just like before. Annika and Nathan, you'll take point. We need you on the ground, gathering intel and mapping out the building's interior. We need to know every room, every corridor, every blind spot."

Annika nodded, her expression focused. "We'll handle it."

"David and I will set up a forward operations base nearby," James continued. "We'll coordinate the strike and provide backup if things go sideways."

"And what about us?" Kane asked, glancing at Sarah.

"You two will be running command and control again," James said firmly. "Kane, you'll be monitoring Lansing's digital communications. I want to know the moment he tries to reach out to anyone. Sarah, you'll be keeping an eye on the building's security systems. If there's even a hint of trouble, I want to know about it."

"We've got it covered," Sarah said softly. She glanced at Kane, who gave a quick nod of agreement.

"Good," James murmured. "Once we have the layout and we know where Lansing is, we move in. No hesitation, no mistakes."

"And what's our objective?" Nathan asked quietly. "Are we taking him alive?"

James hesitated, his gaze distant. Then he shook his head slowly. "No. This isn't about capturing him. This is about ending it. Lansing has too many connections, too many resources. If we take him alive, he'll find a way to wriggle out of it. We take him down. For good."

The silence that followed was heavy, but there was no dissent. Each of them understood what that meant. Each of them had seen the damage men like Lansing could do if they were left breathing.

"Understood," Nathan murmured. "We'll make it clean."

James nodded. "Good. Now let's get to work."

A few hours later, the Patriots moved through the crowded streets of Capitol Hill, blending seamlessly with the hustle and bustle of the city. The air was cool and crisp, carrying the faint scent of freshly fallen leaves and the distant hum of traffic. The sun was setting, casting long shadows across the sidewalks and washing the buildings in a warm, golden glow.

Annika and Nathan walked side by side, their steps casual but purposeful. They were dressed like any other professionals out for an evening stroll—Annika in a tailored gray coat, her hair pulled back in a loose ponytail; Nathan in a dark jacket and slacks, his expression relaxed but alert.

"Perimeter looks clear," Annika murmured softly, her voice barely audible over the buzz of the street. "No sign of increased security presence."

"Copy that," Kane's voice crackled through their earpieces. "I've got eyes on the building from the nearby traffic cameras. No unusual activity. You're good to proceed."

They reached the corner of the block and paused, glancing casually at the unassuming brick building across the street. It was nondescript, blending in with the other townhouses and office buildings that lined the street. But Annika knew it was anything but ordinary. Behind those walls was the nerve center of Lansing's operations—a place where countless lives had been ruined and manipulated.

"Looks quiet," Nathan murmured, his gaze sweeping over the windows. "Too quiet."

"They'll have layers of security inside," Annika said softly. "Cameras, motion sensors, guards in plainclothes. They'll be watching."

"Then let's not give them a reason to look too closely," Nathan said with a faint smile. He glanced at her, his gaze softening slightly. "You ready?"

Annika took a deep breath, then nodded. "Always."

They crossed the street casually, slipping into the alleyway beside the building. A heavy iron gate blocked the entrance to the rear courtyard, but Nathan pulled out a small device and held it against the lock. A soft click echoed in the stillness, and the gate swung open.

"Nice," Annika murmured, stepping through the gate. "You've been practicing."

"Gotta keep my skills sharp," Nathan replied with a grin.

They moved through the courtyard and approached the rear entrance. Annika glanced up at the small camera mounted above the door, its lens turning lazily to scan the area.

"Kane, can you loop the feed?" she whispered.

"Already done," Kane replied, a hint of satisfaction in his voice. "You're invisible."

"Good," Annika murmured. She reached up and disconnected the camera, then slipped inside, Nathan close behind her.

The interior of the building was dark and silent, the only light coming from the faint glow of emergency exit signs. They moved through the narrow hallway, their footsteps muffled against the thick carpet.

"Approaching the main stairwell," Nathan murmured. "Going up to the third floor."

"Copy that," Kane replied. "I'm picking up a couple of heat signatures on that floor. Looks like two guards, possibly more."

"Understood," Annika said softly. "We'll handle it."

They ascended the stairs quickly and quietly, reaching the third-floor landing without incident. The hallway beyond was empty, but Annika could hear the faint murmur of voices drifting from a room at the far end.

"Guards are in there," Nathan whispered, nodding toward the closed door.

Annika nodded and crept forward, her body low and tense. She pressed her ear to the door, listening intently. Two voices, speaking in low, murmured tones. She couldn't make out the words, but the tone was casual, relaxed.

"They're not expecting trouble," Annika whispered. "We move in, quick and quiet."

Nathan nodded, his gaze sharpening. "On three."

One... two... three.

They burst through the door, weapons raised. The two guards barely had time to react before Annika and Nathan were on them, taking them down with swift, precise blows. The guards slumped to the floor, unconscious.

"Clear," Nathan murmured, breathing heavily.

Annika nodded and moved to the nearest console. She plugged in a small device, her gaze scanning the readouts on the screen.

"Kane, I'm in," she whispered. "Uploading the building's layout now."

"Receiving it," Kane murmured. "Give me a second to map out the internal security systems..."

The minutes stretched on in tense silence as they waited, every small sound amplified in the stillness. Finally, Kane's voice crackled through the earpiece.

"Got it," he said softly. "Lansing's in the basement. He's using an old fallout shelter as a command center. You'll need to take the elevator down, but be careful, there's a biometric lock on the doors."

"We'll handle it," Annika murmured. She glanced at Nathan, who nodded.

"Let's get to work," he whispered.

They moved through the building, each step bringing them closer to their target. Every instinct in Annika's body screamed at her to be ready, to expect the worst. But she kept her breathing steady, her gaze focused.

This was it. The moment they'd been fighting for. The endgame.

They reached the elevator and paused, staring at the sleek metal doors. A small keypad and biometric scanner were mounted beside them, the faint glow of the screen casting a blue light over Annika's face.

"Kane, how do we bypass this?" she asked softly.

"You'll need a keycard and a thumbprint," Kane replied.

"Got it." Annika said

Chapter 12

The elevator hummed softly as it descended deep into the basement of the unassuming Capitol Hill building. The Patriots stood shoulder to shoulder in the small space, their expressions grim and focused. The metallic walls reflected their tense faces, and the faint, sterile scent of machinery mixed with the adrenaline that hung thick in the air.

Annika's gaze flicked to the digital display above the elevator doors, watching the numbers count down slowly. Each tick seemed to resonate in her chest, amplifying the silence. Her grip tightened on her weapon, the familiar weight of it grounding her in the moment.

"This is it," Nathan murmured beside her, his voice a low rumble. "We're finally going to finish this."

Annika nodded, her gaze shifting to him briefly. "We're ready. We've come too far to let him slip through our fingers now."

Nathan's lips curved into a faint smile, more a baring of teeth than a gesture of reassurance. "We've been ready for this since the day we signed up. Lansing's going to find out just how big of a mistake he made coming after us."

Across from them, James stood with his back straight, his eyes locked on the doors. He exuded a quiet, lethal calm, the kind that came from years of experience and countless battles fought in the shadows. He glanced at Annika and Nathan, giving them a brief nod.

"Remember, we're not just taking down Lansing," James said softly. "We're dismantling everything he's built. We're severing his ties, burning his bridges, and cutting off every last one of his escape routes. When we're done, there won't be anything left for him to crawl back to."

"Understood," Annika replied, her voice steady.

Nathan nodded as well. "We'll make it clean."

David shifted slightly, his gaze flicking between the others. He reached out and clasped James's shoulder, giving it a firm squeeze. "No matter what happens down there, we've got each other's backs. We always have, and we always will."

James met David's gaze, his expression softening. "I know, David. And that's what's going to see us through this."

Kane's voice crackled softly through their earpieces. "You're almost at the bottom level. I've disabled the alarms and rerouted the camera feeds. They won't know you're there until it's too late."

"Good work, Kane," James murmured. "Sarah, status on external security?"

"Perimeter's clear," Sarah replied. "I've got eyes on all entry points. No signs of reinforcements or additional personnel arriving. Whatever Lansing's got down there, it's all he's got left."

"Perfect," James said, his gaze hardening. "Then let's end this."

The elevator slowed to a stop, a soft chime echoing through the confined space. The doors slid open, revealing a long, dimly lit hallway lined with reinforced steel doors and thick concrete walls. The air was cool and still, carrying the faint scent of antiseptic and old dust.

Annika's eyes narrowed as she scanned the corridor. "Basement's clear. No guards."

"They'll be in the command center," Nathan murmured. "Lansing will have everything he needs to defend himself there."

James nodded. "We take him out first. Without Lansing, the rest of his men will fall apart."

They moved forward, their footsteps soft and controlled. The hallway stretched on for what felt like miles, every shadow and every corner a potential hiding place for an ambush. But there was nothing, no sign of movement, no sounds of life.

Annika's gaze swept the walls, noting the small, discreet cameras mounted high above. "Kane, are you still looping the feeds?"

"Yeah," Kane replied, his voice tinged with a hint of strain. "But it's getting harder. Lansing's systems are reacting to my presence. They know something's wrong, but they can't pinpoint it. You've got about ten minutes before they figure it out."

"Then let's not waste time," James murmured. "Move fast, stay focused."

They reached a set of heavy double doors at the end of the hallway. A small plaque beside it read Command Center - Authorized Personnel Only. James exchanged a glance with Annika and Nathan, his eyes glinting with a cold, steely resolve.

"This is it," he whispered. "No turning back."

Annika nodded, her heart pounding in her chest. "We're with you, James. All the way."

"Always," Nathan added softly.

James reached out, his fingers brushing the biometric scanner beside the door. A soft beep echoed through the stillness, and the doors slid open with a low hiss.

The room beyond was a stark contrast to the rest of the basement. It was large and spacious, filled with rows of monitors and control panels. A massive digital map of the United States dominated one wall, pulsing with red and green markers that represented Lansing's network. The air was thick with the hum of electronics, and the glow of the screens cast a harsh, artificial light over the faces of the men and women seated at the consoles.

But it was the man standing in the center of the room that drew Annika's attention. Robert Lansing.

He looked older than she remembered, his hair graying at the temples, deep lines etched into his face. But his eyes were as sharp and calculating as ever, glittering with a mix of fury and something darker. He was dressed in a tailored suit, his stance rigid and composed.

"Well, well," Lansing drawled, his voice carrying a dangerous edge. "I must say, I'm impressed. I didn't think you'd make it this far."

"Underestimating us has always been your mistake," James replied coolly, his weapon held steady. "But I'm not here for your compliments, Lansing. I'm here to end this."

"End this?" Lansing's lips curled into a mocking smile. "You think killing me will end anything? You think you've won because you've made it this far? You have no idea what's really at stake."

"I know enough," James said softly. "I know you've spent decades corrupting this country, using your power and influence to manipulate governments, destroy lives. That ends today."

Lansing's gaze flicked over the team, his eyes narrowing. "And what then, James? What happens when I'm gone? Do you really think the world will be a better place? Or will someone else just take my place? Someone younger, hungrier, more ruthless?"

"Maybe," James murmured. "But they won't be you. And they won't have your network, your resources. We've burned your empire to the ground. All that's left is to put you out of your misery."

Lansing's smile faded, replaced by a cold, dangerous fury. "You think you're so righteous, don't you? So noble. But you're no better than me. You're just as ruthless, just as willing to do whatever it takes. That's why you've made it this far. That's why you're standing here."

"Difference is," Annika interjected, her voice low and fierce, "we don't destroy innocent lives for power. We protect people. And we protect the values you've spent your life undermining."

Lansing laughed softly, a bitter, mocking sound. "Protect people? Is that what you tell yourselves? Is that what helps you sleep at night?"

"Enough," James snapped, his gaze hardening. "This ends now, Lansing."

Lansing's gaze locked onto James, a dark, twisted smile curving his lips. "You think you've got it all figured out, don't you? But there's one thing you didn't account for."

He reached into his pocket and pulled out a small, sleek device. A remote.

"What are you doing?" David growled, his weapon trained on Lansing's chest.

Lansing's smile widened. "Ending this on my terms."

He pressed the button.

The lights in the command center flickered, then went out, plunging the room into darkness. A series of sharp, mechanical clicks echoed through the silence, followed by the low, ominous hum of machinery powering up.

"What the hell... " Nathan began, but his words were cut off by a deafening alarm that blared through the room.

"Self-destruct sequence initiated," an automated voice droned. "All personnel, evacuate immediately. Three minutes until detonation."

"Damn it!" Annika hissed, her gaze snapping to James. "He's rigged the building!"

"Get him!" James shouted, his voice cutting through the chaos.

They lunged forward, but Lansing was already moving, ducking behind a row of consoles. The Patriots fired, their bullets shattering screens and sparking against metal, but Lansing was fast... too fast. He disappeared through a side door, his laughter echoing through the room.

"Go after him!" James roared. "We can't let him escape!"

Annika and Nathan bolted after Lansing, their footsteps echoing down the narrow corridor. The walls shook as the self-destruct sequence continued to count down, the lights flashing red.

"Two minutes until detonation," the automated voice intoned.

"We're not going to make it out if we don't stop that sequence!" Sarah's voice crackled through their earpieces. "You've got to find Lansing! He's the only one who can shut it down!"

"We're on him!" Annika panted, her eyes scanning the darkened hallway.

They rounded a corner and spotted Lansing ahead, his silhouette a blur in the flashing lights.

"Lansing!" Nathan bellowed. "Stop!"

Lansing didn't stop, he sprinted down the dimly lit corridor, his figure disappearing into the shadows as the lights flickered overhead. Annika and Nathan were on his heels, their breaths coming in short, harsh gasps. The sound of the automated countdown reverberated through the building, each second ticking away like a drumbeat of impending doom.

"Two minutes until detonation," the voice droned again, its calm tone at odds with the chaos unfolding around them.

"Lansing!" Annika shouted, her voice a sharp command that cut through the silence. "There's nowhere left to run!"

But Lansing didn't look back. He darted through a doorway at the end of the hall, and Annika and Nathan followed, their weapons raised and ready. They burst into a narrow stairwell, the air thick with the scent of dust and metal.

"Keep moving!" Nathan growled, his gaze locked on Lansing's retreating form. "We can't let him get away!"

They pounded up the stairs, each step taking them closer to their target. Lansing glanced over his shoulder, his eyes wild with desperation and fury. He stumbled, his foot catching on the edge of a step, but he quickly regained his balance, pushing onward with a frantic energy that bordered on madness.

"He's headed for the roof!" Annika gasped, her lungs burning with exertion. "He's trying to buy time!"

"We're not letting him get away!" Nathan snarled.

They reached the top of the stairs just as Lansing burst through the door leading to the rooftop. The night air hit them like a shock, cool and crisp against their sweat-slicked skin. The rooftop was bathed in the eerie glow of emergency lights, casting long shadows across the concrete.

Lansing stood at the edge of the roof, his chest heaving as he struggled to catch his breath. He looked back at them, his eyes gleaming with a twisted mix of rage and defiance.

"You think you can just walk in here and take everything I've built?" he shouted, his voice hoarse. "You think you can destroy me?"

"You destroyed yourself, Lansing," Annika shot back, her weapon trained steadily on him. "We're just cleaning up the mess you made."

Lansing laughed, a harsh, bitter sound that echoed across the rooftop. "You don't get it, do you? This isn't just about me! It's never been about me!"

"Then what's it about?" Nathan demanded, his gaze narrowing.

"It's about control!" Lansing spat, his voice rising with manic intensity. "It's about power! You think taking me down will change anything? You think it'll make a difference? You're fools! You're fighting against a tide you can't stop!"

"Maybe we can't stop it," Annika said softly. "But we can make damn sure you don't get to ride it."

Lansing's eyes flashed with fury, and he raised the remote again, his thumb hovering over the button. "If I go down, I'm taking you all with me!"

"Lansing, don't!" Annika shouted, but it was too late.

Lansing's thumb pressed down.

The building shook violently, a deep, rumbling tremor that seemed to come from the very bowels of the earth. Annika stumbled, her knees buckling as the ground shifted beneath her feet. The air filled with the sound of cracking concrete and grinding metal.

"Warning," the automated voice droned, louder now. "Structural integrity compromised. One minute until detonation."

"Annika, get out of there!" Kane's voice crackled through her earpiece, filled with panic. "The whole building's going to come down!"

"Not without Lansing!" Annika shouted back. She pushed herself up, her gaze locking onto Lansing, who was swaying dangerously at the edge of the roof.

"Annika!" Nathan roared, his voice filled with equal parts fury and fear. He reached out, his hand closing around her arm in a tight grip. "We need to go! Now!"

"No!" Annika snarled, yanking her arm free. "Not yet!"

She took a step forward, her gaze never leaving Lansing's. "This is your last chance, Lansing. Shut down the sequence. You don't have to die here."

Lansing's laughter was a broken, hysterical sound. "You don't get it, do you?" he whispered. "I'm already dead."

With that, he turned and threw himself off the edge of the roof.

"No!" Annika screamed, lunging forward.

But she was too late. Lansing's body plummeted down, disappearing into the darkness below. The wind howled around them, carrying his final, despairing laugh away into the night.

"Damn it!" Nathan shouted, his voice raw with frustration. "He's gone!"

Annika stood at the edge of the roof, her chest heaving as she stared down into the abyss. For a moment, everything seemed to freeze, the world narrowing to just the sound of her own breathing, the pounding of her heart.

Then, slowly, she turned away.

"Let's go," she whispered, her voice hollow. "We need to get out of here."

Nathan grabbed her arm, pulling her back toward the stairwell. They stumbled down the stairs, their legs burning with the effort. The building groaned and creaked around them, the walls shaking as the self-destruct sequence neared its final countdown.

"Thirty seconds until detonation," the voice intoned.

"Move, move!" Nathan shouted, pushing Annika ahead of him.

They burst out onto the ground floor, the air thick with dust and the acrid scent of burning wires. James and David were waiting for them, their faces pale and drawn.

"Where's Lansing?" James demanded, his gaze snapping to Annika.

"Gone," she panted, shaking her head. "He jumped."

James's face tightened, a flash of something dark crossing his eyes. "Damn it. Alright, we need to move. Now."

They ran for the exit, the ground bucking and swaying beneath them. The sound of crumbling concrete filled the air, and Annika felt a surge of panic rise in her chest.

"Ten seconds until detonation."

They reached the outer doors and burst out into the open, the cool night air hitting them like a shock. Behind them, the building shuddered violently, a deep, rumbling roar reverberating through the ground.

"Get down!" James shouted.

They dove behind a parked car just as the building exploded in a massive fireball of heat and light. The shockwave slammed into them, the force of it lifting them off the ground and hurling them back. The roar of the explosion was deafening, a tidal wave of sound that seemed to crush everything in its path.

Annika hit the ground hard, her ears ringing and her vision blurred. She tasted blood and smoke, felt the rough grit of asphalt against her skin. She blinked, trying to clear the haze from her eyes.

"Annika!" Nathan's voice cut through the ringing in her ears, sharp and panicked. He was beside her in an instant, his hands gripping her shoulders. "Are you okay?"

"I, yeah, I'm fine," she managed, shaking her head. "I'm fine."

Nathan helped her to her feet, his gaze scanning her for injuries. Satisfied, he nodded and turned to the others.

"Everyone good?" he called out.

"Yeah," David grunted, dusting himself off. "That was too close."

"Too damn close," James agreed, his expression grim. He glanced back at the burning wreckage of the building, his eyes narrowing. "But it's over."

"Lansing's dead," Sarah's voice crackled through their earpieces. "I just confirmed it on the external feeds. He didn't survive the fall."

"Then it's over," Kane murmured softly. "It's really over."

There was a long, heavy silence as the reality of what had happened settled over them. They'd done it. They'd taken down Lansing, destroyed his network, and severed the final threads of his control. But the victory felt hollow, the cost of it weighing heavily on each of them.

Annika turned to James, her gaze searching his face. "What now?"

James was silent for a moment, his gaze distant. Then he took a deep breath and nodded slowly.

"Now," he said softly, "we go after Reichter."

The words hung in the air like a promise, a vow that they would see this through to the end, no matter the cost.

"Wherever he is," James murmured, his gaze hardening, "we'll find him. And we'll finish what we started."

And with that, the Patriots turned away from the burning wreckage of Lansing's empire, their steps sure and unyielding as they walked into the night.

They still had a battle to fight.

And they weren't done yet.

Chapter 13

The rain fell in a steady rhythm over Washington, D.C., the droplets tapping softly against the windows of the Patriots' new safe house. It was a quiet neighborhood, the kind of place where people kept to themselves and turned a blind eye to the comings and goings of strangers. The house itself was modest, a two-story brick structure tucked away behind a line of old oaks. It was a temporary base, just a place to regroup, but it felt oddly comforting in its unassuming simplicity.

Inside, the Patriots gathered around the dining room table, which had been converted into a makeshift command center. Maps and documents were spread across the surface, alongside laptops and tablets displaying the latest intel feeds. A soft, yellow glow from the overhead light cast a warm halo over their faces, but there was an underlying tension in the air, a sense of anticipation, of something unresolved.

James stood at the head of the table, his hands braced against the wood as he looked down at the maps. His face was a mask of concentration, eyes narrowed as he absorbed every detail. The others watched him quietly, their expressions mirroring his intensity.

"We took down Lansing, but we haven't finished this," James said softly, his voice carrying a quiet authority. "Lansing was just one piece of a larger puzzle, one cog in Reichter's machine. We know he's going to make a move now. He won't stay in hiding."

"He'll be looking to regain control," Annika murmured, leaning forward slightly. "Consolidate his power base, reorganize his assets. He knows we're coming for him, and he's not the kind of man to wait around and let us do it."

David nodded, his fingers drumming lightly against the table. "Reichter's been pulling strings for decades. He's built an empire that spans continents. Taking down Lansing crippled him, but it didn't break him. If anything, he's going to come out swinging."

"That's why we need to be one step ahead," Nathan said quietly, his gaze sweeping over the group. "We can't let him regroup. We hit him fast and hard, just like we did with Lansing. No mercy, no hesitation."

"Easier said than done," Kane muttered from where he sat at the end of the table, his laptop open in front of him. "Reichter's not some run-of-the-mill corrupt politician or business mogul. He's a ghost. We've got bits and pieces of his operation, but we still don't know where he's hiding. Every lead I've run has hit a dead end."

James nodded slowly, his gaze thoughtful. "That's because Reichter's different. He doesn't rely on the same tactics and resources as Lansing. He's more dangerous because he's more subtle. He knows how to disappear when he needs to."

"But he won't disappear now," Sarah said softly, her voice cutting through the murmur of conversation. She was seated beside Kane, her fingers tapping lightly against the edge of her tablet. "Lansing was his lieutenant, his right hand. Losing him was a huge blow to Reichter's operation. He's going to want to retaliate, to send a message."

"And we'll be ready for him," James said firmly. "But we need to find him first. Kane, I want you to go over everything we have, every contact, every transaction, every piece of data we've pulled from Lansing's servers. Reichter's got to have some kind of fallback, a place where he can regroup. Find it."

Kane nodded, his gaze sharpening with resolve. "I'm on it. I'll cross-reference it all, see if there's any pattern we've missed."

"Good," James murmured. He straightened, his gaze sweeping over the others. "In the meantime, we need to keep pressure on his network. Cut off his resources, disrupt his supply lines, make it impossible for him to operate. We took down Lansing's infrastructure, now we take down Reichter's."

"What's our first target?" David asked, his voice steady.

"We hit his financials," James replied. "Reichter's got his hands in a lot of pies, but his primary base of operations has always been Europe. If we can isolate his accounts and freeze his assets, we'll force him to make a move. And when he does, we'll be waiting."

Annika's eyes narrowed thoughtfully. "Reichter's been using a series of shell companies and front organizations to launder money. We know he funnels it through his charitable foundations, using government grants and donations to cover his tracks. If we can find a way to expose those transactions, we can take away his funding."

"Which means we need more intel," Nathan murmured, his brow furrowing. "We've got fragments, but nothing concrete. How do we get inside his network without tipping him off?"

"We already have an in," James said softly. He reached out and tapped a file on the table, Moreau's dossier. "Vincent Moreau. He was one of Lansing's key operatives, but he's got deep ties to Reichter's European network. He'll know where the money's going and how to get to it."

"Moreau's in protective custody," Annika pointed out. "If we approach him, it could spook him, or worse, alert Reichter that we're onto him."

"That's why we need to be careful," James agreed. "Annika, I want you to reach out to Moreau. Use the cover you established before. Make it clear that we're offering him a way out, a real way out. If he cooperates, we'll make sure he's safe."

Annika nodded slowly, her gaze thoughtful. "I'll handle it. But we need to move fast. The longer we wait, the more time Reichter has to rebuild."

"Agreed," James said softly. "While Annika works on Moreau, the rest of us will start laying the groundwork for our next moves.

Kane, keep digging through the data. David, I want you to map out potential targets for Reichter's next moves. We're going to need to be everywhere at once, and I need you to have a plan for every contingency."

David nodded sharply. "You got it, James. I'll start with his known associates and branch out from there."

"Good," James murmured. He took a deep breath, his gaze sweeping over the group once more. "This is going to be a long fight. Reichter's not going to go down easily. But we're in this together. We've faced worse, and we've come out on top every time."

There was a murmur of agreement around the table, a shared resolve that seemed to pulse through the air. They'd been through hell together, faced enemies that most people couldn't even imagine. And through it all, they'd stood by each other's sides, united by a bond that went beyond loyalty.

"Whatever happens," James said quietly, his gaze lingering on each of them in turn, "we don't give up. We don't back down. We've come too far to let Reichter win now."

He straightened, his shoulders squaring as he glanced down at the map one last time. "Let's get to work."

Over the next few days, the Patriots fell into a familiar rhythm, each of them taking on their assigned roles with a precision born of years spent operating on the edge of danger. The safe house became a hive of activity, the quiet neighborhood outside a stark contrast to the storm brewing within.

Kane spent hours hunched over his laptop, his fingers flying over the keys as he sifted through terabytes of data, cross-referencing names, locations, and financial transactions. Every so often, he'd let out a soft curse or a muttered exclamation, his brow furrowed in concentration.

Sarah moved between the various screens set up around the room, coordinating their efforts and monitoring the latest intel feeds. She worked in silence, her focus unbroken as she tracked Reichter's known associates and kept tabs on potential targets.

David mapped out routes and tactics, his movements precise and deliberate as he planned for every possible scenario. His gaze was intense, his jaw clenched as he considered the best way to counter Reichter's strategies.

Annika spent most of her time reaching out to contacts, using her extensive network to gather information and lay the groundwork for their next move. She was relentless, her voice a calm, controlled force that carried a quiet authority.

Nathan moved between the others, offering support where needed, his presence a steadying influence that kept the team grounded. He spoke little, his gaze always watchful, always alert.

And through it all, James stood at the center, his eyes never leaving the maps and documents spread across the table. He coordinated their efforts, his mind a whirlwind of strategies and possibilities. He knew they were on the brink of something big, something that could change everything.

Finally, on the fourth day, Kane looked up from his laptop, a triumphant grin spreading across his face.

"I've got something," he announced, his voice breaking the tense silence.

The others turned to him, their expressions shifting from exhaustion to sharp focus.

"What is it?" James asked, his gaze intense.

"It's a pattern," Kane said, his eyes bright with excitement. "A series of transactions between one of Reichter's foundations and a bank in Luxembourg. It's buried under layers of false fronts and shell companies, but I traced it back to a central account. That account is being used to fund a network of operatives across Europe, operatives that Reichter's been using to rebuild his organization."

"Where's the account?" Annika asked, leaning forward.

Kane's grin widened as he looked up from his laptop, his fingers tapping a rapid rhythm against the table. "Geneva," he repeated, his voice filled with triumph. "Reichter's got a private account in a discreet financial institution just outside the main banking district. It's where he's funneling most of his liquid assets."

James leaned over the table, his eyes narrowing as he studied the data on Kane's screen. "That's his war chest," he murmured. "If we hit it, we don't just take his money. We cut off his ability to pay his people, to fund his operations. We can cripple him."

"And force him into the open," Annika added quietly. "He'll have no choice but to respond. If Reichter loses access to those funds, he'll have to make a move to secure new assets or risk his entire network collapsing."

Nathan nodded slowly, his gaze thoughtful. "But Geneva isn't some backwater town. It's one of the most secure banking hubs in the world. If we're going to pull this off, we need to be precise. One misstep, and we'll have the entire Swiss security apparatus breathing down our necks."

James straightened, his eyes glinting with determination. "Then we do it right. We go in, get what we need, and get out before anyone knows we were there. No alarms, no attention."

David glanced at the others, his brow furrowing. "We've pulled off high-risk ops before, but this is going to require a level of finesse that even we haven't attempted. We're talking about infiltrating one of the most secure banks in the world. We're going to need a detailed plan, schematics, and a way to bypass multiple layers of security."

"I can handle that," Kane said, his fingers already flying over the keys. "I've been inside their systems before. I can map out the entire building, give us access to their digital infrastructure, and loop the security feeds. But we're going to need someone on the ground to take down the physical barriers, someone to get into the vault and retrieve whatever assets Reichter's hiding there."

Annika's gaze sharpened. "I can do it. I've got experience with high-security systems. And with Nathan providing cover, we can move quickly enough to avoid detection."

James considered her for a moment, then nodded. "You and Nathan will go in. David and I will provide external support and secure the extraction route. Kane, you'll handle everything on the digital front. Sarah, you'll coordinate and monitor any external threats."

"Works for me," Sarah said softly. "I'll set up a secure command center here. We'll have eyes and ears on the ground the whole time."

"Then it's settled," James murmured. He glanced at Kane. "What kind of timetable are we looking at?"

"I'll need at least twenty-four hours to finish mapping out their systems and prepare the backdoors we'll need," Kane said. "After that, it's all about timing. We'll need to go in during a maintenance window, late night, minimal personnel, fewer eyes watching."

"Which gives us enough time to fine-tune the plan," James said, his gaze sweeping over the team. "This is going to be a high-risk operation. We can't afford any mistakes. Everyone needs to be at the top of their game."

There was a murmur of agreement, each of them falling into their familiar roles with a sense of purpose. This was what they did, what they were best at. And though the stakes were higher than ever, they knew they were ready.

"All right," James said softly. "Let's get to work."

· · · ·

Two nights later, the Patriots gathered in a private hotel suite overlooking Lake Geneva. The view outside the floor-to-ceiling windows was breathtaking, snow-capped mountains in the distance, the city's lights reflecting off the water like a thousand shimmering stars. But none of them spared a glance at the scenery. Their attention was focused solely on the large digital display set up in the center of the room, which showed a detailed schematic of their target: the Banque Privée d'Élite.

"The bank's main building is a fortress," Kane said, his voice carrying a note of both admiration and challenge. "They've got every modern security measure you can think of, motion sensors, biometric scanners, armed guards, and a state-of-the-art surveillance system. But I've managed to find a few cracks in their defenses."

He pointed to a section of the schematic highlighted in red. "There's a maintenance tunnel that runs underneath the building, ,part of an old utility system that hasn't been used in years. It's not on any official blueprints, but I found a reference to it in some old city planning documents. It'll get you past the main perimeter and into the lower levels of the bank."

Annika nodded, her gaze intent on the display. "Once we're inside, what are we looking at?"

"Two layers of security before you reach the vault," Kane explained. "The first is a biometric scanner and a passcode-protected door. The second is a series of motion sensors that cover the approach to the vault itself. If any of them are triggered, the vault goes into lockdown, and there's no way to access it without setting off every alarm in the building."

"So we disable the sensors," Nathan said, his tone matter-of-fact. "What about the vault door?"

"Reichter's vault is on a separate system," Kane said, his expression serious. "I've found references to a secondary control room located on the top floor. It's where the bank's most sensitive assets are monitored and controlled. You'll need to access that control room and disable the vault's internal security protocols before you can get inside."

"That's where I come in," Annika said softly. "I can handle the controls."

"And I'll be right there with you," Nathan added, his gaze steady. "We'll get it done."

James nodded, his gaze shifting to David. "Once Annika and Nathan are inside, we'll position ourselves on the outer perimeter. If anything goes wrong, we'll move in and extract them."

"Understood," David said, his voice low and firm. "I'll have a few contingencies in place. If we need to, we can create a distraction and draw security away from their position."

Kane glanced at the clock on his laptop, then back at the group. "We've got a three-hour window, starting at 2 a.m. That's when the security protocols reset, and the night shift changes over. We'll be in and out before they know what hit them."

Annika took a deep breath, her gaze steady. "Let's do this."

The maintenance tunnel was dark and musty, the air thick with the scent of damp earth and rusted metal. Annika and Nathan moved carefully through the narrow passage, their footsteps echoing softly against the concrete floor. The tunnel sloped gently downward, leading them closer to their entry point beneath the bank.

"Tunnel's clear," Nathan murmured, his voice low in the darkness. "Kane, what's our status?"

"All external security feeds are looped," Kane replied through their earpieces. "You're invisible. The tunnel should lead you to an access hatch directly beneath the bank's lower levels. It'll put you about fifty feet from the first layer of security."

"Copy that," Annika whispered. "Moving to the access hatch now."

They reached a rusted metal ladder embedded in the wall and began climbing. The metal creaked softly under their weight, but it held firm. At the top of the ladder, Annika reached out and pushed against the hatch. It opened with a faint squeal, revealing a dark, empty storage room.

"Access point secured," Annika whispered. "We're in."

"Nice work," Kane murmured. "There's a service door on your right that'll take you to the main corridor. Once you're there, head left. The first security door is about thirty feet down."

Annika and Nathan moved through the storage room and slipped into the corridor beyond. The air was cooler here, tinged with the faint hum of machinery. They crept down the hallway, their movements smooth and controlled.

"There's the first door," Nathan murmured, nodding toward a reinforced steel door with a biometric scanner mounted beside it.

Annika pulled out a small device from her belt and attached it to the scanner. The device hummed softly, a series of lights blinking across its surface.

"Disabling the scanner," Annika whispered. "Give me a few seconds..."

The seconds ticked by with agonizing slowness. Then, with a soft beep, the scanner's light turned green, and the door clicked open.

"Nice," Nathan breathed, his lips curving into a faint smile.

Annika returned his smile briefly, then slipped through the door. The room beyond was a small, cramped space filled with rows of wires and control panels. She moved to the nearest panel and began typing rapidly.

"Disabling motion sensors," she murmured. "Almost... there. Sensors are offline."

"Good work," Kane said softly. "Now get to the control room and disable the vault's internal security."

"On our way," Annika replied.

They moved quickly and silently through the bank's lower levels, their hearts pounding in their chests as they approached their objective. Every corner, every shadow seemed to pulse with the promise of danger, but they pressed on, driven by a shared resolve that left no room for hesitation.

Finally, they reached the control room.

Annika slipped inside the control room, her senses attuned to every flicker of light, every hum of machinery. The room was small but dense with technology. A massive wall of screens displayed a dizzying array of feed,hallway cameras, infrared motion detectors, pressure-sensitive floor maps, all showing live data on the bank's security status.

Nathan followed close behind, his gaze sweeping the room. "Looks like a tech nightmare," he murmured. "You sure you can handle all this?"

Annika flashed him a brief, determined smile. "I've dealt with worse. Cover me."

She moved to the main console and began working, her fingers flying over the keys as she accessed the bank's security systems. The screens flickered as she bypassed firewalls and encryption protocols, her focus unbroken.

"Alright, I'm in," she whispered, a bead of sweat trickling down her temple. "I'm bringing the vault's internal security offline, but it's going to trigger a system-wide alert. We'll have about two minutes before they realize something's wrong."

"That's more than enough time," Nathan replied softly, his stance tense as he kept watch. "Do it."

Annika's fingers danced over the keys, each stroke precise and deliberate. The monitors around her flickered, then went dark, replaced by a single message:

SECURITY OVERRIDE. SYSTEMS OFFLINE.

"Vault's unprotected," Annika murmured. "We're clear to proceed."

"Copy that," James's voice crackled softly through their earpieces. "David and I are in position. We've got the external exit covered. Move to the vault and secure the assets. We'll be ready to extract when you're done."

"Roger," Nathan whispered. He glanced at Annika, his eyes gleaming with a fierce light. "Let's go."

They moved out of the control room and down the main corridor, the air humming with a strange, tense energy. Annika's pulse pounded in her ears, each beat matching the countdown in her head. They had to move fast. Every second counted.

They reached the vault door, a massive, reinforced slab of steel and titanium. Annika's gaze swept over the biometric scanners, the keypad, the multiple layers of security that had been rendered useless by her override.

"This is it," she murmured, her breath catching slightly. "The heart of Reichter's empire."

Nathan nodded, his jaw clenched. "Open it."

Annika keyed in the access code she'd retrieved from the control room, her fingers steady despite the adrenaline surging through her veins. There was a low, heavy thunk as the locks disengaged, and the vault door slowly swung open.

The room beyond was a stark contrast to the sterile hallways outside. It was lined with shelves and cabinets, each one meticulously organized and labeled. The faint scent of old paper and polished metal filled the air. Annika's gaze swept over the contents, stacks of cash in various currencies, gold bars, bearer bonds, and, most importantly, a series of black, sealed boxes marked with a discreet insignia.

"That's it," Nathan murmured, his eyes narrowing as he moved to one of the boxes. "Reichter's private assets. Whatever he's been hiding, money, leverage, intelligence, it's all here."

"Grab what we need," Annika said quietly. "Documents, hard drives, anything we can use to track his movements, his contacts."

They moved quickly, pulling open the boxes and sorting through the contents. Nathan extracted a stack of ledgers and a small, encrypted laptop, while Annika focused on a series of flash drives and data discs labeled with various dates and project names.

"Kane, we're collecting the assets now," Annika murmured. "How's our time?"

"Not good," Kane replied, his voice tense. "The bank's systems are starting to reboot. I've managed to delay the alarms, but we're looking at less than a minute before they come back online."

"Understood," Annika said softly. "We're almost done."

She grabbed the last flash drive and slipped it into her pack, her gaze darting to Nathan. "Got everything?"

"Yeah," Nathan replied, his expression fierce. "Let's get out of here."

They turned and moved back to the vault entrance, their steps quick and purposeful. But just as they reached the doorway, a soft chime echoed through the room, followed by the faint whir of machinery.

"Damn it," Nathan hissed. "The system's rebooting."

"Kane?" Annika whispered, her heart pounding.

"I'm working on it," Kane replied, his voice strained. "Just keep moving. I'll do what I can to keep them blind."

Annika and Nathan moved into the corridor, the air thick with the sound of distant alarms beginning to stir. The lights overhead flickered, then stabilized, casting a harsh white glow over the walls.

"They're coming back online," Nathan muttered, his gaze darting to the camera mounted above them. Its red light blinked on, its lens swiveling toward them.

"Kane... " Annika began, but Kane cut her off.

"Got it!" he shouted. "I've got a temporary loop going. You're still invisible, for now. But you need to get out of there. Now."

"We're on our way," Nathan growled. "Move, Annika."

They sprinted down the hallway, the sound of their footsteps echoing off the walls. The building seemed to pulse with a strange, frenetic energy, as if it were coming alive around them. Annika's heart raced, her mind focused solely on the path ahead.

They reached the maintenance tunnel and slipped inside, the air cooler and darker here. The tunnel stretched out before them like a gaping maw, its walls narrowing as they descended deeper.

"Keep going," Annika panted, her lungs burning. "We're almost there."

The tunnel seemed to stretch on forever, every turn and twist blurring together in a haze of adrenaline and exhaustion. But finally, they reached the ladder leading up to the surface.

"Go, go!" Nathan shouted, shoving Annika ahead of him.

She scrambled up the ladder, her muscles trembling with exertion. The hatch above them creaked open, and she hauled herself through, collapsing onto the cool concrete of the alleyway outside the bank.

Nathan was right behind her, his face flushed and sweaty as he pulled himself out of the tunnel. He looked back at the hatch, his chest heaving.

"We made it," he breathed, a fierce grin breaking across his face.

"Not yet," James's voice crackled through their earpieces. "Security's mobilizing. They're on their way. Get to the extraction point. Now."

Annika and Nathan didn't hesitate. They ran through the narrow alleyways, the sounds of distant sirens growing louder. The city seemed to blur around them, each corner a potential ambush, each shadow a threat.

Finally, they rounded a corner and spotted the black SUV parked at the curb, its engine idling. James and David were waiting beside it, their weapons raised and their gazes sharp.

"Get in!" David shouted.

Annika and Nathan dove into the backseat, the doors slamming shut behind them. The SUV roared to life, tires squealing as David floored the accelerator.

"Are we clear?" Annika gasped, glancing back at the rapidly receding bank.

"Not yet," James murmured, his gaze fixed on the rearview mirror. "They're mobilizing a response. We've got a few minutes before they start locking down the city."

"But we've got what we came for," Nathan said fiercely, his eyes gleaming. "Reichter's assets, his plans, it's all here."

"Yeah," Annika murmured, her heart still racing. "We've got him. We've got everything."

The SUV sped through the streets of Geneva, weaving through traffic as they made their escape. The city lights blurred past them, the sound of sirens fading into the distance.

"We're not out of this yet," James said softly, his gaze hard. "But we've taken his money. We've taken his leverage. And now, we're going to take him down."

Annika nodded, a fierce smile curving her lips. "Wherever he runs, we'll be there."

There was a murmur of agreement around the SUV, a shared sense of purpose that pulsed through the air like a living thing.

"We're coming for you, Reichter," James whispered, his voice low and steady. "And when we find you, there won't be anywhere left to hide."

The words hung in the air like a promise, a vow that echoed in the silence as the Patriots drove into the night, ready to finish what they'd started.

Chapter 14

The sun was setting over Zurich, casting a soft, golden light over the city's skyline. The Patriots had relocated to another safe house, a sleek, modern apartment with large windows that offered a sweeping view of the Limmat River. The safe house was located on the top floor of a discreet building in a quiet residential neighborhood, a place where their movements could go unnoticed and their conversations remain private.

Inside, the team gathered around the living room, their expressions a mixture of exhaustion and grim determination. The adrenaline from the heist in Geneva had worn off, leaving behind a quiet intensity that seemed to hum in the air. They were in uncharted territory now, closer than ever to taking down Reichter, but also more vulnerable.

James Donovan stood near the windows, his gaze fixed on the distant mountains. He'd been silent since they'd left Geneva, his mind clearly racing with thoughts and strategies. The room was filled with the low murmur of conversation, but when James finally spoke, all eyes turned to him.

"We have Reichter's financials," James began, his voice low and steady. "We know where his money's been going, who he's been paying, and what he's been funding. But we need more than that if we're going to bring him down. We need to cut off his command structure, isolate him, and force him into the open."

Annika nodded from her position at the dining table, where she and Sarah had been going over the data they'd retrieved from the Geneva bank. "Reichter's been using a series of shell companies to funnel money into covert operations, projects that even his closest associates don't know about. He's got ties to government officials, intelligence agencies, and criminal syndicates all over Europe."

"Which means he's got a deep network of people who are going to do whatever it takes to protect him," David said quietly, his gaze dark. "If we move on him directly, we'll be facing an army."

"That's why we're going to dismantle his network first," James said, his gaze sweeping over the group. "We go after his key operatives, take out his lieutenants, and neutralize his support structure. We make it impossible for him to coordinate a response."

Nathan leaned back in his chair, his arms crossed over his chest. "And where do we start? We've got names, locations, but not much else. These people are scattered all over the place."

"We start with the weakest link," Annika murmured, her eyes narrowing thoughtfully. She tapped a file on the table, pulling up a profile of a man in his early forties with graying hair and a nervous expression. "Thomas Rehnquist. He's Reichter's primary money man in Eastern Europe, handles all the transfers, makes sure the funds keep flowing. He's based in Prague, and he's got a reputation for being cautious. If we can get to him, we can cut off Reichter's access to several major accounts."

"Rehnquist is a key player," Kane added, glancing up from his laptop. "But he's not untouchable. He's kept a low profile, but I've found traces of his movements over the last few weeks. He's been making a lot of trips between Prague and Zurich, probably meeting with Reichter's other financiers."

"Which means he's nervous," Sarah interjected. "He knows something's coming, but he doesn't know what. If we make the right move, we can push him into a corner, make him desperate enough to talk."

"And once we have him," James murmured, his eyes narrowing, "we use him to get to the others."

There was a murmur of agreement around the room, the team's resolve hardening.

"So, what's the plan?" Nathan asked, his gaze locked on James.

"We take a small team to Prague," James replied. "Annika, Nathan, you're with me. We'll track down Rehnquist, figure out his routine, and wait for the right moment to grab him. Kane and Sarah, you'll provide remote support, monitor communications, loop camera feeds, keep us one step ahead."

"And me?" David asked, his brow furrowing slightly.

"I need you to stay here and coordinate with our contacts in Europe," James said. "If anything goes wrong, I want you ready to deploy reinforcements and handle extraction. Reichter's going to know we're moving against him soon, and we need to be prepared for anything."

David nodded, his expression serious. "I've got your back."

"Good," James murmured. He straightened, his gaze sweeping over the team once more. "This isn't just about taking down Reichter anymore. It's about finishing what we started. We've come too far to let him slip away now."

He paused, letting his words sink in, then nodded firmly. "Let's move."

• • • •

The city of Prague was a maze of winding cobblestone streets and narrow alleyways, its architecture a blend of old-world charm and modern efficiency. The Patriots had set up a temporary base in a nondescript apartment overlooking Wenceslas Square, the heart of the city's business and cultural district. From here, they could monitor Rehnquist's movements and plan their approach without drawing attention.

Annika stood by the window, her gaze sweeping over the square below. The streets were filled with tourists and locals alike, their laughter and conversations drifting up through the open window. But Annika's attention was focused on a single figure seated at an outdoor café, a middle-aged man with graying hair and a nervous energy that seemed to radiate from him.

"That's him," Annika murmured into her comm, her eyes narrowing. "Rehnquist. He's been sitting there for the last twenty minutes, nursing the same cup of coffee."

"I see him," James replied from where he and Nathan were positioned in a rented car down the street. "Any signs of backup?"

"None," Sarah's voice crackled through their earpieces. "I've got eyes on all entry points. No one's made contact with him since he arrived."

"He's alone," Nathan murmured, his gaze locked on Rehnquist. "We should move now, while we have the advantage."

"Not yet," James said softly. "Let's see if he makes a move. We need him alive, and willing to talk."

The minutes stretched on, each second a test of their patience. Rehnquist shifted nervously in his seat, glancing around the square as if expecting someone. Then, finally, he pulled out his phone and began typing rapidly.

"Kane, can you see what he's doing?" Annika asked, her voice tight with anticipation.

"Give me a second," Kane replied. "I'm patching into the cell tower... got it. He's sending a message, encrypted, but I'm decrypting it now. Looks like it's going to a burner phone registered in Zurich."

"What's the message say?" James asked, his gaze sharpening.

Kane paused, then his voice came through, edged with tension. "'We need to meet. It's not safe here anymore. They're getting closer.'"

Annika exchanged a glance with Nathan. "He knows we're after him."

"Which means he's going to run," Nathan murmured.

"We can't let that happen," James said firmly. "Annika, Nathan, move in. We take him here, now."

"Copy that," Annika whispered, her gaze locking onto Rehnquist. "We're on him."

She and Nathan slipped out of the apartment and moved through the crowded streets, their movements smooth and unhurried. They approached the café from opposite directions, blending seamlessly with the flow of people around them.

Rehnquist glanced up as Annika approached, his eyes widening slightly. For a moment, he seemed to hesitate, then his hand darted toward his pocket, reaching for something.

"Don't," Annika said softly, her voice calm but edged with steel. "You don't want to do that."

Rehnquist froze, his hand hovering over his pocket. His gaze darted to Nathan, who had appeared at his other side, his expression cool and unyielding.

"Mr. Rehnquist," Nathan said quietly, his voice almost conversational. "We need to have a little chat. Let's not make a scene, alright?"

Rehnquist swallowed hard, his eyes darting between them. "Who... who are you?"

"We're the people who can make all your problems go away," Annika replied, her gaze steady. "Or we can make them a lot worse. It's your choice."

Rehnquist hesitated, his face pale. Then, slowly, he nodded.

"Alright," he whispered, his voice trembling slightly. "Alright, I'll talk."

"Good," Nathan murmured. He glanced at Annika, his eyes glinting. "Let's take him somewhere private."

They guided Rehnquist out of the café and into a waiting car, the city's lights blurring past them as they drove to a secure location on the outskirts of town. Rehnquist sat between Annika and Nathan, his hands trembling slightly as he glanced nervously at them.

"You have no idea what you're getting into," Rehnquist whispered, his voice filled with a mix of fear and desperation. "Reichter, he'll find out. He'll come after you."

Annika leaned forward, her gaze intense. "We're counting on it."

Rehnquist blinked, confusion flickering across his face. "You... you want him to come after you?"

"No," Nathan said softly, his expression dark. "We want him to come to us."

The car came to a stop in the secluded alley, the sound of the engine cutting out echoing softly against the brick walls. The air was cool and still, carrying a faint, musty scent. The narrow passage was shielded from view, a perfect place for a private conversation.

James stepped out of the driver's seat and moved around to the back of the car, his gaze steady as he regarded Rehnquist. The banker's face was pale and drawn, his eyes wide with fear and uncertainty. Annika and Nathan flanked him on either side, their presence a silent reminder that there was no escape.

James nodded to Annika and Nathan, and they stepped back, giving him space. He leaned against the car, his arms crossed over his chest as he looked down at Rehnquist.

"Mr. Rehnquist," James said softly, his voice calm but firm. "You have information that can help us stop a very dangerous man. We need you to tell us everything you know about Reichter's operations, locations, contacts, upcoming plans. The more you tell us, the better your chances are of walking away from this."

Rehnquist's hands fidgeted nervously in his lap, his gaze darting between the Patriots. "I... I already told them what I know," he stammered, his voice shaking. "The bunker outside Vienna, Reichter's been using it to organize his people, move equipment. But I swear, I don't know anything more!"

"Then tell us about the people he's working with," James pressed gently. "You mentioned high-level contacts, politicians, military figures. Who are they?"

Rehnquist swallowed hard, his gaze dropping to the ground. "I-I don't have all the names, but I know some of them. There's Viktor Gregorov, he handles logistics for Reichter's operations in Eastern Europe. He's ex-intelligence, and he's got connections all over the region. There's also a man named Jan Kratochvil, a local arms dealer who's been supplying Reichter with weapons and equipment. They meet regularly in Vienna, at a private club called The Glass House."

James's gaze sharpened. "The Glass House? What else do you know about it?"

Rehnquist hesitated, his fingers twisting together anxiously. "It's... it's not just a club. It's a meeting place for people like Reichter, people with money and influence who don't want to be seen in public. They use it to make deals, share information. Reichter's been going there for years, and he's got people on the inside."

Nathan exchanged a glance with Annika, his brow furrowed. "If Reichter's got people on the inside, it's going to be difficult to get close without tipping him off."

"We don't need to get close to him yet," James said quietly. "We just need to confirm that he's there and see who he's meeting with. If we can identify more of his associates, we'll have leverage, people we can use to push Reichter out into the open."

Rehnquist's head snapped up, his eyes wide with alarm. "Wait, you're not seriously thinking about going there, are you? The Glass House is a fortress! Armed guards, cameras, biometric scanners... if you try to get in, they'll know you're there."

"We're not going in," Annika said softly. "Not yet. We'll set up surveillance outside and monitor the place. If Reichter's there, we'll find a way to track his movements without alerting him."

"Then what happens to me?" Rehnquist asked, his voice barely above a whisper.

"You're coming with us," James replied firmly. "We're not letting you out of our sight until we have what we need. You're too valuable to risk losing."

Rehnquist seemed to deflate, his shoulders slumping as if the fight had gone out of him. He nodded slowly, his expression a mixture of fear and resignation. "Okay. I'll... I'll cooperate. Just... don't leave me out here alone. Reichter's people are everywhere."

James's gaze softened slightly, and he nodded. "We'll keep you safe, Rehnquist. But you need to keep giving us what we need. Understand?"

Rehnquist nodded jerkily. "Yes, yes... I understand."

"Good," James murmured. He glanced at Annika and Nathan, his expression serious. "Let's get him back to the safe house. We'll regroup and make a plan to surveil The Glass House."

The safe house in Prague was located in a quiet residential neighborhood, tucked away behind a row of ivy-covered buildings. It was a modest two-story structure, its exterior blending in seamlessly with the surrounding homes. From the outside, it looked like just another residence, nothing to draw attention. But inside, the Patriots had set up a secure command center, complete with communications equipment and monitoring stations.

They guided Rehnquist into the living room, where he slumped down onto a worn leather armchair, his face pale and his hands shaking. Annika handed him a glass of water, her gaze steady as she watched him drink.

"Take a breath," she murmured softly. "You did the right thing. Just keep cooperating, and you'll get through this."

Rehnquist nodded, swallowing hard. "I don't have much of a choice, do I?"

"No," Nathan said bluntly. "But it's better than the alternative."

Rehnquist shuddered and lowered his gaze to the floor, his shoulders hunched.

James turned to the rest of the team, his expression thoughtful. "We've got a name and a location. That's more than we had before. If Reichter's meeting people at The Glass House, we need to find a way to monitor those meetings and identify everyone he's in contact with."

"Setting up surveillance on a place like that won't be easy," Kane said, his brow furrowing as he considered the challenge. "They'll have all kinds of countermeasures, signal jammers, encrypted communications, possibly even thermal scanners to detect external monitoring."

"Can you get us close enough without being detected?" James asked, his gaze steady.

Kane nodded slowly. "I can find a way. It'll take some time to set up, but I can establish a secure perimeter and deploy some of our more advanced equipment. We'll be able to listen in on conversations and track movements without tripping their alarms."

"Do it," James said firmly. "Sarah, I want you coordinating with Kane. Make sure everything is in place before we make a move."

"Understood," Sarah replied, her expression serious.

"David," James continued, "you'll be on standby with me and Nathan. If anything goes wrong, we'll move in and extract everyone. This is a recon mission for now, but if we get a shot at Reichter, I want to be ready."

David nodded, his jaw set. "You got it."

James glanced around the room, his gaze lingering on each of them in turn. He could see the exhaustion etched into their faces, the weight of everything they'd been through bearing down on them. But there was also a fierce determination, a shared resolve that seemed to bind them together.

"We're almost there," he murmured softly. "Reichter's running out of places to hide. We've crippled his finances, taken out his lieutenants, and now we're closing in on his last strongholds. But this is where he's going to fight back the hardest. We need to be ready for whatever he throws at us."

There was a murmur of agreement, the tension in the room thickening as they all absorbed his words.

"We'll take shifts monitoring the surveillance once Kane's got everything in place," Annika said quietly. "If Reichter's there, we'll spot him. And when we do..."

"We'll take him down," Nathan finished, his voice filled with a quiet intensity. "No more games. No more cat-and-mouse."

James nodded slowly, his gaze hardening. "No more games."

They fell silent then, each of them lost in their own thoughts as the weight of what lay ahead settled over them.

Reichter was still out there, still pulling strings, still plotting. But the Patriots were closing in. They had the skills, the experience, and the unwavering resolve to see this through.

Whatever it took.

Whoever they had to face.

They would finish it.

Chapter 15

T he streets of Vienna were bathed in the warm glow of twilight, the city's historic architecture casting long shadows across the cobblestone roads. The air was cool and crisp, carrying with it the faint scent of roasting chestnuts from street vendors and the low murmur of conversations drifting from nearby cafes. The Patriots had set up their new base of operations in a quiet, unassuming office building on the outskirts of the city, far from the prying eyes of Reichter's network.

Inside, the safe house was a hive of activity. Maps of Vienna and digital schematics of The Glass House were pinned to the walls, with red strings and pins marking key locations. Laptops and monitoring equipment cluttered the long table in the center of the room, their screens flickering with live feeds and encrypted data streams. The tension in the air was palpable, everyone knew they were venturing deeper into enemy territory.

James stood at the head of the table, his gaze focused on a live satellite image of The Glass House projected on the wall. It was an elegant structure nestled in Vienna's industrial district, its sleek glass facade giving it a modern yet discreet appearance. But they all knew it was more than just a place for meetings and business deals. It was a fortress, a place where Reichter's associates gathered under the guise of civility.

"All right, team," James said, his voice low but firm. "Kane's done his magic, and we've got surveillance in place. We've managed to tap into the building's external cameras, so we have eyes on all entrances and exits. The feeds are being looped, so for now, we're flying under the radar."

Kane nodded, his fingers flying over the keyboard as he pulled up a series of camera feeds on the central monitor. "It took some doing, but I managed to bypass their internal security protocols without triggering any alerts. We can see everyone coming and going. The signal's stable, but I can't guarantee how long we'll stay undetected."

"Understood," James replied. He glanced around at the rest of the team, Annika, Nathan, David, and Sarah, all gathered around the table. "We need to identify who's inside and confirm whether Reichter is there. If we see him, we'll monitor his movements and anyone he talks to. Our goal is to get intel on his next move and the people he's meeting with."

"And if we get the chance to grab him?" Nathan asked, his eyes narrowing.

James hesitated, then shook his head. "Not yet. Reichter's too well-protected, and if we make a move too early, we could lose our chance to bring down his entire network. We need to be smart about this."

Nathan's jaw tightened, but he nodded, understanding the reasoning. "Got it. So, we wait."

"Exactly," James murmured. "We wait, we watch, and we gather information. When we're ready, we'll hit them hard."

Annika's gaze shifted to the live feed of The Glass House's entrance. A group of men in tailored suits were approaching, their movements brisk and purposeful. She recognized the lead figure, Jan Kratochvil, the arms dealer Rehnquist had mentioned.

"Looks like our friend Kratochvil has arrived," Annika said softly. "We should get eyes on who he's meeting."

Kane tapped a few keys, zooming in on Kratochvil's face. "Got it. He's heading toward the side entrance. Security's letting him through without any checks. He's definitely a regular."

"Let's see who joins him," James murmured. "Nathan, David, you're up. I want you two on the ground, keeping a low profile. Blend in with the crowd and stay out of sight. If you see anything suspicious, report back immediately."

"Roger that," Nathan replied, his expression focused. He turned to David, who gave a quick nod.

"We'll be ghosts," David said softly. "They won't even know we're there."

They moved quickly, slipping out of the safe house and into a nondescript sedan parked down the street. As they drove through the city, Nathan's gaze flicked to the rearview mirror, scanning for any sign of a tail. But there was nothing, just the steady flow of evening traffic and the soft glow of streetlights reflecting off the wet pavement.

"Think Reichter's got eyes on us?" David asked quietly, his gaze fixed on the road ahead.

"Always," Nathan murmured. "But he doesn't know how close we are. Not yet."

David nodded, his grip tightening on the steering wheel. "Then let's keep it that way."

Back at the safe house, the atmosphere was thick with anticipation as the team monitored the feeds. The Glass House's main lobby was filled with well-dressed men and women, their expressions a mixture of determination and wariness. Annika leaned forward, her eyes narrowing as she scanned the faces.

"Kane, run facial recognition," she murmured. "I want to know who these people are."

"Already on it," Kane replied, his fingers flying over the keyboard. A series of data points appeared on the screen, matching faces to names and affiliations. "Let's see... that's Karl Hennings, a German industrialist with ties to Reichter's old network. Next to him is Marta Schreiber, a former lobbyist turned private consultant. She's been linked to several covert political campaigns in Eastern Europe."

"Looks like we're dealing with more than just business associates," Sarah murmured, her gaze intent. "These people have influence. They can move money, make deals... shape policy."

"Which means Reichter's building more than just a criminal network," Annika said softly. "He's building a coalition, people who can protect him and help him operate in the shadows."

"And destabilize governments if necessary," James added, his expression grim. "He's not just a threat to us, he's a threat to national security."

"We need to get a complete list of everyone at that meeting," Annika said, her voice low and urgent. "If we can identify them all, we'll have leverage. We can put pressure on them, isolate Reichter even further."

Kane nodded, his gaze locked on the screen as he continued scanning the crowd. "I'm on it. Give me a few minutes."

The minutes stretched on in tense silence, the team watching as more people arrived at The Glass House. Each new face was cataloged, cross-referenced, and added to the growing list of Reichter's potential allies.

"There," Kane murmured suddenly, his voice filled with tension. "That man, entering through the rear entrance."

Annika's eyes snapped to the screen, her heart skipping a beat. The man was tall and broad-shouldered, his face partially obscured by the brim of his hat. But there was something unmistakable about his presence, something that sent a chill down her spine.

"Is that...?" she whispered, her voice trailing off.

Kane zoomed in, the image sharpening. The man glanced up briefly, his eyes flashing in the light.

"It's Viktor Gregorov," Kane confirmed softly. "Reichter's logistics man."

James straightened, his gaze locked on the screen. "If Gregorov's here, then Reichter's close. He wouldn't leave his right-hand man exposed unless he was nearby."

"Agreed," Annika murmured. "We need to find out what Gregorov's doing here. Who's he meeting with?"

"Kane, can you tap into their communications?" Sarah asked, her voice urgent. "Even if we can't get audio, we might be able to intercept text messages or emails."

"I'm trying," Kane replied, his brow furrowed in concentration. "Their systems are layered with encryption. I've managed to get partial access, but, wait."

"What is it?" James asked sharply.

Kane's gaze flicked to the side as a new window opened on his screen. "I've got a text message. It's heavily encrypted, but I can see the sender and recipient."

"Who's it from?" Annika asked, leaning forward.

"Sender is Gregorov," Kane murmured. "Recipient is... Reichter."

Annika's heart pounded in her chest. "What does it say?"

"I'm decrypting it now," Kane whispered, his fingers flying over the keys. "Just a few more seconds... got it."

The message appeared on the screen, its meaning chilling in its simplicity.

"All assets in place. Ready to move forward. Awaiting your signal."

James's gaze hardened, his voice dropping to a deadly whisper. "He's about to make his move."

"We need to intercept Gregorov," Nathan's voice crackled through the comms. "He's our best shot at finding out what Reichter's planning."

"Agreed," James replied. "But do it quietly. If Reichter gets wind that we're onto him, he'll disappear, and we'll lose our chance."

"Understood," Nathan murmured. "We're on it."

Nathan and David moved swiftly through the back alleys, their steps silent as they approached the rear entrance of The Glass House. The air was thick with tension, every shadow seeming to pulse with the promise of danger.

"Gregorov's on the move," Kane's voice murmured through their earpieces. "He's leaving through the service exit. You've got about thirty seconds before he's outside."

"Copy that," Nathan whispered, his gaze locked on the exit.

The door swung open, and Gregorov stepped out, his head down as he typed rapidly on his phone. He didn't notice Nathan and David standing in the shadows until it was too late.

In a fluid, precise motion, Nathan closed the distance between them. He grabbed Gregorov by the collar and yanked him into the alley, slamming him against the wall with just enough force to make his point without knocking the man out.

"Not a sound," Nathan growled, his face inches from Gregorov's. "If you want to live, you're going to cooperate."

Gregorov's eyes widened, a flicker of panic crossing his features. He glanced around, his mouth opening as if to shout, but David stepped forward, the cold steel of a handgun pressing lightly against Gregorov's ribs.

"I'd think twice about that," David murmured, his voice low and deadly calm. "We can do this the easy way, or we can do it the hard way. Either way, you're coming with us."

Gregorov's gaze darted between them, his mind clearly racing. He swallowed hard, his breath coming in short, panicked bursts. "You... you don't know who you're dealing with," he whispered, his voice trembling.

"No," Nathan murmured, his grip tightening on Gregorov's collar. "You don't know who you're dealing with. We're giving you one chance to walk away from this alive. Don't waste it."

For a moment, Gregorov seemed to consider his options. Then, slowly, his shoulders slumped, and he nodded jerkily.

"All right, all right," he whispered, his voice tight with fear. "I'll come quietly. Just... don't hurt me."

Nathan exchanged a glance with David, then nodded. "Good. Now, we're going to take a little walk. No sudden moves, no funny business. Got it?"

Gregorov nodded frantically. "Yes, yes, I understand."

"Let's go," David murmured, stepping back just enough to let Gregorov move. He kept his weapon discreetly trained on Gregorov's side, his gaze never wavering.

They moved through the darkened alley, Nathan and David flanking Gregorov on either side. The narrow passage was empty, the air thick with the scent of damp brick and asphalt. Every step seemed to echo through the silence, a reminder of how precarious their position was.

"Sarah, status on external security?" Nathan murmured into his earpiece as they made their way toward the extraction point.

"Perimeter's clear," Sarah's voice crackled softly through the comms. "No signs of anyone tailing you. You're good to go."

"Roger that," Nathan replied. He glanced at Gregorov, his expression hard. "Keep moving."

They reached the end of the alley, where a black SUV was parked in the shadows. Nathan opened the back door and gestured for Gregorov to get in.

"Inside," Nathan ordered, his voice cold.

Gregorov hesitated, his gaze flickering to the dark interior of the vehicle. For a moment, it looked as if he might try to run, but Nathan's eyes locked onto his with a look that promised swift retribution if he so much as twitched the wrong way.

With a resigned sigh, Gregorov climbed into the back seat. Nathan followed him in, the door closing with a soft click. David slipped into the driver's seat, his gaze flicking to the rearview mirror as he started the engine.

"Let's get him back to the safe house," Nathan murmured, his gaze never leaving Gregorov's face. "We've got questions, and I think he's finally ready to answer them."

Back at the safe house, the Patriots reconvened in the secure basement room they'd designated for interrogations. The space was stark and functional, with concrete walls and a single overhead light that cast harsh shadows across the floor. A sturdy metal chair was bolted to the center of the room, and it was there that they placed Gregorov, his hands cuffed to the armrests.

James stood at the far end of the room, his arms crossed over his chest as he regarded Gregorov with a cool, assessing gaze. Annika and Nathan flanked him, their expressions equally unyielding.

Gregorov shifted uncomfortably in the chair, his eyes darting around the room. "You... You can't do this," he stammered, his voice trembling. "I'm a protected asset. I have rights... "

"Your rights are the last thing you need to worry about right now," James said softly, his voice carrying a lethal edge. "You're going to tell us everything we need to know about Reichter's operation. And if you cooperate, maybe, just maybe, you'll get to walk out of here alive."

Gregorov swallowed hard, his gaze flickering between them. "I already told you everything I know. The bunker outside Vienna, Reichter's using it to organize his people, move equipment. I don't know what else you want from me."

"We want specifics," Annika said, her voice calm but firm. "What kind of equipment? How many people? What's his endgame?"

Gregorov licked his lips nervously, his eyes widening. "I don't, I don't have all the details. Reichter compartmentalizes everything. I only see a piece of the puzzle."

"Then tell us about your piece," Nathan growled, his gaze hard. "Start talking, or this is going to get a lot more unpleasant."

Gregorov hesitated, his mouth opening and closing as if he were struggling to find the words. Then, with a resigned sigh, he nodded slowly.

"All right," he whispered. "I'll tell you what I know."

The room fell silent, the Patriots leaning in slightly as Gregorov began to speak.

"Reichter's been funneling assets into that bunker for months, equipment, weapons, supplies. He's brought in mercenaries, former special forces... people who know how to fight and aren't afraid to get their hands dirty. But that's just the start."

He glanced around the room, his eyes filled with a mix of fear and desperation. "He's not jus, a place where he can coordinate operations across Europe without being detected. He's planning something big, something that will destabilize governments and create chaos on a massive scale."

"Like what?" James asked sharply. "What's he planning to do?"

Gregorov shook his head frantically. "I don't know the details! All I know is that he's been meeting with key figures, people with influence, power. Politicians, business leaders, even rogue elements from intelligence agencies. He's got something up his sleeve, something that will give him leverage over all of them."

"Leverage?" Annika murmured, her gaze narrowing. "What kind of leverage?"

"I don't know," Gregorov whispered, his voice breaking. "But whatever it is, it's big. Big enough to make people fall in line. Reichter's always had his fingers in a lot of pies, but this... this is different. He's consolidating power, making moves that even his old allies are wary of."

The Patriots exchanged grim looks, the weight of Gregorov's words settling over them like a dark cloud.

"If he's consolidating power, then he's preparing for something imminent," James murmured. "We need to get to that bunker and find out what's going on. If Reichter's setting up a command center there, it could be our only chance to take him down once and for all."

"But it's going to be heavily guarded," Nathan said quietly. "We'll need more than just the five of us to breach a fortified bunker."

"We'll need to be smart," Annika agreed. "Find a way in without alerting his entire network. And if we can't do that... we go in fast and hard, take out his people before they can react."

James nodded slowly, his gaze shifting back to Gregorov. "You've done the right thing by talking, Gregorov. But if you're holding anything back, now's the time to tell us. Because once we're in that bunker, there won't be any turning back."

Gregorov's shoulders slumped, his face pale. "I... I've told you everything I know," he whispered. "Just... don't let him find me. He'll kill me if he knows I talked."

"We'll keep you safe," James said quietly. "But you're staying under our watch until this is over. You're too valuable to let go."

Gregorov nodded numbly, his gaze dropping to the floor.

James straightened, his expression hardening. "We move tonight. Kane, start gathering everything we have on the bunker. Annika, Nathan, David, prep for infiltration. We're going to hit Reichter where it hurts."

There was a murmur of agreement, the Patriots falling into action with the precision of a well-oiled machine. They'd been pushed to their limits, tested in ways most people couldn't imagine. But they weren't backing down.

Not now.

Not ever.

Reichter's reign was coming to an end.

And the Patriots were going to make sure of it.

Chapter 16

The night air around the outskirts of Vienna was cold and damp, the kind of chill that seemed to seep into your bones. The Patriots had gathered in a small clearing just outside the forest surrounding the bunker's entrance, their dark clothing blending seamlessly with the shadows. The low hum of insects and the rustling of leaves were the only sounds that filled the silence as they prepared for the mission ahead.

James stood at the center of the group, his gaze steady as he reviewed the final plan. The soft glow from the tactical tablet in his hand cast faint shadows across his face, highlighting the lines of concentration etched there.

"All right, listen up," he murmured, his voice barely audible over the whispering wind. "The bunker is surrounded by multiple layers of security. We're looking at perimeter guards, motion sensors, and a closed-circuit surveillance system. Kane's managed to bypass the cameras for now, but we'll need to be quick and quiet. Once we're inside, we split into two teams. Annika and Nathan, you're with me. We'll go for the command center and gather as much intel as we can on Reichter's operations."

He glanced at David and Sarah. "You two will secure the exits and cover our extraction. If we're compromised, we'll need a clear route out, no matter what. Understood?"

David nodded firmly, his jaw set. "Got it. We'll keep the door open."

"Good," James murmured. "This isn't just about taking down Reichter's bunker. It's about getting the information we need to dismantle his entire network. We find out what he's planning, who he's working with, and we shut it all down."

Nathan shifted slightly, his expression tense. "And if Reichter's there?"

James's gaze hardened. "If we have a shot at taking him, we do it. But only if it's safe. The mission comes first."

Annika nodded slowly, her eyes steady. "Understood."

There was a long moment of silence as the Patriots exchanged glances. They'd faced impossible odds before, but this mission felt different, more dangerous, more uncertain. But the bond between them, forged through years of fighting side by side, held strong. They trusted each other with their lives, and that trust would see them through.

"All right," James murmured finally. "Let's move out."

The team moved through the dense forest with the grace and precision of seasoned hunters, their steps soundless against the soft underbrush. The trees closed in around them, the canopy above blocking out most of the moonlight, leaving only faint slivers of silver to guide their path.

Annika led the way, her sharp eyes scanning the shadows for any sign of movement. She raised her hand, signaling for the others to halt as they neared the first line of security, a tall, chain-link fence topped with barbed wire. Beyond it, the entrance to the bunker was just visible through the trees, a massive concrete structure partially buried in the side of a hill, its exterior lit by floodlights.

"There," Annika whispered, pointing to a small guard post positioned near the gate. Two guards stood outside, their rifles slung over their shoulders as they exchanged quiet words.

Nathan crouched beside her, his gaze locked on the guards. "Take them out quietly?"

James nodded. "No gunfire. We can't afford to alert anyone inside."

Annika pulled out a small, sleek knife from her belt, the blade glinting faintly in the dim light. She glanced at Nathan, who gave her a brief nod.

"On three," she murmured softly. "One... two... three."

They moved as one, slipping through the underbrush and closing the distance to the guard post in a matter of seconds. Annika struck first, her hand flashing out to cover the nearest guard's mouth as her blade found its mark. The guard's eyes widened in shock, his body going limp as she lowered him silently to the ground.

Nathan was just as quick, his arm wrapping around the second guard's neck in a tight chokehold. The guard struggled for a moment, then slumped forward, unconscious.

"Clear," Nathan whispered, his voice barely a breath in the night air.

James and the others moved forward, their eyes scanning the area for any sign of alarm. But the night remained still and silent, the guards' disappearance unnoticed.

"Good work," James murmured. "Let's get through the fence."

Kane's voice crackled softly through their earpieces. "I've disabled the sensors on the gate. You're clear to cut through."

Annika pulled a pair of wire cutters from her pack and quickly snipped a section of the fence, creating a narrow opening just wide enough for them to slip through.

"Sarah, David, you're up," James said softly. "Secure the perimeter and keep an eye out for any patrols."

"Copy that," Sarah replied. She and David moved to the edges of the clearing, their weapons at the ready as they scanned the treeline for any sign of movement.

"Let's move," James murmured to the others.

They slipped through the opening and made their way toward the entrance of the bunker, keeping low and using the shadows for cover. The entrance was a massive steel door set into the concrete wall, flanked by two more guards. Annika's gaze narrowed as she sized up the situation.

"Kane, can you disable the door's security?" she whispered.

"Working on it," Kane replied, his voice tense. "The door's on a separate system. Give me a minute."

The seconds ticked by in tense silence, every sound seeming magnified in the stillness. Then, with a soft beep, the red light above the door flickered to green.

"Door's unlocked," Kane whispered. "You're good to go."

"Move in," James ordered softly.

They slipped through the door and into the bunker, the cool air of the interior hitting them like a wave. The hallway was dimly lit, the overhead lights casting long shadows across the concrete floor. The faint hum of machinery filled the silence, the sound reverberating through the narrow passage.

"Annika, Nathan, you're with me," James murmured. "We'll head for the command center. Sarah, David, secure the exits and set up a fallback point in case things go sideways."

"Roger," David replied. "Stay sharp."

They moved swiftly and silently through the bunker's corridors, their senses attuned to every flicker of light, every whisper of sound. The walls seemed to close in around them, the narrow hallways twisting and turning like a labyrinth.

"Command center's two levels down," Kane murmured through their earpieces. "I've got a partial map of the facility. You're looking for a room labeled 'Operations'... should be heavily guarded."

"We'll find it," Annika whispered, her eyes scanning the corridor ahead. "How many people are in the bunker?"

"Hard to say," Kane replied, his voice edged with frustration. "I'm picking up at least a dozen heat signatures on the lower levels, but I can't pinpoint their locations. Be careful."

"Copy that," James murmured. "Let's go."

They descended a narrow staircase, their footsteps soundless against the metal steps. The air grew colder as they moved deeper into the bunker, the walls lined with cables and conduits. Annika's heart pounded in her chest, every nerve on edge as they reached the bottom of the stairs.

Ahead, the corridor widened into a larger, open space. A heavy metal door marked "Operations" loomed at the far end, flanked by two guards armed with submachine guns. Annika's eyes narrowed as she studied the guards' positions, the way they shifted their weight, their gaze sweeping the hallway.

"They look alert," Nathan murmured softly. "No way we're getting past them without taking them out."

"Agreed," James said quietly. "Annika, you take the one on the left. Nathan, you're on the right. I'll cover you."

They moved with the lethal grace of seasoned professionals, slipping through the shadows and closing the distance to the guards in a matter of seconds. Annika's knife flashed, a blur of silver as she struck, the guard crumpling to the ground without a sound. Nathan's takedown was just as quick, his arm locking around the second guard's neck and cutting off his air.

"Clear," Annika whispered, wiping the blade clean.

"Good," James murmured. "Now let's see what's behind that door."

They moved to the entrance, Annika carefully sliding a thin device into the door's access panel. The small screen on the device blinked, and with a soft click, the door slid open.

The room beyond was a stark contrast to the utilitarian corridors outside. It was filled with high-tech equipment, monitors displaying live feeds, consoles covered in blinking lights, and a massive central table covered in maps and documents. Two men in dark suits stood at the far end, their backs to the door as they spoke in low, urgent tones.

James raised his weapon, his voice calm and steady. "Don't move."

The men froze, their hands hovering in midair. Slowly, they turned, their expressions shifting from shock to anger as they took in the sight of the Patriots.

"Who the hell are you?" one of them demanded, his voice tight with fear.

"We're the people who are going to put an end to this," James said softly. "Now, you're going to tell us everything we need to know about Reichter's plans."

The men exchanged a glance, then one of them sneered. "You think you can stop him? You have no idea what you're dealing with."

James's gaze remained steady, his weapon trained on the man who had spoken. "Enlighten us, then. What is Reichter planning? And who are you meeting with here?"

The man's sneer deepened, his eyes flicking over each of them, assessing, calculating. "Even if I told you, it wouldn't matter. Reichter's already set things in motion. You're too late to stop it."

"Why don't you let us decide that?" Annika said softly, taking a step forward. "We're giving you a chance to talk. Don't make us regret it."

The second man's gaze darted nervously between Annika and James, his fingers twitching at his sides. "We... we're just analysts," he stammered, sweat beading on his forehead. "We don't know everything. We just process information and pass it along to the field teams."

"Field teams?" Nathan echoed, his eyes narrowing. "What kind of information?"

"Movement orders, logistics, supply routes... " the man began, but his voice faltered as the other man shot him a furious glare.

"Shut up, Rudy," the first man snapped. He turned his glare on the Patriots, defiance simmering in his eyes. "If you think we're going to betray Reichter, you're wasting your time. He's got eyes everywhere. He'll know if we talk."

James's expression didn't change, but a dangerous edge crept into his voice. "And if you don't talk, you'll wish you had. You think Reichter's dangerous? You haven't seen what we can do."

Rudy swallowed hard, his gaze shifting to the first man. "Karl, please... they're going to kill us if we don't cooperate."

"Reichter will do worse," Karl spat, his lips curling in a sneer. "You know that."

Annika exchanged a glance with Nathan, her eyes narrowing. "What's worse than death, Karl? Because that's what you're looking at right now."

Karl's jaw tightened, but he didn't respond. The silence stretched on, thick and tense, until finally, Rudy let out a shuddering breath.

"All right, all right," he whispered, his shoulders slumping in defeat. "I'll tell you what I know. But you have to promise... you have to promise you'll keep us safe."

"We'll protect you as long as you're honest with us," James said softly. "But if you hold back, or if we find out you're lying..."

Rudy nodded frantically, his face pale. "I get it. I get it. I'll talk."

The Patriots exchanged glances, then James gave a short nod. "Start with what Reichter's planning."

Rudy hesitated, glancing once more at Karl. But when the other man remained silent, he took a deep breath and spoke in a low, trembling voice.

"Reichter's not just consolidating power, he's planning to create chaos across Europe. He's going to destabilize governments, undermine economies, and force entire regions into conflict. He's using his network of operatives to coordinate attacks, bombings, assassinations, sabotage, anything that will weaken the existing power structures."

Annika's eyes widened slightly. "He's trying to create a power vacuum."

"Exactly," Rudy whispered. "He's been gathering support from radical groups, mercenaries, anyone who's willing to cause disruption. He's even recruited rogue elements from various intelligence agencies, people with experience in covert operations. Once the chaos starts, Reichter's going to step in with his own people, his own version of order, and establish himself as a new power broker."

"And the command center here?" Nathan pressed. "What's its role in all this?"

"It's a hub," Rudy explained, his voice shaking. "They're coordinating everything from here. Reichter's lieutenants come and go, delivering updates, receiving new orders. It's all being managed from this location."

"Who's here now?" James demanded, his gaze sharp. "Who's running things?"

Rudy shook his head frantically. "No one big. Just lower-level operatives. The key players, Reichter's closest allies, don't stay here for long. They come in for briefings, then leave. Reichter's been in and out, but I haven't seen him in weeks. Last time he was here, he mentioned something about 'the final phase.'"

"The final phase of what?" Annika asked quietly.

"I don't know," Rudy murmured, his eyes filled with desperation. "But it's happening soon. Whatever it is, it's going to cause chaos on a scale we've never seen before. He's been focusing on Eastern Europe, Russia, Ukraine, Poland, the Baltics... that's where it's all going to start."

A chill ran down Annika's spine. "Why those regions?"

"Because they're already unstable," Rudy explained, his voice gaining a frantic edge. "There are existing tensions, political, economic, ethnic. Reichter's going to exploit those tensions, push them to the breaking point. And when everything collapses, he'll have the leverage he needs to install his own people in positions of power."

James exchanged a grim look with Nathan and Annika, the weight of Rudy's words settling over them like a lead blanket.

"We need to stop this now," James murmured. "If Reichter pulls this off, it'll be more than just a few governments falling. It could destabilize all of Europe."

Nathan's jaw clenched. "So we hit him where it hurts. We destroy this command center, take out his people, and gather as much intel as we can. Then we go after him, wherever he's hiding."

Rudy's eyes widened in panic. "Wait, you can't! If Reichter finds out you've been here, he'll activate his backup plans. He's got contingencies, hidden operatives... he'll go underground, and you'll never find him again."

"We'll take that risk," Annika said coldly. "We're not letting him get away. Not this time."

Karl finally spoke up, his voice a low, defiant growl. "You don't understand. Reichter's been planning this for years. He's got allies you can't even imagine, people who will cover for him, protect him. Even if you take down this place, he'll rebuild somewhere else."

"Then we'll find him again," James said softly. "And we'll take him down again. Until there's nowhere left for him to run."

There was a long, tense silence, the air crackling with unspoken threats and promises. Then, finally, Karl let out a harsh, bitter laugh.

"You're all fools," he spat. "But I suppose that's what makes you dangerous. You actually think you can stop him."

"We've already started," Nathan said evenly. "And we're not stopping until Reichter's done."

James stepped forward, his gaze locking onto Rudy's. "Tell us everything you know about the bunker's defenses. We're going to disable every single piece of technology Reichter has in this place, and then we're going to rip his network apart."

Rudy nodded shakily, his expression filled with fear and resignation. "Okay. I'll tell you. But once you're inside... you're on your own."

"Just show us the way," James murmured. "We'll handle the rest."

With Rudy's guidance, the Patriots moved deeper into the bunker, their every step calculated and deliberate. The hallways were empty, the air thick with tension as they approached the central operations room, a massive chamber filled with servers, communication terminals, and security monitors.

"Place is a fortress," Nathan muttered, his gaze sweeping over the rows of equipment. "How are we going to take all this out?"

"We don't need to destroy it," Kane's voice crackled through their earpieces. "Just give me access to one of the main terminals. I'll plant a data spike that will disable their systems and siphon off all their intel. They won't even know what hit them."

"On it," James murmured.

Annika moved to one of the main terminals and connected a small, sleek device to the console. Lights blinked across its surface, and a soft beep signaled the start of the upload.

"Kane, you're live," Annika whispered. "Make it quick."

"I'm in," Kane replied, his voice tense. "Just need a few minutes..."

The minutes stretched on, the Patriots standing guard as the data spike did its work. The faint hum of the servers filled the air, the lights flickering softly as Kane's program moved through the system.

"Got it," Kane murmured finally. "Their entire network's been compromised. We've got everything, names, locations, contingency plans... everything."

"Perfect," James murmured. "Now let's get out of here."

They moved swiftly and silently through the bunker, the walls seeming to close in around them as they made their way back to the entrance. The sense of urgency hummed through the group like an electric current, they'd hit Reichter where it hurt, but they still had a long way to go.

As they reached the outer door, James paused, his gaze sweeping over the team. "We did good work tonight," he said quietly. "But this is just the beginning. Reichter's going to know we were here, and he's going to come at us with everything he has."

"Let him," Nathan growled, his eyes flashing with determination. "We'll be ready."

James nodded slowly, his gaze filled with a fierce resolve. "Yeah. We will."

They slipped through the bunker's outer door, the cold night air a stark contrast to the stifling, controlled environment inside. The forest surrounding the bunker seemed darker, the shadows thicker as if the trees themselves were holding their breath. The Patriots moved swiftly and silently, making their way back to the perimeter fence where Sarah and David were waiting.

The two sentinels were positioned behind a thick stand of trees, their eyes scanning the surroundings as the rest of the team approached.

"Any movement?" James asked quietly as they reached the spot where Sarah and David were concealed.

"Nothing yet," Sarah replied, her voice low and controlled. "Looks like we managed to slip in and out without triggering any alarms."

David nodded, his gaze still locked on the treeline. "But it's only a matter of time before they realize something's wrong. We should be gone before that happens."

"Agreed," James murmured. He turned to Annika, Nathan, and the others, his expression serious. "We've got what we came for. Let's get back to the safe house and review the data. Every second counts now."

They moved in a tight formation, their weapons held at the ready as they navigated through the forest. The faint rustle of leaves and the soft crunch of dirt underfoot were the only sounds that broke the silence. The tension was palpable, each of them acutely aware of how vulnerable they were in the open.

But they moved with the confidence of a team that had been through the worst and survived. Their bond, their trust in one another, was unshakeable. It was what had carried them through missions like this before, and it would carry them through again.

After what felt like an eternity, they reached the clearing where their vehicles were hidden. The dark SUVs were parked under a thick canopy of trees, blending in with the shadows.

"Load up," James ordered softly, his gaze sweeping the area one last time. "Let's get out of here."

They climbed into the vehicles, the doors closing with soft, controlled clicks. Annika slipped into the passenger seat of the lead SUV, her eyes scanning the darkened forest as Nathan started the engine.

"Everyone ready?" James's voice came through the comms.

"Ready," Nathan replied, his voice steady.

"Let's move."

The SUVs pulled out of the clearing and onto a narrow, gravel road that wound through the forest. The tires crunched softly over the dirt and rocks, the vehicles' headlights off as they navigated by the pale light of the moon. The tension in the air was thick, every nerve on edge as they made their way toward the main road.

They drove in silence for several miles, the only sound the low rumble of the engines. The forest around them gradually gave way to open fields, the distant glow of city lights appearing on the horizon.

Then, just as they approached the edge of the forest, Kane's voice crackled through the comms, urgent and filled with tension.

"Guys, we've got a problem."

James straightened, his gaze snapping to the rearview mirror. "What is it?"

"I'm picking up chatter on the local channels," Kane replied. "Someone's flagged a breach at the bunker. They haven't pinpointed you yet, but they know something's wrong. They're mobilizing security teams to sweep the area."

"Damn it," Nathan muttered under his breath. "How long do we have?"

"Not long," Kane said grimly. "They're moving fast. You need to get out of there now, before they lock down the roads."

James's mind raced as he considered their options. "We stick to the plan. Get back to the safe house and go dark. We're not ready for a confrontation yet."

"Copy that," Nathan replied, his grip tightening on the steering wheel. He glanced at Annika, who gave him a quick, reassuring nod.

"Just drive," she murmured softly. "We'll get through this."

The SUVs sped up, the dark landscape blurring past them as they left the forest behind. The roads were empty, the quiet hum of the tires on the pavement the only sound that broke the silence. But each of them knew that time was running out. Reichter's men would be closing in, searching for any sign of the intruders who had dared to infiltrate their stronghold.

"We'll take the back route," James said quietly, his voice calm despite the urgency in the air. "Avoid the main roads. We need to stay off the grid until we're clear."

The vehicles veered off onto a narrow side road, the headlights off as they navigated through a series of winding paths. The minutes stretched on, each one filled with a tense, charged silence. But gradually, the distant sounds of the city grew louder, the glow of streetlights appearing ahead.

"We're almost there," Nathan murmured, his gaze flicking to the rearview mirror. "No sign of pursuit."

"Good," James replied. "Let's keep it that way."

They reached the outskirts of Vienna, the darkened streets deserted at this late hour. The SUVs wound through the quiet neighborhoods, moving with the practiced ease of a team that knew how to blend in, how to disappear.

Finally, they pulled up to the nondescript office building that served as their temporary safe house. The Patriots exited the vehicles quickly but quietly, their movements smooth and efficient as they entered the building.

Once inside, they made their way to the secure command center on the second floor. The room was filled with the soft glow of computer screens, the hum of electronics filling the air.

Kane was already there, his fingers flying over the keyboard as he brought up the data they'd retrieved from the bunker. He glanced up as they entered, his expression grim.

"Bad news," he murmured, his gaze locking onto James's. "Reichter's people are onto us. They've flagged all the routes leading out of the area. Roadblocks, checkpoints... they're sweeping everything."

James nodded slowly, his jaw tightening. "We expected this. What about the intel? Did we get anything useful?"

Kane's lips twitched in a faint, humorless smile. "Oh, we got more than useful. We've got everything. Locations, names, schedules. Reichter's entire operation, laid out in black and white."

"Then what's the problem?" Nathan asked, his brow furrowing.

Kane tapped a key, bringing up a detailed map on the central screen. Red markers dotted the map, each one indicating a key location in Reichter's network.

"The problem is this," Kane said quietly. "Reichter's planning something big, and it's going down in less than 48 hours. He's mobilizing his forces, pulling in assets from all over Europe. Whatever he's planning, it's going to hit hard and fast."

James's gaze swept over the map, his mind racing as he processed the information. "What's the target?"

"That's the thing," Kane murmured, his eyes darkening. "It's not just one target. It's multiple. Coordinated strikes in four major cities, Warsaw, Budapest, Berlin, and Prague. Political leaders, infrastructure, financial institutions... he's aiming to create chaos and panic on an unprecedented scale."

A heavy silence settled over the room, the weight of Kane's words hanging in the air like a dark cloud.

"He's launching a campaign of destabilization," Annika whispered, her voice filled with disbelief. "This isn't just about power. He's trying to tear Europe apart."

"Exactly," Kane said softly. "And if we don't stop him, it's going to work."

James took a deep breath, his gaze sweeping over the team. "We've got less than 48 hours to stop Reichter. We're going to have to split up, hit each of the cities and neutralize his assets before they can carry out their attacks."

"We're talking about multiple ops across four countries," David murmured, his eyes narrowing. "This is going to be a logistical nightmare."

"Then let's make a plan," James said firmly. "Because if we don't stop this... it's not just Europe that's going to feel the impact."

He turned to the map, his gaze hardening with resolve. "Let's get to work."

The Patriots gathered around the table, their expressions filled with grim determination as they began laying out their strategy. They knew the stakes, knew that the coming hours would test them in ways they hadn't been tested before.

But they were ready.

Because they weren't just fighting to bring down a corrupt network.

They were fighting to prevent a catastrophe.
And they would stop at nothing to see it through.

Chapter 17

The secure command center in their safe house buzzed with activity as the Patriots prepared for the most crucial mission of their careers. Each member of the team was focused, their movements precise and deliberate as they reviewed intelligence reports, laid out maps, and checked their gear. The atmosphere crackled with tension, 48 hours to stop a coordinated assault on four major cities was a monumental task, but the Patriots had faced seemingly impossible odds before.

James stood at the head of the table, his gaze sweeping over his team. There was a new intensity in his eyes, a fire that had only grown brighter as they'd gotten closer to Reichter. He knew what was at stake, and he could see that same understanding in each of their expressions.

"All right, everyone," he began, his voice calm and steady. "We've got less than 48 hours before Reichter's plan goes live. That means we're splitting into four teams to hit each of the target cities. We're going to break up his network, neutralize his assets, and stop the chaos before it starts."

He gestured to the large map pinned to the wall, where each of the four cities was marked with red circles. "Kane's gathered as much intel as possible, but we're still missing pieces. We know the targets are high-profile, but we don't have exact details on each operation. We'll have to adapt on the ground. Stay sharp, communicate frequently, and trust your instincts."

Nathan stepped forward, his eyes scanning the map. "What's the team breakdown?"

James nodded. "Nathan, you and Annika will take Berlin. There's an old weapons depot on the outskirts of the city that Reichter's been using as a staging ground. We believe he's stockpiling arms and explosives there. Your mission is to locate and neutralize the weapons cache. If possible, capture anyone with direct knowledge of Reichter's movements."

"Roger that," Nathan murmured, his gaze flicking to Annika. She gave him a brief, determined nod.

"David, you and Sarah will handle Warsaw," James continued. "Reichter's got connections in the Polish government people who can shield him from repercussions. There's a meeting scheduled with a key contact in the energy sector. We need to intercept and shut it down. Cut off his political ties and make sure he has no support when everything goes sideways."

David exchanged a glance with Sarah, his expression serious. "We'll take care of it. If we can sever his political connections, we'll cripple his ability to operate in Eastern Europe."

"Good." James turned to Kane, who was watching the proceedings from behind his array of monitors. "Kane, you'll be running operations remotely from here. You're our eyes and ears. Make sure each team has the support they need, and keep monitoring communications. If Reichter's people get wind of what we're doing, I want to know about it before they can react."

"Don't worry," Kane said quietly, his fingers tapping over the keys. "I'll keep everyone in the loop. We've got one shot at this, and I'm not letting Reichter slip through our fingers."

"And what about you?" Annika asked, her gaze steady as she looked at James. "Which city are you taking?"

"Budapest," James replied, his tone firm. "I've already reached out to a few old contacts in the city. They've confirmed Reichter's been using a private estate outside the city for meetings with some key players in the arms trade. If I can disrupt that, I'll force him to change his strategy. He won't have the resources he needs to keep pushing his operations."

Silence fell over the room as each of them absorbed the plan. It was risky, four simultaneous missions, each with its own unique challenges and threats. But they didn't have a choice. This was the only way to stop Reichter before he could execute his plans.

"We're a family," James said softly, his gaze sweeping over the group. "We've fought together, bled together, and faced down some of the most dangerous people in the world. But this... this is bigger than any of us. We're not just fighting for each other, we're fighting for everything we believe in. For the people who don't even know what's coming."

The silence in the room deepened, the weight of his words settling over them like a tangible force. Each of them felt the truth of it, the enormity of what lay ahead.

"Stay safe," James murmured, his voice filled with quiet intensity. "Watch each other's backs. And remember, no matter what happens, we're in this together."

Nathan stepped forward, a fierce smile curving his lips. "You're not getting rid of us that easily, Donovan. We'll see this through, every last one of us."

"Damn right," David murmured, his gaze locked on James's. "We've come too far to back down now."

Annika nodded slowly, her eyes softening as she looked at each of them in turn. "We'll make it through this. And when we do, we'll make sure Reichter never has the chance to hurt anyone again."

James's gaze swept over them one last time, his chest tightening with a mix of pride and determination. "Let's move out."

The flight to Berlin was silent, each of them lost in their own thoughts as they prepared for what was to come. Annika sat beside Nathan in the dimly lit cabin, her gaze fixed on the darkened sky outside. The hum of the plane's engines filled the silence, a steady rhythm that seemed to match the pounding of her heart.

"You okay?" Nathan asked softly, his voice barely audible over the noise of the engines.

Annika glanced at him, a faint smile tugging at her lips. "I should be asking you that."

Nathan chuckled quietly, shaking his head. "You know me, always ready to dive headfirst into the fire."

"Yeah," Annika murmured, her gaze softening. "But this time, the fire's hotter than ever."

Nathan's expression grew serious, his eyes locking onto hers. "We'll get through this, Annika. We always do."

She nodded slowly, reaching out to place her hand over his. "I know. I just... it feels different this time. Like we're standing on the edge of something huge, and once we step off, there's no going back."

Nathan's hand tightened around hers, his gaze fierce. "That's because we are. But we're not doing it alone. We've got each other, and we've got James, David, Sarah... We're a team. A family."

Annika's smile widened slightly, warmth blooming in her chest. "Yeah. We are."

The rest of the flight passed in a blur of tactical discussions and last-minute checks. By the time the plane touched down at a private airstrip outside Berlin, they were ready.

Nathan led the way as they exited the plane, the cold night air biting at their skin. A black SUV was waiting at the edge of the tarmac, its headlights casting long shadows across the ground.

"We've got transport," Nathan murmured, glancing at Annika. "Let's get to the weapons depot and see what we're up against."

Annika nodded, her gaze sharpening as they climbed into the vehicle. "Kane, do you have eyes on the target?"

"Roger that," Kane's voice crackled through their earpieces. "Satellite feed shows minimal movement around the perimeter. A couple of guards, but nothing heavy. Either they're trying to keep a low profile, or they're hiding something big inside."

"Let's hope it's the latter," Nathan murmured as he started the engine. "Because we're about to knock on the door."

The drive to the weapons depot was tense, the city lights blurring past them as they navigated through Berlin's winding streets. The depot was located in a rundown industrial area on the outskirts of the city, its entrance hidden behind a crumbling brick wall.

They parked a few blocks away and approached on foot, their senses attuned to every sound, every shadow. The depot loomed up before them, a dark, hulking structure surrounded by rusting fences and abandoned machinery.

"There," Annika whispered, pointing to a small side entrance. "That's our way in."

Nathan nodded, his gaze sweeping the area. "Let's make it quick. In and out before they know what hit them."

They slipped through the entrance and into the depot, the air thick with the scent of oil and metal. The interior was dimly lit, shadows pooling in the corners as they moved deeper into the building.

Annika's gaze swept over the rows of crates and containers stacked haphazardly throughout the space. "This place is huge. How are we supposed to find the weapons cache?"

"Leave that to me," Kane murmured. "I've got the layout of the building. Head to the east corner, there's a storage area that's been flagged as restricted access. That's your target."

"Copy that," Nathan whispered. He glanced at Annika, his eyes glinting in the low light. "Ready?"

"Always," she murmured.

They moved silently through the depot, their weapons held at the ready as they approached the designated storage area. The air seemed to hum with tension, every sound amplified in the stillness.

When they reached the storage area, Nathan signaled for Annika to take position at the door. She nodded, her heart pounding as she prepared to breach the entrance.

"On three," Nathan whispered. "One... two... three."

Annika kicked the door open, her weapon raised as she swept the room. But what she saw inside made her freeze, her breath catching in her throat.

The storage area wasn't filled with weapons or ammunition like they'd expected. Instead, it was lined with rows of large metal containers, each one connected to a series of cables and monitors that hummed softly in the dim light. The walls were covered in complex schematics, maps of Berlin, and documents marked with coded symbols.

"What the hell...?" Nathan breathed, stepping inside behind her. He moved cautiously, his eyes narrowing as he took in the strange equipment. "This isn't a weapons cache. This is... something else."

Annika's gaze swept over the containers, her mind racing. "Kane, we've got a situation here. There are no weapons, no explosives. Just... these containers. Can you identify what we're looking at?"

"Hold on," Kane murmured, his voice tense with concentration. "I'm pulling up schematics of the building. Give me a second... Okay, I see it. Those containers, they're not weapons. They're advanced communication nodes. Reichter's using them to establish a secure, encrypted network. He's creating a digital command center that can control his entire operation remotely."

"Damn it," Nathan muttered, glancing at Annika. "He's using Berlin as a communications hub. That's how he's coordinating everything in the other cities. If we don't take this place down, he'll be able to keep his network operational, even if we disrupt his assets in Warsaw, Budapest, and Prague."

"Which means we need to destroy it," Annika said firmly. She moved to one of the containers, studying the tangled mess of cables and wiring. "But it's not going to be easy. This setup is advanced, if we just start ripping out wires, we could trigger some kind of failsafe."

"Can you disable it remotely, Kane?" Nathan asked, his gaze locked on the rows of equipment.

Kane's voice crackled through the comms, edged with frustration. "I can try, but it'll take time. This system is layered with encryption. If I push too hard, I could trip an alarm and alert Reichter's people that we're here."

"We don't have time," Annika murmured, glancing at Nathan. "We need to destroy it now, before anyone realizes we've breached the facility."

Nathan's jaw tightened, his gaze sweeping over the equipment. "Then we do it the old-fashioned way. Set charges, blow the place sky-high."

"Agreed," Annika said softly. She glanced at her watch, calculating the time they had left. "We'll plant the charges and set a timer. Five minutes should be enough to get clear and out of range."

"Make it quick," Kane urged, his voice low and tense. "I'm picking up increased activity on local comms. Reichter's people are starting to mobilize. If they converge on your location, you'll be trapped."

"Copy that," Nathan murmured. He turned to Annika, his expression hardening. "Let's do this."

They moved swiftly, their hands working with practiced efficiency as they planted small explosive charges on the containers. The soft clicks and beeps of the timers being set filled the air, each sound a reminder of how little time they had.

Annika's fingers moved nimbly over the last charge, securing it to the base of one of the central nodes. "That's the last one," she whispered, straightening. "Timers are set. We have five minutes to get out."

"Let's go," Nathan replied, his gaze sharp. "Kane, keep us updated on external movements. If anyone's heading our way, we need to know."

"Roger that," Kane murmured. "I'll guide you out."

They moved quickly through the storage area and back into the main corridor, their steps swift and silent. The faint hum of the equipment faded behind them as they retraced their path through the depot, every shadow seeming to pulse with potential danger.

"Two guards ahead," Kane's voice crackled softly through their earpieces. "They're patrolling the exit corridor. You'll have to take them out quietly."

"Copy that," Annika whispered.

She and Nathan slowed their pace as they approached the corner, peeking around to spot the two guards walking side by side, their rifles slung casually over their shoulders. They seemed relaxed, unaware of the impending explosion just a few dozen feet away.

Nathan motioned to Annika, signaling that he would take the guard on the left. She nodded, her grip tightening on her weapon as they moved in tandem.

It took only seconds. Nathan's arm wrapped around his target's neck, cutting off his air and dragging him into the shadows. Annika followed suit, a swift strike to the side of her target's neck sending him crumpling to the ground.

"Clear," Nathan murmured.

They reached the outer entrance, the cool night air brushing against their faces as they slipped outside. The darkened depot loomed behind them, its silent presence almost oppressive. They moved swiftly across the open ground, their breaths misting in the cold air.

"Three minutes," Kane's voice crackled through the comms. "You need to get clear."

"We're almost out," Nathan replied, his gaze scanning the perimeter. "Any sign of movement?"

"Negative," Kane murmured. "You're in the clear... wait, hold on. I'm picking up something... a vehicle. It's approaching fast from the north. Could be a patrol or... "

An explosion of light and sound shattered the stillness as headlights blazed across the clearing. A black SUV screeched to a halt just outside the depot's entrance, its doors flying open as armed men poured out, their weapons raised.

"Contact!" Annika hissed, her pulse spiking as she and Nathan ducked behind a stack of rusting barrels.

"Damn it," Nathan muttered, peering around the corner of their cover. "Looks like they sent a response team. How many do you see?"

"Six, maybe more," Annika whispered. She glanced at her watch. "Two minutes left. We need to hold them off until the charges blow."

Nathan's eyes narrowed, a fierce light flashing in his gaze. "Copy that. Let's give them hell."

They moved in unison, rising from their cover and opening fire in controlled bursts. The sharp crack of gunfire echoed through the night as they engaged the response team, their weapons flashing in the darkness.

The guards scrambled for cover, shouting commands as they returned fire. Bullets whizzed past Annika's head, splintering the wood of the barrels beside her. She ducked low, her breath coming in quick, controlled bursts as she aimed and fired again.

"We need to draw them back," Nathan growled, his voice tight with concentration. "Get them closer to the building. If they're too far out, the blast won't take them."

"On it," Annika replied, shifting her position to draw the guards' attention. She fired a series of rapid shots, the bullets sparking off metal and concrete as she moved to the left.

The guards reacted, their focus shifting to her as they began advancing, moving closer to the depot's entrance.

"Now!" Nathan shouted, his voice cutting through the chaos.

Annika ducked behind a metal crate as Nathan opened up with his rifle, laying down suppressive fire that drove the guards back toward the depot. The seconds ticked down, each one seeming to stretch into an eternity.

Then, with a deafening roar, the charges detonated.

The shockwave slammed into them, a wall of heat and sound that knocked them to the ground. Flames erupted from the depot's interior, the force of the blast shattering windows and sending debris flying in all directions. The guards were thrown back, their bodies crumpling under the force of the explosion.

Annika gasped for breath, her ears ringing as she struggled to her feet. Smoke billowed from the ruined structure, the acrid scent of burning electronics and scorched metal filling the air.

"Are you okay?" Nathan's voice was rough, his hand reaching out to steady her.

"Yeah," Annika panted, blinking through the haze. "I'm good. Let's get out of here."

They moved quickly, leaving the blazing ruins of the depot behind as they made their way back to the extraction point. The sound of sirens filled the night, growing louder as emergency responders converged on the scene.

"Kane, we're clear," Nathan murmured into his comms. "Get us a route out of here."

"On it," Kane replied, his voice tight with relief. "I'm sending coordinates now. I've got a safehouse in the Tiergarten district. Head there and lay low until the heat dies down."

"Copy that," Nathan replied. He glanced at Annika, his lips curving into a faint smile. "One down, three to go."

Annika nodded, her chest still heaving with exertion. "And Reichter's going to know we're coming for the rest."

"Let him," Nathan growled softly, his gaze fierce. "We're not stopping until we finish this."

With a final glance at the burning depot, they turned and disappeared into the night, leaving destruction and chaos in their wake.

Back at the safe house, Kane's fingers flew over the keyboard, his gaze locked on the screens as he monitored the other teams. David and Sarah were in position in Warsaw, their voices calm and steady as they reported on the movements of Reichter's contacts.

"We've got visual on the target," David's voice came through the comms, calm and professional despite the tension simmering beneath. He and Sarah were crouched on the roof of a nondescript office building overlooking a sleek, glass-fronted restaurant in the heart of Warsaw's business district. The restaurant was dimly lit, its interior a shadowy blur of high-end decor and polished steel. Patrons sat at candlelit tables, the low murmur of conversation drifting up to where David and Sarah watched from above.

"Who's in there?" James asked, his voice low and steady through the comm link.

Sarah adjusted her scope, the crosshairs settling on a group of men seated at a table in a private corner of the restaurant. "I count three primary targets. The man in the center is Jacek Wozniak, a senior advisor to the Minister of Energy. The others are unknown, but they look like private security. Heavily armed."

"Wozniak's the one we want," James murmured. "He's been funneling money from the Polish government into Reichter's front companies, giving Reichter a backdoor into the energy sector. If we take him out, we cut off a major source of funding."

David nodded, his gaze steady as he observed the scene below. "What's the play, James? Extraction or neutralization?"

"Extraction, if possible," James replied. "We need information more than we need bodies. But if he won't cooperate... you know what to do."

"Understood," David murmured. He glanced at Sarah, his lips curving into a faint smile. "Ready?"

"Always," Sarah whispered, her eyes still locked on the targets. "I'll cover you from here. Get in, grab Wozniak, and get out. Clean and quick."

"Roger that," David murmured. He adjusted his gear, his movements smooth and controlled as he prepared for the descent. "See you on the ground."

He slipped over the edge of the roof, his silhouette blending seamlessly with the shadows as he rappelled down the side of the building. The faint whisper of the rope and the soft thud of his boots landing on the ground were the only sounds that marked his arrival.

David moved silently through the alley behind the restaurant, his senses sharp as he approached the rear entrance. He paused, his gaze sweeping the area for any sign of security. There were two men stationed at the back door, their stances relaxed but their eyes watchful.

"Two guards at the rear," David whispered into his comm. "Taking them out now."

He moved like a shadow, his steps soundless on the cobblestones as he closed the distance. With a swift, precise motion, he struck, one guard crumpled silently to the ground, followed quickly by the other. David caught their bodies, lowering them gently to the pavement.

"Guards down," he murmured. "Moving inside."

He slipped through the back door and into the dimly lit corridor that led to the restaurant's kitchen. The low hum of voices and the clatter of dishes filled the air, but David's focus was on the far end of the hall, where a door marked "Private" stood slightly ajar.

"Sarah, what's the situation inside?" he whispered.

"Wozniak and his men are still seated," Sarah replied. "No movement. You're clear to enter."

"Copy that," David murmured.

He approached the door, his hand hovering over the knob. Then, with a deep breath, he pushed it open and stepped inside.

The private dining room was a small, elegantly appointed space, its walls lined with dark wood paneling and expensive artwork. Wozniak looked up as David entered, his expression shifting from surprise to shock.

"What... who the hell are you?" Wozniak demanded, his voice rising.

David didn't respond. He moved forward in a blur of motion, his hand flashing out to grab Wozniak by the collar and slam him against the wall. The other two men at the table scrambled to their feet, their hands reaching for their weapons.

"Don't," David growled, his voice a low, dangerous rumble.

The two men hesitated, their gazes flicking to Wozniak. David tightened his grip on the advisor's collar, his eyes boring into the man's.

"Tell your men to stand down," David murmured softly. "Or I will put them down. Your choice."

Wozniak swallowed hard, his face pale. "D-Don't shoot," he stammered. "Stand down, both of you!"

The two men froze, their hands hovering in midair. David's gaze remained locked on Wozniak's, his expression hard.

"Good," David murmured. "Now, you and I are going to have a little chat."

Wozniak's breath hitched, his eyes wide with fear. "I don't know anything... "

"Wrong answer," David interrupted, his voice deadly calm. "You're going to tell me everything about your dealings with Reichter. How you've been funneling money, who you've been working with, and what the next step in his plan is. And you're going to do it now."

"Or what?" Wozniak whispered, his voice trembling.

David leaned in closer, his eyes cold and unblinking. "Or I'll make sure you never get another chance to betray your country."

There was a long, tense silence as Wozniak stared up at him, his chest heaving with panic. Then, slowly, he nodded.

"All right," he whispered. "I'll talk."

"Good choice," David murmured. He gestured to the table. "Sit down."

Wozniak stumbled back to his seat, his hands shaking as he pulled out a chair. The other two men remained frozen, their eyes locked on David.

"Start with Reichter's plan," David said softly. "What's he trying to accomplish?"

Wozniak took a deep, shuddering breath. "Reichter's... he's planning to disrupt the energy markets. He wants to destabilize the supply chain, create shortages, drive up prices, force governments to compete for resources. Once the chaos starts, he'll use his influence to manipulate the market and control distribution."

"And how's he going to do that?" Sarah's voice crackled through David's earpiece.

Wozniak licked his lips nervously. "He's already put operatives in place at key facilities, power plants, refineries, distribution hubs. They're going to sabotage the infrastructure, make it look like a series of coordinated attacks by extremists. No one will be able to trace it back to him."

David's gaze darkened. "When is this happening?"

"Soon," Wozniak whispered. "Within the next 24 hours. He's already given the go-ahead to his people. Once the attacks begin, it'll be too late to stop it."

"Where are the attacks going to happen?" David demanded. "Give me locations."

Wozniak hesitated, his gaze flickering to the two men standing nearby. But when David's grip tightened on the back of his chair, he swallowed hard and nodded.

"Okay, okay," he whispered. "There are four main targets, one in Warsaw, one in Berlin, one in Prague, and one in Budapest. They're all critical nodes in the energy grid. If they go down, it'll create a cascading failure that could cripple entire regions."

David exchanged a grim look with Sarah through the comms. "We've got what we need," he murmured. "But we're not done yet."

"Let's move him," Sarah replied. "We'll extract and interrogate him further once we're out of the hot zone."

David nodded and grabbed Wozniak by the arm, pulling him to his feet. "You're coming with us."

The two security guards tensed, but David's cold glare stopped them in their tracks.

"Stay where you are," he growled. "Unless you want to join him."

The guards froze, their expressions tight with anger and fear. David dragged Wozniak out of the dining room and into the corridor, his gaze sweeping the area.

"Sarah, I've got him. Where's the extraction point?"

"Rooftop," Sarah replied. "I'm covering you. Go."

They moved quickly through the restaurant's back corridors, their footsteps silent on the polished floors. The faint sound of conversation and laughter drifted from the main dining area, but no one noticed as David and Wozniak slipped through a side door and into a narrow stairwell.

"Up," David murmured, shoving Wozniak forward. "Keep moving."

They reached the rooftop access door, where Sarah was waiting, her rifle slung over her shoulder. She nodded to David, her gaze shifting briefly to Wozniak.

"Got the package," she murmured. "Let's go."

David and Sarah guided Wozniak across the rooftop and to the edge, where a small helicopter was waiting, its rotors turning slowly. The pilot glanced up as they approached, his expression calm.

"We're good to go," David called over the sound of the rotors.

"Get in," the pilot replied curtly.

They climbed into the helicopter, Wozniak wedged between David and Sarah, his face pale with fear. The pilot lifted off, the aircraft rising smoothly into the night sky.

As the lights of Warsaw blurred beneath them, David glanced at Sarah, a grim smile curving his lips.

"One more target neutralized," he murmured. "

Chapter 18

The dim glow of the early morning sun cast long shadows over Budapest's cityscape, its golden light reflecting off the rooftops and casting a soft, ethereal haze over the Danube River. The city was just beginning to wake, the streets still quiet and the air cool with the lingering chill of night. But James Donovan's focus wasn't on the picturesque view of the Hungarian capital. His mind was on the mission, on the stakes that hung over them like a guillotine blade poised to drop.

He sat in a small café in Pest, the sprawling, flat district across the river from Buda's hilly terrain. From where he sat, he could see the Parliament Building in the distance, its neo-Gothic spires piercing the sky. But James's gaze was locked on the front door of a nearby apartment building, an inconspicuous four-story structure nestled between two larger office buildings. It looked ordinary enough, but according to their intel, it was far from it.

Reichter's people had turned the building into a secure meeting place, a temporary hideout for some of his key operatives. Taking it down would be another major blow to Reichter's network, disrupting his ability to coordinate the destabilization of the energy grid.

James lifted his cup of coffee to his lips, his eyes never leaving the building as he took a slow sip. He wore a dark jacket and a simple cap pulled low over his eyes, his appearance carefully chosen to blend in with the early morning crowd of commuters and café patrons. He looked like any other traveler enjoying a quiet morning in the city, but beneath the calm exterior, his senses were on high alert.

"Status report," James murmured softly, his voice barely more than a breath.

Kane's voice crackled through his earpiece, calm and steady. "I've got eyes on the building from multiple angles. No unusual movement so far. Looks like the targets are still inside."

"Any signs of additional security?" James asked, his gaze scanning the windows of the apartment building.

"Negative," Kane replied. "There are two men stationed at the front entrance and a third patrolling the rear. No cameras on the exterior that I can detect. It's a low-profile setup, but don't let that fool you. If Reichter's key operatives are inside, they'll have internal security measures in place."

"Understood," James murmured. He shifted in his seat, glancing at the time on his watch. "Where's the rest of the team?"

"Annika and Nathan are en route to Berlin's next target," Kane reported. "David and Sarah are airborne, headed back to their staging point in Warsaw. They've confirmed extraction of Wozniak and have a wealth of intel to review once we're secure. Everyone's in position and ready for the next phase."

"Good," James murmured, his gaze sharpening as he spotted a figure emerging from the apartment building's entrance. The man was dressed in a plain suit, his face partially obscured by sunglasses and a heavy beard. He paused on the front steps, glancing around as if checking his surroundings before turning and heading down the street.

"I've got movement," James whispered. "One male, mid-forties, exiting the building. Could be a courier or a lower-level operative."

"Got him," Kane replied. "I'll track his movements. Focus on the primary targets inside."

James nodded slightly, his attention returning to the building's entrance. He knew the risks of making a move here in the open, but they couldn't afford to let this opportunity slip by. Reichter's operatives were on high alert, and if they didn't act now, they might never get another chance.

He took a deep breath, then activated his comm again. "I'm moving in. Kane, keep the feeds up and give me a heads-up if you see any changes in the building's security."

"Roger that," Kane murmured. "Stay sharp, James."

James rose from his seat, leaving a few bills on the table as he slipped out of the café and made his way toward the apartment building. He moved with a casual stride, his hands tucked into his jacket pockets as he navigated the narrow sidewalk. To any passerby, he looked like just another pedestrian enjoying the morning air.

But as he neared the building, his pace slowed, his gaze narrowing as he approached the front entrance. The two guards stationed outside glanced at him briefly, their expressions disinterested. James offered them a faint smile and a nod, as if acknowledging their presence before moving past.

Once he was out of their line of sight, he slipped into the alley that ran alongside the building. The alley was dark and narrow, the faint smell of damp concrete and trash lingering in the air. He moved quickly and quietly, his steps soundless on the uneven pavement as he reached the rear entrance.

"Back entrance is clear," James whispered into his comm. "I'm going in."

"Copy that," Kane replied. "I've looped the camera feed in the stairwell. You're good to go."

James pulled out a small device from his jacket, a digital lockpick, and attached it to the keypad beside the rear door. The device hummed softly, its lights blinking as it worked to bypass the electronic lock. After a few tense seconds, there was a faint click, and the door swung open.

He slipped inside, his eyes adjusting to the dimly lit hallway. The interior of the building was plain and unremarkable, white walls, tiled floors, and a faint hum of fluorescent lights overhead. But James knew that appearances could be deceiving. Somewhere in this building, Reichter's operatives were coordinating attacks that could cripple Europe's energy infrastructure.

He moved swiftly down the hallway, his footsteps muffled by the thin carpet. Kane's voice guided him through his earpiece, each instruction precise and clear.

"Take the stairwell to the third floor," Kane murmured. "The targets are in a conference room near the back. There's a guard stationed outside the door, should be alone."

"Understood," James replied.

He reached the stairwell and slipped inside, moving up the steps with practiced ease. As he ascended, his mind raced through the possible scenarios he might encounter. The guard outside the conference room would be his first obstacle, but he had to assume there were more men inside. He couldn't afford to make a mistake.

When he reached the third floor landing, he paused, his ear pressed against the door as he listened for any sound on the other side. The muffled murmur of voices drifted through the wood, low and indistinct, but clear enough to confirm activity inside.

"Kane, how many targets in the conference room?" James whispered.

"Four heat signatures," Kane replied. "Two seated, one standing near the door, and the fourth... hard to say, but it looks like he's moving around the room."

"Got it," James murmured.

He eased the door open and slipped into the hallway, his gaze locking onto the guard stationed outside the conference room. The man was tall and broad-shouldered, his posture tense as he stared straight ahead. He didn't see James until it was too late.

James moved like a shadow, his hand flashing out to cover the guard's mouth as he drove a swift, precise strike into his throat. The guard's eyes widened in shock, his body convulsing once before going limp. James lowered him gently to the floor, his movements controlled and silent.

"One down," he whispered. "Moving in."

He approached the conference room door, his hand hovering over the handle. With a deep breath, he turned the knob and pushed it open.

The room was larger than he'd expected, its walls lined with maps and charts detailing energy distribution networks and key infrastructure points. Four men stood around a central table, their expressions shifting from surprise to alarm as James stepped inside.

"Who the hell?" one of them began, but James was already moving.

He brought his weapon up, the silenced shots barely more than faint pops as he took down the two men closest to him. The third man reached for his gun, but James was faster, a single shot dropping him to the ground.

The fourth man, the one standing near the back, stumbled backward, his face pale with shock. "Wait... wait! Don't shoot!"

James hesitated, his gaze narrowing. "You have two seconds to tell me everything you know about Reichter's plans."

The man's hands shot up, his breath coming in rapid gasps. "Okay, okay, I'll talk! Just, don't kill me."

"Start talking," James growled, his weapon still trained on the man.

The man swallowed hard, his gaze flickering to the bodies on the floor. "Reichter's planning to create a massive blackout across Europe. He's going to hit the power grids in all four cities simultaneously, Warsaw, Berlin, Prague, and Budapest. It'll cause a domino effect, knocking out the entire energy infrastructure."

"And what's he hoping to accomplish with that?" James demanded, his voice cold.

"Chaos," the man whispered. "Pure chaos. Governments will be scrambling to restore power, the markets will crash, and Reichter's people will be in position to exploit the fallout. He's going to step in as the only one with the resources to restore order."

James's jaw tightened. "How do we stop it?"

"You can't!" the man gasped. "It's already set in motion. His operatives are in place at key facilities in each city. They're just waiting for the go-ahead. Once the blackout starts, it'll be too late…"

James's finger tightened on the trigger. "Where are the facilities?"

"Here, the main control centers are in government energy facilities," the man stammered, his eyes darting between the bodies on the floor and James's cold gaze. "They've rigged each location with devices to overload the power grid. It'll look like a system failure, a cascade of surges that will take down every major facility. The only way to stop it is to disable the devices before they're triggered."

"Where's Reichter?" James pressed, his voice low and deadly calm.

"I, I don't know!" The man's voice cracked, his face pale and slick with sweat. "He's not in the city. He's keeping his distance, watching from a secure location. He'll only show himself once the plan is complete."

James's jaw clenched. "Then give me something I can use. Who's coordinating the attacks?"

The man hesitated, his gaze flickering with indecision. But as James stepped closer, his weapon never wavering, the man's resolve crumbled.

"Gregorov," he whispered hoarsely. "Viktor Gregorov. He's in charge of the logistics. He's been traveling between the cities, overseeing everything. If you find him, you can disrupt the entire operation."

"Where is he now?" James demanded.

"Prague," the man breathed. "He's in Prague, at a safe house near the city center. But he's only there to monitor the final setup. He'll be moving soon, heading to Berlin to ensure the detonations go off as planned."

James felt a surge of adrenaline, his mind racing. Gregorov, the same man they'd encountered in Zurich, was at the heart of this entire operation. If they could take him out, they'd have a real shot at stopping Reichter's plan.

"Good," James murmured. "You did the right thing."

The man sagged with relief, a faint smile tugging at his lips. "So... I'm free to go?"

"Not quite," James replied softly.

With a swift motion, he brought his weapon up and struck the man on the side of the head. The man crumpled to the floor, unconscious.

"Status, James?" Kane's voice crackled through the comms, a note of concern lacing his tone.

"Got the information we needed," James replied, his voice tight. "Gregorov's in Prague. He's coordinating the attacks and will be moving to Berlin soon."

"Damn," Kane murmured. "Then we're running out of time. Annika and Nathan are already in Berlin, but if Gregorov makes it there before we take him out, he could accelerate the timeline."

"Understood," James said quietly. He glanced at the unconscious man at his feet, then turned toward the door. "I'm heading back to the extraction point. Patch me through to Annika and Nathan."

"Copy that," Kane replied.

James moved swiftly through the building, his footsteps silent as he made his way back to the rear entrance. The morning light was brighter now, casting long shadows across the alley as he slipped outside. He pulled out his phone, the secure line connecting to Annika and Nathan's comms.

"Annika, Nathan, do you read me?" James murmured, his voice low and urgent.

"Loud and clear, James," Annika's voice crackled softly through the comm. "What's going on?"

"Change of plans," James said. "Gregorov's in Prague, but he'll be moving to Berlin soon to oversee the attacks. We need to intercept him before he gets there."

"Prague?" Nathan echoed, his tone sharpening. "That's going to complicate things. If he makes it to Berlin, we'll lose our window to take him down."

"I know," James murmured. "Which is why I'm going to Prague to deal with him. I need you two to stay in Berlin and monitor the situation there. If anything changes, I want you in position to respond."

Annika hesitated, her voice filled with concern. "Are you sure, James? Going after Gregorov alone?"

"I won't be alone," James interrupted gently. "I'll have Kane feeding me intel. But we don't have a choice. Taking down Gregorov is our best shot at stopping this before it starts."

There was a long pause, then Nathan's voice came through, steady and filled with determination. "All right, James. We'll hold down the fort here. Just... be careful."

"You too," James murmured. "I'll be in touch."

He ended the call and made his way to the extraction point, his mind already shifting to the next phase of the mission. They were playing a dangerous game, one that could spiral out of control at any moment. But they'd come too far to back down now.

"Kane," James murmured into his comm, his voice calm and measured. "Get me a flight to Prague. We're taking this to the next level."

• • • •

T he flight to Prague was uneventful, the hours passing in tense silence as James reviewed the intel Kane had gathered. Every piece of information pointed to the same conclusion: Gregorov was the key. If they could take him out, Reichter's network would be thrown into disarray.

James touched down at a private airfield just outside the city, where a car was waiting for him. He drove into Prague's bustling city center, his gaze sweeping over the historic buildings and winding cobblestone streets. The city was a maze of narrow alleys and hidden passageways, a perfect place for someone like Gregorov to hide.

"James, I've got eyes on the safe house," Kane's voice crackled through the comms as James navigated the crowded streets. "It's an old townhouse in the Mala Strana district, overlooking the river. I'm picking up at least four heat signatures inside, probably more."

"Any sign of Gregorov?" James asked, his gaze narrowing as he pulled the car to a stop a few blocks from the target location.

"Negative," Kane replied. "But there's a black SUV parked outside. Matches the description of the vehicle Gregorov was using in Zurich. He's got to be there."

"Understood," James murmured. He exited the car and moved quickly down the street, his eyes scanning the area for any sign of surveillance. The townhouse loomed ahead, its exterior dark and unassuming. But James knew that appearances could be deceiving.

"Kane, I need eyes on the rear entrance," James whispered. "Any way to access the building from behind?"

"Let me check," Kane murmured. A few seconds later, his voice came through again, edged with urgency. "There's a narrow alley that runs behind the townhouse. Leads to a service entrance. It's not on the main security grid, could be your way in."

"Copy that," James whispered.

He slipped into the alley, his steps soundless on the cobblestones as he approached the rear of the building. The service entrance was a plain wooden door, weathered and worn. James reached for his lockpick, his fingers moving quickly as he worked to bypass the simple lock.

The door swung open with a faint creak, and James slipped inside, his weapon held at the ready. The interior of the building was dimly lit, the air thick with the scent of dust and old wood. He moved through the narrow hallway, his senses alert for any sign of movement.

"Kane, what's the layout?" James whispered.

"First floor is mostly storage and common areas," Kane replied. "Targets are on the second floor, main conference room. I'm picking up six heat signatures now. Gregorov could be one of them."

"Understood," James murmured.

He reached the base of the stairs and paused, his gaze flickering upward. The faint murmur of voices drifted down from above, low and indistinct, but clear enough to confirm that the room was occupied.

James took a deep breath, then moved silently up the stairs, his weapon raised. As he reached the top, the voices grew louder, punctuated by the occasional laugh or murmured command.

He crept toward the conference room door, his heart pounding as he listened.

"... everything is in place," a familiar voice was saying. "Reichter will be pleased. Once the blackout starts, there will be no stopping the chaos."

James's eyes narrowed. Gregorov.

He took a step closer, his hand hovering over the door handle.

"Stay calm, James," Kane's voice whispered in his ear. "Wait for the right moment."

James nodded slightly, his grip tightening on his weapon.

He waited, every nerve on edge.

And then, with a single, fluid motion, he pushed the door open and stepped inside.

The room fell silent as every eye turned to him.

Gregorov stood at the far end of the room, his gaze widening in shock.

"Hello, Viktor," James said softly, his voice cold as steel. "We need to talk."

Chapter 19

The conference room's sudden silence was almost deafening, broken only by the faint ticking of a wall clock and the muffled sound of the city outside. Six pairs of eyes were locked on James as he stood in the doorway, his weapon raised and his stance steady. Gregorov's expression shifted from shock to fury, his face flushing red as he took a step back, his hands trembling.

"Donovan," Gregorov spat, his voice a low, dangerous growl. "You've made a serious mistake coming here."

James's eyes narrowed, his weapon trained steadily on Gregorov's chest. "The only mistake was thinking you could hide from us. It's over, Viktor. Tell me where Reichter is and what the final steps of his plan are, or I will end this right here and now."

Gregorov glanced around the room, his eyes flicking to the other men. They were all well-dressed, wearing suits that spoke of power and wealth. But James could see the fear in their eyes, the slight tremor in their hands as they watched the confrontation unfold.

"You really think I'm going to talk?" Gregorov sneered, his lips curling into a mocking smile. "You're outnumbered, Donovan. Even if you take me down, these men will have you before you make it out the door."

James didn't flinch. "Then why aren't they reaching for their guns?" he asked softly. "You see, they know something you don't. They know I didn't come here alone."

As if on cue, the door behind him swung open, and Nathan and Annika stepped inside, their weapons raised. Nathan's gaze was hard and unyielding, his finger resting lightly on the trigger. Annika moved with the lethal grace of a predator, her eyes locked on Gregorov.

"You didn't think we'd let James have all the fun, did you?" Nathan murmured, his voice low and dangerous. "We're here to make sure you don't leave this room unless you give us what we want."

Gregorov's expression faltered, his eyes widening as he realized the trap he was in. He glanced at the men flanking him, but they remained still, their faces pale with fear.

"Don't look to them for help," Annika said coldly. "They're not going to risk their lives for you, Gregorov. They're just lackeys, paper tigers. You're alone in this."

James stepped forward, his weapon still trained on Gregorov's chest. "Tell us where Reichter is. Tell us how to stop the attacks. Or I promise you, Viktor, you'll regret ever setting foot in this room."

There was a long, tense silence as Gregorov stared at them, his breath coming in short, angry bursts. Then, slowly, a twisted smile spread across his face.

"You want to know where Reichter is?" he whispered, his voice low and mocking. "He's everywhere. He's in every shadow, every corner of Europe. You can stop me, but it won't matter. Reichter's plan is already in motion. There's no stopping it now."

"Maybe not," Annika said softly, her gaze steady. "But we're going to try."

In one swift motion, she brought her weapon down and struck Gregorov across the face. He staggered back, a gasp of pain escaping his lips as he clutched his cheek. Blood trickled from a split in his skin, staining his expensive shirt.

"Enough games," Nathan growled, his voice a low rumble. "You're going to talk, Gregorov. And you're going to tell us everything we need to know, or I swear I'll make sure your last moments are spent wishing you had."

Gregorov's smile wavered, his eyes darting around the room as if seeking a way out. He glanced at the other men, but none of them moved to help him. They were frozen in place, their gazes locked on Nathan and Annika's weapons.

"I... " Gregorov began, his voice trembling slightly.

The silence stretched on, thick and suffocating.

"I'll talk," he whispered finally. "But you have to promise me protection. You have to get me out of here, away from Reichter. He'll find me if I tell you anything."

"Tell us what we need to know first," James said quietly. "Then we'll decide whether you're worth protecting."

Gregorov hesitated, his face pale and drawn. He glanced at the other men, then back at James, and finally, he nodded slowly.

"Reichter's plan is to bring down the entire energy grid across Europe," he murmured, his voice barely above a whisper. "He's targeting four main nodes, control centers that oversee the distribution of power to the entire continent. If those nodes go down, the grid collapses. Governments will be paralyzed, and Reichter's people will step in to take control of the chaos."

"Where are the nodes?" Annika demanded, her gaze fierce.

"Berlin, Warsaw, Prague, and Budapest," Gregorov whispered. "Each city has a primary and secondary node. The primary nodes are heavily guarded, military-grade security. But the secondary nodes... they're less obvious, hidden within civilian infrastructure. Those are the ones Reichter's people are targeting."

James exchanged a grim look with Annika and Nathan. This was the confirmation they needed, the final piece of the puzzle.

"What's Reichter's timeline?" Nathan asked, his voice tight with urgency.

"Forty-eight hours," Gregorov whispered. "He's set everything to go off in forty-eight hours. Once the nodes are compromised, it'll look like a coordinated cyberattack, something that'll take weeks, maybe months to fix. By then, the damage will be done. Governments will be at each other's throats, and Reichter will be in position to swoop in and offer his solution."

James's gaze hardened. "And where is he coordinating all this from?"

"I don't know exactly," Gregorov said, his voice breaking. "He's been moving around constantly, always staying one step ahead. But... I've heard him mention a place. A facility somewhere in the Carpathian Mountains. Remote, secure... like a fortress."

"The Carpathian Mountains," Annika murmured, her brow furrowing. "That's a vast area. Do you have any more specific information?"

"No, but... there's a man," Gregorov whispered, his eyes darting nervously around the room. "Reichter's most trusted lieutenant, Emil Krause. He's the one who handles all the logistics, all the travel arrangements. If anyone knows where Reichter is, it's him."

"Where can we find Krause?" James asked sharply.

"He's... he's in Berlin," Gregorov stammered. "He's overseeing the final preparations for the attacks on the grid. But be careful, Krause isn't like me. He's ex-military, special forces. He's dangerous, and he won't hesitate to stop you if he thinks you're a threat."

"Thanks for the warning," Nathan said dryly. "But we'll take our chances."

Gregorov swallowed hard, his gaze flickering with desperation. "So... you'll get me out of here? You'll keep me safe from Reichter?"

James regarded him for a long moment, his expression unreadable. Then, slowly, he nodded. "We'll keep you safe. But first, you're coming with us."

"Where... where are we going?" Gregorov asked nervously.

"To Berlin," James said softly. "We're going to have a little chat with your friend Krause."

The Patriots moved quickly, their actions smooth and efficient as they secured Gregorov and escorted him out of the conference room. The other men remained seated, their faces pale and drawn as they watched the Patriots leave.

Once they were outside, Nathan glanced at James, his gaze serious. "What's the plan?"

"We head to Berlin," James replied. "Annika, you stay with Gregorov. Keep him secure and keep an eye on him. Nathan and I will make contact with Krause and see what we can get out of him."

Annika nodded, her gaze steady. "What if Krause won't talk?"

James's expression hardened. "Then we make him talk. One way or another."

They moved swiftly through the alley, their steps soundless as they made their way to the extraction point. The faint sounds of the city buzzed around them—cars honking, people talking, the distant wail of a siren—but none of it registered. Their focus was absolute.

"Kane, we've got Gregorov," James murmured into his comm. "Set up a secure line with Annika. We need to keep him isolated."

"Copy that," Kane replied. "I've already scrambled the local feeds. No one's going to know you were here."

"Good work," James said softly. He glanced at Annika and Nathan, his gaze filled with a fierce resolve. "Let's finish this."

The Patriots moved as one, their bond unshakeable as they disappeared into the early morning light, the shadow of Reichter's looming plan hanging over them like a dark cloud.

• • • •

The flight to Berlin was tense, the air inside the private jet thick with anticipation. James sat across from Gregorov, his gaze never wavering as he watched the man fidget nervously in his seat. Annika and Nathan sat nearby, their expressions unreadable as they prepared for the confrontation with Emil Krause.

"Kane," James murmured softly into his comms, his gaze focused on Gregorov's uneasy expression. "What's the latest on Krause's movements? Any indication of where we can find him once we touch down?"

Kane's voice came through steady, yet urgent. "I've tracked Krause's activities. He's operating out of an abandoned industrial complex in Marzahn, a district on the outskirts of Berlin. From what I've gathered, it's more than just a temporary hideout it's a command center. He's got his people coordinating the last stages of the attacks from there."

James nodded, his expression thoughtful. "That means he's staying close to the action. If we take him out, we cut the head off the entire Berlin operation. What about security?"

"There's plenty," Kane replied, his fingers tapping over his keyboard. "I'm seeing heavy patrols on the ground, snipers positioned on rooftops, and a central hub of armed men inside. It's not impossible to breach, but it'll be tough."

"We don't need to storm the place," Annika interjected, her voice calm and controlled. "If we can draw Krause out, we'll have a better chance of taking him down without stirring up a hornet's nest."

"How do we draw him out?" Nathan asked, his brow furrowed as he considered their options.

"Gregorov," James said simply, his gaze shifting back to their captive. "He's a high-level operative. Krause will want to know what happened to him. If we use Gregorov as bait, we might be able to force Krause into a vulnerable position."

Gregorov's face drained of color, his eyes widening with fear. "Wait, no, you can't! Krause won't fall for it. He's too smart, he'll see through it. And if he thinks I've betrayed him... "

"Relax," Nathan said dryly, though his gaze remained sharp. "We're not handing you over on a silver platter. We'll keep you close, make it look like you've still got leverage. Krause doesn't need to know we've already squeezed everything out of you."

"I... I don't know..." Gregorov stammered, his hands trembling slightly.

James leaned forward, his gaze intent. "Listen, Viktor. This is your best shot at survival. You help us get to Krause, and you prove you're willing to cooperate. If we take down Krause, it'll make it a lot easier for us to keep you safe from Reichter's people."

Gregorov swallowed hard, then nodded jerkily. "Okay. Okay, I'll do it. But you have to protect me."

"We will," James said softly, his voice laced with steel. "As long as you do exactly what we tell you."

The rest of the flight passed in tense silence, each of them lost in their own thoughts as the jet cut through the dark sky, carrying them closer to Berlin, and to Krause. James's mind was already spinning with potential strategies, each one fraught with danger and uncertainty. They were playing a high-stakes game, and one misstep could unravel everything they'd fought for.

But that was the risk they'd accepted the moment they decided to stand against Reichter.

The jet touched down at a private airstrip on the outskirts of Berlin, where a black SUV was waiting for them. The air outside was crisp and cool, a faint breeze rustling through the trees that lined the runway. As they climbed into the vehicle, Kane's voice crackled through their earpieces.

"I've been monitoring Krause's communications," Kane murmured. "He's cautious, but I managed to pick up some chatter. He's expecting a report from Gregorov's team in Prague. If we time it right, we can make it look like Gregorov is contacting him with urgent news."

"Let's set it up," James replied. He glanced at Gregorov, his gaze sharp. "You're going to talk to Krause, tell him you've uncovered some new information and you need to meet in person."

Gregorov's eyes widened. "What if he doesn't believe me?"

"Make him believe you," Annika said firmly. "You know how to talk to him. If he gets suspicious, this whole thing falls apart."

Gregorov swallowed hard, then nodded. "I'll... I'll do my best."

They drove through the quiet streets of Berlin, the city's imposing architecture rising around them like dark sentinels. The industrial complex in Marzahn loomed ahead, its tall fences and crumbling walls a testament to the building's abandonment and subsequent repurposing. The soft glow of floodlights illuminated the entrance, casting long shadows that seemed to shift and flicker in the breeze.

They parked a few blocks away, out of sight from any prying eyes. James glanced around the darkened interior of the SUV, his gaze lingering on each of his teammates.

"Here's the plan," he murmured softly. "Gregorov, you're going to contact Krause and tell him you have vital information that needs to be delivered in person. Try to get him to meet you outside the complex, if we can isolate him, it'll give us the upper hand."

"And if he doesn't take the bait?" Nathan asked quietly.

"Then we go in and get him ourselves," James replied, his gaze hardening. "But let's try to avoid a direct assault if we can."

Gregorov took a deep, shuddering breath, then pulled out his phone. He glanced at James, who gave him a short nod.

"Go ahead," James murmured.

Gregorov dialed the number and pressed the phone to his ear. The faint sound of ringing filled the silence, each second dragging out as they waited.

Then, finally, a voice answered. Gruff and wary.

"Gregorov," Krause's voice growled. "What's going on? You're supposed to be in Prague."

"I know," Gregorov said quickly, his voice trembling slightly. "But something's come up. Something big. I need to meet with you, face to face. There's... there's a problem with the timeline."

There was a long pause, then Krause's voice came through again, sharper this time. "What kind of problem?"

"It's too complicated to explain over the phone," Gregorov said, his gaze flickering to James. "I need to show you something. It's... sensitive."

Another pause, then a faint, irritated sigh. "Fine. Meet me at the loading bay entrance in ten minutes. But this better be worth my time, Viktor."

"It will be," Gregorov whispered. "I promise."

The line went dead.

Gregorov lowered the phone, his face pale and drawn. "He's... he's going to meet us."

"Good work," James murmured. "Now, remember, stay calm, and let us handle the rest."

They moved quickly, making their way to the edge of the industrial complex. The faint hum of machinery filled the air, the glow of floodlights casting long shadows across the ground.

Krause was waiting at the loading bay entrance, his figure partially hidden in the shadows. He glanced around warily, his hand hovering near his side as if ready to draw a weapon at the first sign of trouble.

Gregorov stepped forward, his movements hesitant. "Krause... "

But before he could finish, James and Nathan emerged from the shadows, their weapons trained on Krause's chest. Krause's eyes widened, his hand freezing in place.

"Don't," James said softly, his voice steady. "It's over, Krause. Put your hands where I can see them."

For a long moment, Krause remained still, his gaze locked on James's. Then, slowly, he raised his hands, his expression shifting from shock to fury.

"You think this changes anything?" Krause hissed. "Reichter's plan is already in motion. You're too late."

"We'll see about that," Nathan murmured, his voice cold. "Right now, you're going to tell us everything you know about Reichter's location."

"Never," Krause spat, his eyes blazing with defiance. "You'll have to... "

But before he could finish, James stepped forward, his gaze hard. "I don't have time for your loyalty games, Krause. You're going to talk, one way or another."

Krause stared at him, his chest heaving with each rapid breath. Then, slowly, a twisted smile spread across his lips.

"Go ahead," he whispered, his voice low and mocking. "Do your worst, Donovan. It won't matter. Reichter's already won."

James's gaze never wavered as he stared into Krause's eyes. "We'll see who wins in the end."

With that, the Patriots closed in, their resolve unbreakable as they prepared to extract the final pieces of information that would lead them to Reichter, and to the ultimate showdown that would decide the fate of everything they'd fought for.

Chapter 20

The dark interior of the abandoned factory echoed faintly with the distant sounds of machinery, a low, mechanical hum that seemed to pulse through the walls like the heartbeat of a beast lying in wait. James stood a few feet away from Krause, his gaze cold and unyielding as he watched the man's every move. Krause's shoulders were tense, his jaw clenched tight, but his eyes remained defiant. He hadn't broken, yet.

Nathan paced a few steps away, his footsteps slow and deliberate as he circled Krause like a predator assessing its prey. Annika stood just inside the doorway, her expression calm but watchful, while Gregorov huddled against the wall, his eyes darting nervously between them.

The tension in the room was palpable, thick enough to cut through. Every breath seemed to echo, every movement felt magnified.

"Where is Reichter?" James asked softly, his voice carrying a quiet intensity that cut through the silence like a knife.

Krause's lips twitched into a faint, mocking smile. "I already told you, you'll never reach him. By now, he's far away, safely hidden in his mountain fortress. He's watching, waiting... and when the time is right, he'll make his move. You're too late."

James's gaze didn't waver. "Maybe. But you're still going to tell us everything you know."

Krause's smile faltered slightly, a flicker of uncertainty crossing his eyes. He glanced at Nathan, who had paused in his pacing, his gaze locked on Krause's face.

"Don't make this harder than it needs to be," Nathan said quietly, his voice laced with a dangerous calm. "You think you're protecting him, but all you're doing is sealing your own fate. Tell us where

Reichter is, and maybe, just maybe, we'll let you walk away from this."

Krause's eyes flashed with anger, his mouth tightening. "Walk away? You really think you can threaten me, like I'm some low-level thug? I've been by Reichter's side for years. I know things that would make you..."

"Enough," Annika interrupted softly, stepping forward. "We don't need your bravado. We need facts. Where. Is. Reichter?"

There was a long silence, the air crackling with unspoken tension. Krause shifted slightly, his gaze flicking to Gregorov, who was staring at him with a mixture of fear and desperation.

"You... you can't hold out forever, Krause," Gregorov stammered, his voice a low, trembling whisper. "Just tell them what they want to know. It's not worth it, Reichter's not worth it. He'd sell you out in a heartbeat if it meant saving himself."

"Shut up, Viktor," Krause snarled, his gaze blazing with fury. "You're nothing but a coward. You were always weak. That's why Reichter never trusted you."

"Maybe," Gregorov murmured, his voice shaking. "But I'm still here. I'm still alive. And I'm willing to do whatever it takes to stay that way. You should be too."

Krause's eyes narrowed, his expression hardening. He glanced at James, his lips curling into a sneer.

"You think you've got it all figured out, don't you?" Krause spat. "You think you're the heroes, the ones who can save the world from the big, bad villain. But you don't know anything. You don't know how deep this goes, how many people are involved. Reichter's just the beginning. He's the tip of the iceberg."

"Then tell us about the rest," James said softly, his voice deadly calm. "Tell us everything, and we'll make sure you get out of this alive."

Krause's expression wavered, his gaze shifting between the Patriots. For a moment, it seemed as if he might relent, as if he might give them what they wanted. But then, his lips twisted into a cruel smile.

"You'll never win," he whispered. "Even if you take down Reichter, there will always be someone else. Someone smarter, stronger... someone willing to do whatever it takes to reshape the world. You can't stop it. You're just fighting a losing battle."

"Maybe," Annika murmured. "But we're still going to fight."

Krause stared at her, his chest heaving with each labored breath. Then, slowly, he shook his head.

"You're all fools," he whispered, his voice filled with contempt. "But I suppose that's what makes you dangerous."

James exchanged a glance with Nathan and Annika, a silent conversation passing between them. They had dealt with men like Krause before, men who thought they were untouchable, men who believed their loyalty would protect them. But they all broke eventually.

"We're not leaving here until you talk, Krause," James murmured softly. "You can keep playing games, or you can make this easy on yourself. Your call."

The silence stretched on, heavy and suffocating. Krause's gaze flickered, uncertainty warring with defiance in his eyes. He opened his mouth as if to speak, but before he could say a word, the sound of a door slamming echoed through the factory.

All eyes turned toward the entrance as a figure stepped into the room, a tall, broad-shouldered man with close-cropped hair and a hard, weathered face. He was dressed in black tactical gear, a pistol holstered at his side and a faint smirk on his lips.

"Well, well," the newcomer drawled, his voice low and mocking. "Looks like I'm just in time for the party."

Kane's voice crackled urgently through their earpieces. "James, we've got company, local reinforcements just showed up. Armed units. You need to get out of there."

James's gaze locked onto the newcomer, his eyes narrowing. "Who are you?"

The man's smirk widened. "Me? I'm just here to clean up the mess. Krause, Viktor, you boys really thought you could slip away unnoticed? You should know better."

"Lukas," Krause whispered, his voice filled with a mixture of shock and fear. "What, what are you doing here?"

"Making sure you don't talk," Lukas replied coldly. He drew his weapon, his gaze flicking to James. "Step aside, Donovan. This doesn't concern you."

"The hell it doesn't," Nathan growled, his weapon snapping up to aim at Lukas. "You're not going anywhere near him."

Lukas's smile faded, his expression hardening. "You think you can stop me? I have backup on the way, heavily armed backup. If you don't want this to turn into a bloodbath, you'll walk away. Now."

James's mind raced as he considered their options. They were outnumbered, outgunned, and deep in hostile territory. But they couldn't afford to lose Krause, not now, not when they were so close.

"Backup or not, you're not taking him," James said softly, his voice filled with quiet resolve. "We're leaving here, and Krause is coming with us."

Lukas's gaze darkened, his finger twitching near the trigger of his pistol. "You really want to do this?"

Before anyone could respond, Gregorov took a step forward, his voice trembling. "Please, Lukas, just let me go. I won't say anything, I swear. Just let us leave."

Lukas's gaze flicked to Gregorov, his lips curling into a sneer. "Pathetic, Viktor. You were always spineless. Reichter should've gotten rid of you a long time ago."

"Lukas," Krause whispered urgently, his eyes wide with fear. "Don't..."

But Lukas didn't respond. He raised his weapon, his gaze locked on Gregorov's face.

And then, everything happened at once.

James moved first, his arm flashing out to knock Gregorov to the ground as he fired a single, precise shot at Lukas's weapon hand. The bullet struck true, knocking the pistol from Lukas's grasp as Nathan and Annika moved in tandem, their weapons trained on the doorway.

Lukas staggered back, a snarl of pain escaping his lips as he clutched his bleeding hand. But his expression was filled with fury, his eyes blazing with hatred.

"You think this is over?" Lukas hissed. "You think taking me down will change anything?"

James stepped forward, his gaze hard. "We're taking Krause, and we're leaving. If you want to stop us, you'll have to go through me."

Lukas's lips curled into a twisted smile. "Gladly."

The factory seemed to erupt into chaos as more armed figures poured into the room, their weapons raised and ready. The Patriots moved as one, their weapons flashing in the dim light as they engaged the newcomers.

The air filled with the sharp crack of gunfire, the sound reverberating off the walls as James and his team fought their way through the hostile forces. Krause remained crouched behind a stack of crates, his face pale with fear as the bullets whizzed overhead.

"Go!" Annika shouted, her voice cutting through the noise. "I'll cover you, get Krause out of here!"

James nodded sharply, his gaze locking onto Krause. "Move!"

They sprinted toward the rear exit, their footsteps pounding against the concrete floor. The door burst open under Nathan's shoulder, and they stumbled out into the cool night air, the sounds of gunfire and shouts echoing behind them.

"We need to keep moving," James urged, his voice tense but calm as they bolted through the dark alleyway behind the factory. Krause stumbled, his breath coming in ragged gasps, but James grabbed his arm and hauled him forward.

Nathan and Annika flanked them, their weapons sweeping in precise arcs as they covered every angle. They were exposed out here, vulnerable in the narrow corridor of cracked pavement and dilapidated walls. But there was no other way out, Kane's voice crackled through their earpieces, providing directions as he monitored the unfolding chaos inside the factory.

"Keep going straight, then take a left," Kane murmured urgently. "There's a side street that'll lead you to a secondary exit point. My drone's picking up movement, Lukas's reinforcements are closing in fast."

James's jaw tightened as he glanced back at Krause. "You hear that? We've got one shot at getting you out of here alive. Don't slow us down."

Krause nodded frantically, his face slick with sweat. "I... I understand. Just don't leave me behind!"

They rounded the corner and emerged onto a narrow, dimly lit street. The buildings on either side were dark and abandoned, their windows shattered and doors boarded up. It was a perfect place for an ambush, and every instinct screamed at James to move faster, to get out of the open.

"There!" Annika called softly, pointing to a side alley just ahead. "We can cut through there."

"Go," James ordered, his gaze sweeping the shadows. "I'll cover the rear."

Annika led the way, her steps swift and sure as she guided Krause into the alley. Nathan stayed close, his gaze flicking over every door and window, every darkened corner where an enemy might be hiding.

They were halfway through the alley when the first shots rang out, sharp cracks that shattered the silence and sent them all diving for cover. Bullets slammed into the brick walls around them, sending shards of concrete flying through the air.

"Ambush!" Nathan shouted, his voice carrying over the roar of gunfire.

James pressed his back against a rusting metal dumpster, his heart pounding as he assessed the situation. The attackers were positioned at both ends of the alley, cutting off their escape routes. He could see the muzzle flashes, hear the shouts of orders being barked, but the darkness and smoke made it impossible to get a clear shot.

"Kane, we're pinned down!" James called into his comms, his voice tight with strain. "We need options, now!"

"Hold on, I'm working on it," Kane replied, his fingers flying over the keys. "I've got eyes on your position. There's a fire escape ladder about twenty feet up on your left, if you can get to the rooftop, you'll have a clear path to the extraction point."

"Copy that," James murmured. He turned to Nathan, his gaze sharp. "We're going up. Cover Annika and Krause, make sure they reach the ladder."

"On it," Nathan growled, his weapon snapping up as he fired a series of rapid shots down the alley, forcing the attackers to duck for cover.

"Move!" James shouted.

Annika grabbed Krause's arm and pulled him toward the fire escape. The metal ladder hung high above their heads, just out of reach. Annika glanced around, her eyes narrowing as she spotted an overturned crate nearby. She dragged it over and boosted Krause up, his hands scrabbling at the rungs as he pulled himself up.

"Go, go, go!" Annika urged, her gaze sweeping the alley as more gunfire erupted around them.

Krause climbed as fast as he could, his body trembling with exertion. Annika followed close behind, her movements fluid and precise despite the chaos. Nathan and James laid down cover fire, their weapons barking in sharp, controlled bursts.

"Kane, any sign of Lukas's men getting closer?" Nathan called through the comms, his voice strained.

"Not yet, but they're fanning out," Kane replied. "They're trying to cut you off. Once you're on the roof, head west. There's a footbridge two blocks over that'll take you to the extraction point. I've got a vehicle waiting there."

"Understood," James murmured. He turned his gaze upward, watching as Annika reached the top of the ladder and swung herself onto the rooftop. She turned and extended a hand to Krause, pulling him up beside her.

"Come on!" Annika called, her voice urgent. "You're clear!"

James and Nathan exchanged a brief glance, then turned and sprinted toward the ladder, their footsteps pounding against the pavement. They reached it in seconds, scaling the rungs with practiced ease. As soon as they were both on the roof, they took off, their boots thudding softly against the gravel-covered surface.

The rooftop was a maze of ventilation units and crumbling brick chimneys, but they moved with the surefootedness of men who had done this a hundred times before. Krause stumbled, his breath coming in ragged gasps, but Annika caught him, her grip firm as she pulled him along.

"Keep moving," Annika murmured softly. "We're almost there."

They reached the far edge of the rooftop and peered over. The footbridge Kane had mentioned was visible in the distance, a narrow metal structure spanning a dark, empty street. Beyond it, the outline of a dark SUV could be seen, its engine idling softly.

"Clear path," Nathan murmured. "Let's go."

They descended the fire escape on the far side of the building, their movements swift and controlled. The street below was deserted, the only sound the faint hum of the city in the distance.

"Stay close," James whispered, his gaze sweeping the shadows as they moved toward the footbridge. "Kane, are you picking up anything?"

"Negative," Kane replied, his voice tight with concentration. "But I don't like this. It's too quiet. They should've been on you by now."

"Stay sharp," James murmured. "This could be a setup."

They reached the base of the footbridge and started across, their footsteps echoing softly on the metal grating. Krause stumbled again, his face pale and slick with sweat. Annika caught his arm, her grip firm but gentle.

"You're okay," she murmured softly. "Just a little further."

They were halfway across the bridge when a sudden flash of movement caught James's eye. He spun, his weapon snapping up as a dark figure stepped out from the shadows at the far end of the bridge.

Lukas.

He stood there, his silhouette framed against the dim glow of the streetlights, his weapon raised and aimed directly at Krause.

"You're not leaving here with him," Lukas growled, his voice carrying across the empty street. "Hand him over, or I'll drop you all where you stand."

"Lukas, don't do this," Nathan called, his voice calm but edged with warning. "You don't have to die for Reichter."

"Maybe not," Lukas murmured, his lips curling into a grim smile. "But I'm sure as hell not going to let you take him."

The silence stretched on, a tense, crackling energy filling the air.

"Last chance, Donovan," Lukas growled. "Leave Krause, or this ends right here."

James didn't hesitate. He stepped forward, his gaze locking onto Lukas's.

"Take the shot," he whispered into his comms.

A sharp crack echoed through the night, and Lukas staggered back, a look of shock crossing his face as he clutched at his shoulder. He stumbled, his weapon slipping from his grasp and clattering to the ground.

"Kane?" Annika whispered.

"Sniper drone," Kane replied tersely. "Non-lethal round. You're clear to move."

"Go!" James ordered.

They surged forward, sprinting past the fallen form of Lukas and racing across the bridge. The SUV's headlights flared to life as they approached, the driver's door swinging open.

"Get in!" the driver shouted, his voice urgent.

They piled into the vehicle, the doors slamming shut as the SUV roared to life and peeled away from the curb. The city blurred past in a whirl of lights and shadows, the tension inside the vehicle almost suffocating.

"We're clear," Kane's voice crackled through the comms. "I've got local feeds blocked, they won't be able to track you. Head to the extraction point, and I'll have another vehicle waiting to take you to the airfield."

"Roger that," James murmured.

He glanced at Krause, who was huddled in the corner of the backseat, his face pale and eyes wide with fear.

"You did good back there," James murmured softly. "Now, tell us everything about that facility in the Carpathians. We're going to end this."

Krause swallowed hard, then nodded. "It's... it's a fortress. Hidden deep in the mountains. But I can get you inside. There's a back entrance, an access tunnel Reichter uses. If we can reach it, we can bypass most of the security."

"Then that's where we're going," Nathan said quietly, his gaze hard. "Time to put an end to this, once and for all."

The SUV sped through the darkened streets of Berlin, carrying the Patriots toward their final confrontation with Reichter, a confrontation that would determine the fate of everything they'd fought for, everything they'd sacrificed.

And this time, there would be no turning back.

Chapter 21

The dense forests of the Carpathian Mountains loomed in front of them like a vast, impenetrable wall. The thick canopy of trees stretched as far as the eye could see, dark and foreboding beneath the overcast sky. The narrow, winding road that led them deeper into the mountains was slick with recent rain, the tires of their black SUV humming softly against the wet pavement.

Inside the vehicle, the Patriots sat in tense silence, their eyes scanning the landscape, their minds focused on the mission ahead. This was it, the culmination of months of planning, of countless sacrifices and dangerous maneuvers. Everything had led them to this point, to Reichter's hidden fortress buried deep within the rugged terrain of the Carpathians.

"Twenty miles to Retezat," Kane's voice crackled through their comms, calm and steady despite the gravity of the situation. He was back at the safe house, monitoring their movements through satellite feeds and live drone footage. "There's a turnoff up ahead that'll take you to an old logging road. It's not on any maps, but it'll get you close to the access tunnel Krause mentioned."

"Copy that," James murmured, his hands steady on the steering wheel. He glanced in the rearview mirror, his gaze locking onto Krause's pale, nervous face. "You still sure about this? If you're leading us into a trap..."

"It's not a trap," Krause interrupted quickly, his voice tight with fear. "I swear. The tunnel's real. It's an old mining shaft that was repurposed as an escape route. Reichter uses it to move in and out of the facility without drawing attention."

"Then we'll find it," Nathan murmured from the passenger seat, his gaze hard as he scanned the road ahead. "And once we're inside, you're going to show us the way to Reichter. No more games."

Krause nodded jerkily, his hands trembling as he wiped sweat from his brow. "I... I understand. Just... be careful. The facility's security is no joke. They'll know we're coming long before we reach the main entrance."

"We know the risks," Annika said softly, her voice calm and steady as she turned to look at Krause. "You've done your part getting us this far. Now it's up to us to finish it."

The vehicle continued its steady climb through the winding mountain pass, the forest closing in around them like a living, breathing entity. The trees were tall and ancient, their gnarled branches reaching out like skeletal hands. Mist clung to the undergrowth, swirling in ghostly tendrils as they drove deeper into the wilderness.

James glanced at Annika, his eyes reflecting the unspoken understanding that passed between them. They had been through so much together, every mission, every fight had only strengthened the bond that held the team together. There was a fierce determination in her gaze, a fire that mirrored his own resolve.

"We're close," Kane murmured. "I'm picking up the faint outline of the tunnel entrance on satellite imagery. About a mile up the road, on the right. You won't be able to see it from the road, it's covered by dense brush."

"Got it," James murmured. He eased off the gas, slowing the SUV as they approached the designated location. The road narrowed, the trees pressing in on eithe side, and James's grip tightened on the wheel as he scanned the foliage for any sign of the hidden turnoff.

"There," Nathan said suddenly, pointing to a barely visible gap in the trees. "That's it."

James nodded and turned the wheel sharply, guiding the SUV off the main road and onto the narrow, overgrown path. The branches scraped against the sides of the vehicle, the underbrush crunching beneath the tires as they bumped along the uneven terrain.

They emerged into a small clearing, the ground littered with fallen leaves and debris. At the far end of the clearing, half-hidden behind a tangle of vines and brush, was the entrance to the tunnel, a dark, gaping maw in the side of the mountain.

James killed the engine, the sudden silence almost deafening in the stillness of the forest. He turned to the team, his gaze sweeping over each of them.

"Listen up," he said quietly. "This is it. We go in fast and quiet. Krause will lead us through the tunnel, and Kane will guide us with real-time intel from the drone. We don't know how many guards we're going to encounter or what kind of defenses Reichter's got in place, so stay sharp. No mistakes."

Nathan nodded, his gaze hard. "We get in, take out Reichter, and get out. No distractions."

"Right," Annika murmured. She glanced at Krause, her eyes narrowing. "And if anything feels off, we neutralize it immediately. Understood?"

Krause swallowed hard, his gaze darting between them. "I... I understand. I'll cooperate. Just... don't leave me behind."

"Stay close, and you won't have to worry about that," James replied, his voice low but firm.

They exited the vehicle and moved toward the tunnel entrance, their steps soundless on the leaf-covered ground. The air was thick and damp, the scent of moss and earth filling their lungs. James pushed aside the tangled vines, revealing a rusting metal gate that covered the entrance.

"Looks like it hasn't been used in a while," Nathan muttered, his gaze sweeping the darkened interior of the tunnel.

"That's because Reichter doesn't use it often," Krause whispered. "Only in emergencies."

"Let's hope this doesn't turn into one," Annika murmured.

James tested the gate, the hinges creaking softly as he pushed it open. The darkness beyond was almost absolute, the faint smell of stale air and old earth drifting out. He pulled out a small flashlight, the beam cutting through the blackness as he led the way inside.

The tunnel was narrow and cramped, the walls rough-hewn stone and the floor uneven with scattered rocks and debris. The sound of their footsteps echoed softly, the faint drip of water somewhere in the distance the only other noise.

"Kane, status?" James whispered, his voice barely more than a breath.

"I'm tracking your position," Kane replied, his voice a calm presence in their ears. "You're making good progress. The tunnel branches off about five hundred feet ahead. Take the left fork, it'll lead you closer to the lower levels of the facility."

"Copy that," James murmured.

They moved in silence, their breaths soft and controlled as they navigated the winding tunnel. The darkness pressed in around them, the air growing colder and more stagnant the deeper they went. The tunnel forked as Kane had indicated, and they took the left path, the walls narrowing even further.

After what felt like an eternity, the tunnel began to widen, the air thick with the scent of metal and machinery. Faint lights flickered in the distance, casting long shadows that danced across the walls.

"We're close," Krause whispered, his voice trembling. "This leads to the maintenance access, there's a hatch that opens into one of the lower storage rooms. From there, we can access the control room."

"Good," James murmured. He glanced at Nathan and Annika, their eyes reflecting the same resolve that burned in his chest. "Once we're inside, we move quickly. No hesitation. Kane, keep us updated on any changes."

"Will do," Kane replied. "But be advised, security feeds are showing increased activity in the lower levels. They might know you're coming."

"Doesn't matter," Nathan growled softly. "We finish this. Today."

James nodded sharply. They reached the end of the tunnel, where a large metal hatch was set into the stone wall. He tested the handle, then glanced back at Krause.

"Is it alarmed?"

Krause shook his head. "No. But once we're inside, we'll be in the facility's security grid. They'll know we're there."

"Then we go in hot," Annika murmured, her gaze fierce.

James nodded and pushed the hatch open.

The room beyond was dimly lit, filled with metal shelves and stacks of crates. The faint hum of machinery filled the air, along with the distant murmur of voices and the clank of metal on metal.

"Move out," James whispered.

They stepped through the hatch, their movements swift and soundless as they spread out, covering each corner of the room. Nathan moved to the door, peering through the small glass window set into the metal.

"Clear," he murmured.

James turned to Krause. "Which way?"

Krause pointed down the hallway. "The control room is on the second sublevel. We'll need to take the service elevator at the end of this corridor. But be careful, they might have guards posted."

"Let's go," James murmured.

They moved as one, slipping through the doorway and into the hallway beyond. The facility was a maze of concrete and steel, the air filled with the faint scent of oil and coolant. They reached the elevator, the metal doors gleaming dully in the dim light.

Krause pressed the button, his hand trembling slightly. The doors slid open with a soft chime, revealing the small, sterile interior.

"Once we're down there, it's a straight shot to the control room," Krause whispered, his voice tight with tension. "But if they see us... "

"They won't," Annika murmured. "Just stay close."

They stepped into the elevator, the doors sliding shut behind them. The soft hum of the machinery filled the silence as they descended, the numbers above the doors blinking steadily.

James glanced at each of his teammates, his gaze lingering on their faces for a moment longer. Annika, with her calm, steady focus, her eyes burning with determination. Nathan, his jaw set, muscles coiled like a tightly wound spring, ready to explode into action at any moment. And Krause, pale and trembling, but holding himself together by a thread, fear and desperation etched across his features.

"We've made it this far," James murmured softly, his voice carrying an unshakeable resolve. "We finish what we started."

Nathan nodded, his gaze unflinching. "Together. We see this through, no matter what."

The elevator came to a halt with a soft chime, the metal doors sliding open to reveal a stark, concrete hallway lit by harsh fluorescent lights. The hum of machinery was louder here, a steady thrum that seemed to vibrate through the walls.

They stepped out of the elevator, their weapons raised as they moved in a tight formation down the corridor. The walls were lined with exposed pipes and wiring, the air cool and sterile. Faint voices echoed from somewhere up ahead, and James signaled for the team to stop.

"Wait," he whispered, his voice barely audible. "Kane, what's the status?"

"I'm seeing a patrol moving down the corridor toward you," Kane replied softly. "Two guards, armed. Looks like they're heading to the control room. If you don't want to engage, you'll need to find cover, now."

James glanced around, his gaze settling on a small alcove set into the wall. He motioned for the team to move, and they pressed themselves against the cold concrete, hidden in the shadows just as two guards rounded the corner.

The guards were speaking in low voices, their weapons slung casually over their shoulders. They wore black tactical gear, the insignia of Reichter's private security forces emblazoned on their chests. They looked confident, unaware of the danger lurking just a few feet away.

James held his breath, his finger hovering over the trigger of his rifle as he watched them pass. One of the guards paused, glancing back down the hallway, his brow furrowing slightly.

"Did you hear something?" the guard asked, his voice low and wary.

The second guard shook his head. "No. Come on, we're already late for the briefing."

They continued down the corridor, their footsteps echoing softly in the stillness. James waited until they disappeared around the next corner, then motioned for the team to move.

"Close call," Nathan whispered, his gaze flicking to James. "We'll have to be more careful."

"Agreed," James murmured. He turned to Krause, his eyes narrowing. "How far to the control room?"

"Not far," Krause whispered. "Just through the next set of doors and down one more hallway. The control room is at the end."

"Let's go," James said softly.

They moved quickly, slipping through the double doors and into a wider corridor lined with reinforced metal doors on either side. The air felt heavier here, charged with an almost palpable tension. They could sense it, Reichter's presence, his control over everything that happened in this facility.

The hallway seemed to stretch on forever, each step taking them closer to the heart of Reichter's operations, closer to the man who had orchestrated so much chaos and destruction. The man they had come here to stop, once and for all.

They reached the end of the hallway, where a large, reinforced door stood closed, a keypad mounted on the wall beside it. Krause stepped forward, his hands trembling slightly as he punched in a series of numbers.

"Is it alarmed?" Annika asked quietly, her gaze scanning the walls for any hidden sensors.

"No," Krause replied, his voice tight with tension. "This is just a secondary access code. The main security systems are inside the control room."

The door slid open with a soft hiss, revealing a spacious room filled with rows of computer terminals and monitors. The walls were covered in screens displaying live feeds from security cameras throughout the facility, each one showing a different area, the entrances, the tunnels, the storage rooms, and the central command area.

At the far end of the room, a group of technicians sat hunched over their workstations, their eyes glued to the screens. A few guards were stationed near the back wall, their postures relaxed as they chatted quietly among themselves.

"Perfect," Nathan murmured, his gaze sweeping the room. "They're distracted."

"Let's keep it that way," James whispered. He turned to Krause, his expression hard. "What's the quickest way to disable the security systems?"

"The central console," Krause replied, pointing to a large terminal in the middle of the room. "If we can access it, we can shut down the automated defenses and lock down the facility. But there's a failsafe, if anyone tries to tamper with the system without the correct access codes, it'll trigger an alarm."

"And you have the codes?" Annika asked, her gaze piercing.

Krause nodded quickly. "Yes, yes, I have them. Just... give me a chance to input them."

"We'll give you a chance," James murmured, his voice low but firm. "But don't try anything. I won't hesitate to put you down if you do."

Krause swallowed hard, then nodded. "I... I understand."

"Annika, Nathan, cover him while he works," James ordered. "I'll keep an eye on the guards."

They moved into the control room, their footsteps soundless on the polished floor. The technicians didn't look up, too engrossed in their screens to notice the intruders slipping past them. Krause moved to the central console, his fingers trembling as he tapped in a series of commands.

The monitors flickered, then shifted, the live feeds replaced by a series of warning messages. A soft chime echoed through the room, and the guards stiffened, their eyes narrowing as they glanced around.

"What's going on?" one of the guards muttered, his hand drifting toward the holstered weapon at his side.

"System glitch, probably," another guard replied, his voice wary. "Stay sharp. I don't like this."

James's grip tightened on his weapon as he watched them. They were on edge now, one wrong move and the entire room would erupt into chaos.

"Hurry up, Krause," Nathan whispered urgently, his gaze darting between the guards and the console. "What's taking so long?"

"I'm almost there," Krause murmured, his voice trembling. "Just... a few more seconds..."

The tension in the room was unbearable, each second stretching out like an eternity. James's heart hammered in his chest, his finger hovering over the trigger as he watched the guards exchange uneasy glances.

"Come on," Annika whispered softly, her gaze locked on Krause's shaking hands. "Come on, come on..."

There was a faint beep, and the screens shifted again, the warning messages replaced by a single prompt: SYSTEMS DISABLED. SECURITY OVERRIDE ENGAGED.

Krause let out a shuddering breath, his shoulders slumping in relief. "It's done. The defenses are down. We have full control."

James nodded sharply, his gaze sweeping the room. "Good. Now, let's move. We need to find Reichter before they realize what's happening."

"What about them?" Annika asked, nodding toward the guards and technicians who were still looking around, confusion etched on their faces.

"Lock them in," James replied. "We don't need them raising the alarm."

Annika and Nathan moved quickly, securing the doors with a heavy metal bar and locking the technicians in place. The guards shouted in surprise, their hands going to their weapons, but before they could react, James raised his rifle.

"Don't," he growled, his voice cold and commanding. "You're not dying today. Sit down, keep your hands where I can see them, and you'll walk out of here in one piece."

The guards hesitated, then slowly raised their hands, stepping back from their weapons.

"Good call," Nathan murmured. "Now let's go."

They exited the control room and moved deeper into the facility, their footsteps echoing softly in the silent halls. Krause led the way, his gaze flicking nervously over his shoulder every few steps.

"The central command area is just ahead," he whispered. "That's where Reichter will be."

"Lead the way," James said softly.

They reached a set of heavy double doors, the metal surface gleaming under the harsh lights. Krause paused, his hand trembling as he reached for the access panel.

"He's... he's in there," Krause whispered, his voice barely audible. "But be careful. He'll have guards with him. And he's not going to go down without a fight."

James nodded, his gaze hardening. "We're ready."

Krause took a deep breath, then pressed his hand against the panel. The doors slid open with a soft hiss, revealing a large, spacious room filled with computer terminals and towering screens.

And there, standing in the center of it all, surrounded by armed guards, was Klaus Reichter.

"Well, well," Reichter murmured, his lips curling into a thin smile. "I was wondering when you'd show up."

Chapter 22

The atmosphere in the central command room was thick with tension, every heartbeat pounding like a drumbeat of impending violence. Klaus Reichter stood in the center of the room, his face calm and composed as he looked at the Patriots, a faint, knowing smile playing on his lips. His pale blue eyes flicked over each of them, studying their faces with a dispassionate gaze that sent a chill down James's spine.

"I have to admit," Reichter murmured softly, his voice carrying a faint German accent that seemed to cut through the silence like a blade, "I'm impressed. You've managed to make it this far, further than anyone else ever has. But tell me, James... what do you really think you're going to accomplish here?"

James tightened his grip on his rifle, his gaze locked on Reichter's face. "We're here to shut you down. You've played your last hand, Reichter. It's over."

Reichter's smile widened, his gaze flicking to the armed guards flanking him. The men stood at attention, their weapons raised and aimed steadily at the Patriots. There were at least a dozen of them, all wearing black tactical gear, their faces obscured by masks. Each one looked ready to fire at a moment's notice.

"Over?" Reichter echoed, his tone almost amused. "No, my friend. This is just the beginning. You see, everything I've done, everything I've set in motion, has been leading to this moment. And now, you've brought yourselves right into the heart of it."

He spread his arms wide, gesturing to the screens that lined the walls of the command room. Each one displayed a different feed, live footage of power plants, energy grids, and critical infrastructure sites across Europe. Numbers and data scrolled rapidly across the monitors, a chaotic web of information that seemed to pulse with a life of its own.

"Do you see?" Reichter murmured, his gaze gleaming with a cold intensity. "The energy grid, the power supply, the very lifeblood of this continent... all of it is under my control. One command, one signal, and I can plunge entire nations into darkness. Chaos will spread like wildfire, and when the dust settles, I'll be there to pick up the pieces."

"That's your grand plan?" Nathan growled, his voice filled with barely suppressed rage. "To tear everything down so you can build it back up in your image?"

"Precisely," Reichter replied, his smile widening. "The world is broken, my dear Patriots. Corruption, greed, and incompetence have driven it to the brink of collapse. I'm simply accelerating the process. And when I step in to restore order, I'll reshape it into something... better. Stronger. A new world, built on a foundation of control and discipline."

"You're insane," Annika whispered, her voice trembling with anger. "You think you can just destroy everything and rebuild it? Millions of people will suffer, innocent lives will be lost."

"Sacrifices must be made for the greater good," Reichter said softly, his gaze turning almost wistful. "History is shaped by those who are willing to make the hard decisions, to do what others are too weak to do. That's why you'll fail, and I will succeed."

"Not today," James murmured, his voice low and steady. "This ends here, Reichter."

Reichter tilted his head slightly, his smile fading as he regarded James with a thoughtful expression. "You really believe that, don't you? That you can stop me? You and your little band of Patriots?"

"We don't just believe it," Nathan growled. "We know it."

The room seemed to pulse with a charged energy, every muscle coiled tight, every breath held in anticipation of what would come next. The guards' fingers twitched near their triggers, their gazes locked on James and his team. One wrong move, and the entire room would explode into violence.

But before anyone could react, Reichter raised his hand, a faint smile tugging at his lips.

"Lower your weapons," he ordered softly.

The guards hesitated, glancing at one another in confusion. But Reichter's gaze was unyielding, and slowly, reluctantly, they lowered their rifles, stepping back from their positions.

James's eyes narrowed. "What are you playing at, Reichter?"

"I want to talk, James," Reichter said quietly. "Just you and me. No weapons, no guards. Just a conversation. I believe you owe me that much, after everything we've been through."

Annika stepped forward, her gaze fierce. "You're out of your mind if you think we're going to let you... "

"It's okay," James interrupted softly. He turned to Annika and Nathan, his gaze steady. "Stand down. I'll handle this."

"James..." Nathan began, his voice tight with concern.

"Trust me," James murmured. "This is the only way."

Nathan hesitated, his jaw clenched, but finally he nodded, stepping back. Annika's gaze lingered on James's face, her eyes filled with worry, but she, too, stepped back, her weapon lowered but still ready.

James turned back to Reichter, his expression hard. "All right. Let's talk."

Reichter nodded, a faint smile tugging at his lips. "Follow me."

He turned and walked toward the far end of the command room, where a small, glass-walled office overlooked the banks of monitors and terminals. The room was sparsely furnished, just a single desk and two chairs, the walls lined with maps and schematics.

James followed him inside, his gaze never leaving Reichter's face. The door slid shut behind them with a soft hiss, sealing them off from the rest of the command room.

Reichter gestured to one of the chairs. "Please, have a seat."

"I'll stand," James murmured.

Reichter shrugged, then lowered himself into the chair opposite James, his hands folded neatly on the desk in front of him. For a long moment, neither of them spoke, the silence stretching out between them like a taut wire.

"You've been a worthy adversary," Reichter said softly, his gaze steady. "I've had many opponents over the years, but none have come as close as you have. It's almost... a shame that it has to end this way."

"It doesn't have to end this way," James replied quietly. "You can still stop this, Reichter. Shut down the grid attacks, dismantle your operations, and turn yourself in. You can still make this right."

Reichter chuckled softly, shaking his head. "You really believe that, don't you? That I'd throw away everything I've worked for, everything I've sacrificed, just because you ask me to?"

"It's your only chance," James said evenly. "You might think you've got it all under control, but you're wrong. We've got your men scattered, your command centers compromised. It's over."

"No, James," Reichter murmured, his gaze hardening. "It's only over when I say it is."

Before James could react, Reichter reached under the desk and pressed a hidden button. The walls of the office seemed to ripple, the glass turning opaque as heavy metal shutters slid down, sealing the room off completely.

"Damn it!" James hissed, spinning toward the door, but it was too late. The locks engaged with a heavy, mechanical clunk, trapping him inside.

Outside, Nathan and Annika sprang forward, their weapons raised as they shouted orders at the guards. But the guards didn't move, their expressions blank and uncomprehending as the alarms began to blare throughout the facility.

"Kane, what's going on?" Nathan shouted into his comm.

"Kane?" Annika echoed urgently.

There was no response, just the blaring of the alarms, the red emergency lights flashing through the command room like a heartbeat.

Inside the office, James turned back to Reichter, his gaze blazing with fury. "What did you do?"

Reichter's smile was cold and triumphant. "I've locked us in, James. This room is shielded, cut off from the rest of the facility. No signals in or out. And in a few minutes, the self-destruct sequence will engage, bringing the entire command room down on top of us."

"You're willing to die?" James growled, his fists clenching at his sides.

"I'm willing to do whatever it takes," Reichter replied softly. "But you're not leaving here, James. Neither of us are."

"James, we can breach the door!" Nathan's voice crackled faintly through the comms, distorted but still audible. "Just hang on!"

"No," Reichter murmured, his gaze never leaving James's face. "No one's getting in. No one's getting out."

James took a deep breath, his gaze never wavering. "You really want to die here, Reichter? That's your endgame?"

"My endgame?" Reichter whispered, his smile widening. "This isn't my endgame, James. This is just the beginning. I'll die knowing that I set the world on a new path, one that you and your Patriots can never stop."

He leaned back in his chair, his gaze calm and unblinking. "So, what now, James? Are you ready to watch it all burn?"

The room trembled as the first explosion rocked the facility, the lights flickering overhead. James felt the ground shift beneath his feet, the roar of collapsing metal and concrete reverberating through the walls.

He took a step forward, his gaze hardening. "I'm not going to let you win, Reichter," James said, his voice as steady as granite despite the chaos erupting around them. He stepped closer to Reichter, feeling the vibrations of the distant explosions reverberating through the floor, the heat of adrenaline coursing through his veins. He knew he was racing against time now. "You think locking us in here means I'll just stand by and watch you destroy everything?"

Reichter's smile remained calm, almost serene, as if he were in control of every second that passed. "What other option do you have? The countdown's begun, and soon, this entire facility will be buried under tons of rock and debris. You've lost, James. There's no one left to save you."

"James!" Annika's voice crackled over the comm, faint but insistent. "We're trying to override the system from here. Give us a minute."

"I'm not leaving you in there!" Nathan's voice followed, filled with a raw intensity that carried over the static. "Hang on!"

James's gaze shifted momentarily to the door, where he knew his team was fighting to break through, fighting to reach him. He took a slow, measured breath and turned back to Reichter, his expression calm.

"You're wrong, Reichter," he murmured. "I'm not alone. I never have been."

Reichter's eyes narrowed, a faint shadow of uncertainty crossing his face. "What are you talking about?"

"I'm talking about my team," James said softly, his gaze fierce and unrelenting. "The people I trust with my life, the people who never give up, no matter how hopeless things seem. You think you can break us? Think again."

There was a loud, metallic groan from the door, and Reichter's gaze snapped toward it, his eyes widening in surprise. A moment later, the door buckled inward with a resounding crash, metal shrieking as it was forced open. Smoke and dust filled the room as the Patriots burst through, weapons raised and expressions grim.

"James!" Nathan shouted, his gaze locking onto his friend. "We're getting you out of here!"

Reichter took a step back, his face twisting with anger. "No, no! This isn't how it's supposed to happen!"

But before he could react, Nathan was on him, his fist swinging out in a blur of motion. The punch connected with Reichter's jaw, sending him sprawling to the floor, a cry of pain escaping his lips.

"Stay down!" Nathan growled, his voice low and dangerous. "You're not in control anymore, you son of a... "

"Nathan!" Annika shouted, her gaze darting around the room. "James, we need to disable the self-destruct. Where's the control panel?"

"There," James said, pointing to a console on the far wall, half-hidden behind a mess of cables and debris. "But Reichter said it's isolated. We need to find a way to override it."

"I can do it," Kane's voice crackled through the comms, sharp and urgent. "Patch me in. I'll walk you through it."

Annika raced to the console, her fingers flying over the keys as she connected Kane to the system. The screens flickered, lines of code streaming across them as Kane worked from his remote location.

"Okay, I'm in," Kane murmured. "The self-destruct is on a two-minute countdown. Reichter wasn't lying, it's completely isolated from the rest of the facility's systems. But... there's a manual override. It's risky, but it's our only shot."

"Do it," James ordered, his voice steady.

"Annika, listen carefully," Kane said, his tone serious. "You need to input the following sequence. It'll force the system into a diagnostic loop, which should delay the countdown long enough for me to disable it remotely. But you have to be precise, one mistake, and it'll trigger an immediate detonation."

Annika nodded, her expression focused. "Tell me the sequence."

As Kane dictated the series of commands, Annika's fingers moved with lightning speed, entering the code with the precision of a surgeon. The screen blinked, then flashed red, an angry error message splashing across the monitor.

"Invalid input," Annika read aloud, her voice tight with frustration. "Kane, what... "

"No, it's fine," Kane interrupted, his voice strained but controlled. "That's part of the loop. It's testing the input parameters. Keep going, don't stop."

Annika's brow furrowed, but she continued typing, the error messages blinking and flashing with increasing intensity. The room seemed to pulse with a frantic energy, each second ticking away like a bomb waiting to explode.

"Come on, come on..." Nathan muttered under his breath, his gaze locked on the monitor.

Reichter pushed himself up to his knees, his eyes blazing with fury. "You won't make it in time!" he shouted. "You'll all die here, and my legacy will... "

"Shut up!" Nathan snapped, his fist driving into Reichter's stomach. Reichter doubled over, gasping for breath, but the look of triumph never left his face.

"Almost... there..." Kane murmured, his voice tight with concentration.

The monitor flashed green, then blue, the error messages disappearing as the countdown timer froze on the screen, 00:35 seconds remaining.

"Yes!" Annika breathed, her face flushed with relief. "Kane, you did it!"

"Not yet," Kane replied, his tone urgent. "The diagnostic loop will hold it for a few seconds, but I need to manually sever the power link from here. James, you have to shut down the primary power conduit in the control room. It's the only way to keep it from resetting."

"Where is it?" James asked sharply.

"The conduit is behind that panel on the left wall," Kane said quickly. "There's a manual override switch. Flip it, and it'll cut power to the self-destruct."

James didn't hesitate. He moved to the panel, yanking it open to reveal a mess of wires and circuits. His fingers found the switch, a heavy metal lever nestled between two red emergency lights.

"Got it," James murmured. He wrapped his hand around the lever, bracing himself. "Kane, you're sure about this?"

"Yes," Kane replied, his voice filled with confidence. "Do it, James. Now!"

James took a deep breath and pulled the lever.

There was a loud, metallic clang as the power conduit disengaged, the lights flickering overhead. The countdown timer froze for a second, then blinked off, the numbers disappearing from the screen.

Silence fell over the room, the alarms cutting off abruptly, leaving only the sound of their ragged breathing echoing in the stillness.

"It's done," Kane murmured, his voice filled with relief. "The self-destruct is disabled. You did it."

Annika let out a shuddering breath, her shoulders sagging with exhaustion. Nathan took a step back, his chest heaving as he glared down at Reichter's crumpled form.

James turned, his gaze locking onto Reichter's face. The old man looked up at him, his eyes filled with a strange mixture of rage and resignation.

"You really thought you could beat us," James said softly, his voice carrying a quiet, unshakeable resolve. "But you were wrong. We're stronger than you ever imagined."

Reichter's lips twisted into a bitter smile. "This... doesn't change anything. There will be others. Others who believe in my vision. You can't stop what's coming."

"We'll see about that," James murmured. He glanced at Nathan and Annika, their expressions mirroring his own fierce determination. "But for now, it's over. Take him."

Nathan and Annika moved forward, securing Reichter's hands behind his back with zip ties. He didn't resist, his gaze distant as he stared at the floor.

"What now?" Annika asked quietly, her gaze shifting to James.

"Now we get him out of here," James replied. He turned back to the monitors, his gaze sweeping the darkened screens. "Kane, what's the status outside?"

"Security's still in disarray," Kane said, his voice steady once more. "They're not sure what's happening. I've disabled the facility's communications grid, so they won't be able to call for reinforcements. You've got a clear path to the exit."

"Good," James murmured. He turned to Reichter, his gaze hard. "You're going to face justice, Reichter. And you're going to watch everything you've built come crashing down."

Reichter's smile faded, his eyes narrowing. But he didn't say a word, just stared at James with a cold, calculating gaze.

"Let's go," James ordered.

They moved out of the command room, Reichter in tow, their steps steady and confident as they made their way through the facility. The hallways were empty, the lights flickering as if the entire building were trembling in fear.

They reached the surface, the cool night air washing over them like a breath of freedom. The stars glittered overhead, the distant peaks of the Carpathian Mountains silhouetted against the dark sky.

A helicopter was waiting for them, its rotors spinning slowly, the soft thrum filling the silence. Kane's voice crackled through their comms one last time.

"You did it, James. You really did it."

James glanced at his team, Annika, Nathan, and the rest of the Patriots, each of them battered but unbroken, their expressions filled with quiet resolve. The journey had been long and brutal, marked by impossible choices and dangerous missions, but they had made it through together. And now, standing in the cool mountain air with Reichter bound and at their mercy, it almost felt surreal.

"Load him up," James ordered, his voice low but firm.

Nathan and Annika moved quickly, hauling Reichter toward the helicopter. The old man didn't struggle, his gaze distant and empty as if he were lost in his own thoughts. James watched him closely, searching for any sign of defiance or resistance, but Reichter remained silent, his expression blank.

They secured him in the back of the helicopter, his wrists bound to the seat with thick straps. James climbed in beside him, his gaze never leaving Reichter's face as the rest of the team took their positions.

"Annika, Nathan," James said quietly, nodding toward the cockpit. "Get us out of here. Kane, keep monitoring the perimeter. I don't want any surprises."

"Roger that," Kane replied through the comms. "I've got your back. I'm seeing no movement outside the facility, looks like they're still scrambling to figure out what happened. You've got a clear window."

Annika nodded and moved to the pilot's seat, her hands moving deftly over the controls. The helicopter's engine roared to life, the rotors spinning faster as it lifted off the ground, the landscape below shrinking away. The facility that had once been a fortress of power and control now seemed small and insignificant, a mere blip on the radar.

James leaned back in his seat, his gaze shifting from Reichter's face to the dark expanse of the mountains beyond. The soft hum of the helicopter's engine filled the silence, mingling with the faint rush of the wind outside. It should have felt like a victory, a hard-won triumph over a man who had caused so much pain and suffering, but instead, there was only a heavy, lingering sense of unfinished business.

"We did it," Nathan murmured, his voice carrying over the comms. "We actually did it."

"Yeah," James replied softly, his gaze distant. "But it's not over yet."

Reichter stirred slightly, his eyes flicking to James's face. There was a faint, mocking smile on his lips as if he could sense James's uncertainty.

"You think you've won, don't you?" Reichter whispered, his voice a rasping murmur that barely carried over the hum of the helicopter. "You think capturing me will change anything?"

James's jaw tightened. "It's a start."

"A start?" Reichter chuckled softly, shaking his head. "I'm just one man, James. A symbol, yes, but nothing more. You can bring me down, but my work... my vision... it will live on. There are others, people you've never even heard of, waiting to take up the mantle. You've only delayed the inevitable."

"We've done more than that," James murmured, his gaze hardening. "We've exposed you, dismantled your operations, and stopped your plan before it could take root. You're not some untouchable figure anymore, Reichter. You're just a man facing justice for your crimes."

"Justice?" Reichter's smile widened, his eyes gleaming with a faint, almost manic light. "You think the world cares about justice?

The world craves power, control. And those who understand that will always rise to the top. My followers will continue what I started. You've only cut off one head, many more will grow in its place."

"Then we'll cut them off too," Nathan said firmly, his voice cutting through the tension. "One by one, until there's nothing left."

"Such resolve," Reichter murmured, his gaze drifting to Nathan. "But tell me, Nathan... how long can you keep this up? How many more battles will you fight before you realize that you're only prolonging the inevitable? There will always be more men like me, men with the vision and will to shape the world as it should be."

Nathan's gaze hardened, but he didn't respond, his jaw clenched tight.

Annika glanced back from the cockpit, her expression troubled. "James, what do we do with him now? Taking him to the authorities is risky, he has connections everywhere. They could turn this against us."

"We have to make sure he can't manipulate his way out of this," Nathan added. "Whatever it takes."

"I know," James murmured. He turned his gaze back to Reichter, his expression cold and unreadable. "But we're not going to kill him. He's going to face the consequences of everything he's done. Every life he's destroyed, every crime he's committed... it's all going to come out. And he's going to rot in a cell for the rest of his miserable life, knowing that he failed."

"Failed?" Reichter's smile faded, his eyes narrowing. "I haven't failed, James. I've already won."

James leaned forward, his voice low and filled with a quiet intensity. "Then why are you sitting here, bound and beaten, while everything you built falls apart around you?"

Reichter didn't respond, his gaze dropping to the floor. For a moment, the only sound was the steady thrum of the helicopter's rotors, the wind rushing past the windows.

"Kane," James said quietly, his gaze never leaving Reichter's face. "Contact the nearest secure facility. We're turning Reichter over to the highest authorities. No loopholes, no hidden allies. We're going to do this by the book."

"Copy that, James," Kane replied. "I'll make the arrangements. But... be careful. You know how deep his influence goes. We can't afford to lose him now."

"We won't," James murmured softly. He sat back, his gaze steady as he watched Reichter. "We're going to see this through, Reichter. You're going to face everything you've done. And you'll have nothing left, no power, no followers, no empire. Just a cell and the knowledge that you lost."

Reichter's smile returned, faint and mocking. "We'll see, James. We'll see."

Arrival at the Secure Facility

The helicopter touched down at a remote airstrip outside a heavily guarded facility, a high-security prison designed to hold the most dangerous and influential criminals in the world. The perimeter was lined with layers of fencing and patrolled by armed guards, each one alert and watchful as they scanned the skies.

The Patriots exited the helicopter, their expressions grim and determined. Reichter was hauled out last, his wrists bound tightly as he was marched toward the entrance of the facility. He walked with a strange, almost regal grace, his head held high as if he were a king being escorted to his throne.

James, Nathan, and Annika followed close behind, their eyes never leaving Reichter's back. The guards at the entrance nodded to them, their expressions wary but respectful. They knew who Reichter was, knew what he was capable of.

"Identification?" one of the guards asked, his voice clipped and professional.

"James Donovan, Patriot team leader," James replied, holding out his ID. "We're turning over Klaus Reichter. He's been classified as a national security threat, and we have authorization for full transfer to your custody."

The guard's eyes widened slightly as he glanced at the ID, then at Reichter's impassive face. He nodded sharply and gestured for them to proceed.

"This way, sir."

They moved through a series of security checkpoints, each one more stringent than the last. Biometric scanners, metal detectors, and armed guards lined every hallway, every corner. The air was thick with tension, the hum of security equipment filling the silence.

Finally, they reached a reinforced door at the end of a long, sterile hallway. The guard stepped forward and swiped his ID card, the door sliding open to reveal a small, windowless room with a single metal chair bolted to the floor.

"Put him in here," the guard instructed.

Nathan and Annika led Reichter to the chair, securing him in place with thick metal restraints. The old man sat calmly, his gaze drifting around the room as if he were studying every inch of it, every detail.

James stepped forward, his gaze hard. "This is where it ends, Reichter. You're going to stay here, under guard, until you're put on trial for everything you've done."

Reichter's eyes flicked up to meet James's, a faint smile tugging at his lips. "You really think this is the end?"

"I know it is," James replied, his voice steady. "You've lost."

Reichter's smile widened, his gaze gleaming with a dangerous light. "Then why don't I feel defeated?"

James stared at him, his expression unchanging. "Because men like you never know when to give up. But it's over, Reichter. We're done here."

He turned and nodded to Nathan and Annika. "Let's go."

They exited the room, the heavy door sliding shut behind them with a soft hiss. The sound of the locks engaging echoed through the hallway, sealing Reichter inside.

Nathan glanced back, his brow furrowed. "You think that's really it?"

James took a deep breath, his gaze distant. "I don't know. But whatever comes next, we'll face it together."

Annika placed a hand on James's shoulder, her touch light but steady. "We made it through this. We'll make it through whatever comes next," Annika said softly, her voice filled with quiet assurance.

James turned to her, his gaze softening for a moment. "Yeah, we will." He glanced at Nathan, and then back at Annika, allowing himself a rare moment of relief. "We did what we came here to do. He's locked away now, with no chance of getting out."

"But you know as well as I do," Nathan murmured, his gaze lingering on the reinforced door behind them, "that this is just one battle in a much bigger war."

James nodded slowly. "We've cut off the head, but the body's still thrashing. Reichter's network, his influence, runs deep. There will be people scrambling to pick up where he left off."

"So we keep going," Annika said firmly, her voice steady. "We stay vigilant. We track down every one of his allies and bring them to justice. We don't stop until this whole mess is cleaned up."

James glanced at Annika and then at Nathan, his chest tightening with a surge of gratitude for these people who had stood by his side through everything. They had faced dangers, made impossible choices, and fought with a courage that few possessed. Each of them had their own reasons for joining the fight, their own scars and losses that had driven them to this moment.

Annika Valdez, former CIA operative, brilliant strategist, and the heart of their group. She had joined James after losing her closest friend in an operation that had gone wrong. Her resolve to see justice done, to expose corruption and make the world a safer place, was unbreakable. And through it all, she had become James's most trusted ally, the one person who always seemed to know what needed to be done, no matter how difficult the choice.

Nathan Cross, former Marine, hardened by combat and shaped by years of serving in some of the world's most dangerous places. Nathan's sense of loyalty and honor had brought him to James's side after he'd uncovered Reichter's role in the death of his unit during a covert operation. Nathan's rage had been fierce, but he'd learned to channel it into something greater, a relentless drive to take down those who abused power, no matter the cost.

And the rest of the Patriots, each with their own stories, their own battles. Oliver Kane, the tech genius who had once been an NSA hacker, disillusioned by the government's abuse of power and determined to turn his skills against those who sought to control others. Jackson Moore, the logistics and operations expert who had spent years working for private military contractors before he'd had enough of the dirty dealings and corrupt motives that drove the industry.

And Jennifer Cruz, their medic and survivalist, who had spent her career in the military's elite medical units, saving lives on the battlefield. She had joined the team after witnessing the human cost of Reichter's illegal arms trades and money laundering operations that funded conflicts across the globe.

These people, these Patriots, had become more than just a team. They were a family, bound together by shared purpose and shared pain. And together, they had brought Klaus Reichter to his knees.

"What now?" Nathan asked quietly, his gaze shifting back to James.

James took a deep breath, his gaze drifting toward the small window at the end of the hallway, where the first light of dawn was beginning to creep over the horizon. "Now, we get some rest. We regroup. We analyze everything we've gathered and make sure there aren't any loose ends."

"And after that?" Annika asked softly.

James turned to her, his gaze steady. "Then we take the fight to the rest of them. We dismantle every piece of Reichter's network. We find every corrupt politician, every dirty operative, and we tear them down. We make sure this can never happen again."

Annika nodded slowly, a faint smile tugging at her lips. "I'm with you. Always."

"Me too," Nathan added, his voice filled with quiet determination. "We're not backing down."

James allowed himself a small smile, the weight of the moment settling over him like a mantle. He glanced around the sterile hallway, the hum of security equipment and the distant murmur of guards' voices filling the silence. It felt like the calm after a storm, the brief, fragile stillness before the next wave hit.

"Let's get back to the safe house," James said softly, his voice carrying a note of finality. "We've earned a little bit of peace."

They turned and made their way down the hallway, their footsteps echoing softly in the silence. The guards at the security checkpoint watched them with curious gazes, their expressions a mixture of respect and wariness.

"Good job in there," one of the guards murmured as they passed. "Reichter's a monster. You did the world a favor today."

"Thanks," James replied quietly, his gaze flickering with a hint of something unspoken. "But it's not over yet."

They exited the facility and stepped out into the crisp morning air, the first light of dawn casting long shadows across the tarmac. The helicopter was waiting for them, its rotors spinning lazily in the early morning breeze.

As they climbed aboard, James paused, glancing back at the facility one last time. Reichter was in there now, locked away in a cell where he could no longer manipulate, no longer scheme. But James knew that it wasn't the end, not by a long shot.

There were still people out there people who believed in Reichter's twisted vision, people who would stop at nothing to continue what he had started. The fight was far from over. But for now, for this brief, fleeting moment, they had won.

James settled into his seat as the helicopter lifted off the ground, the landscape falling away beneath them. The Patriots sat in silence, the weight of everything they'd been through hanging between them like an unspoken bond. They had faced the darkness together, fought against impossible odds, and come out on the other side.

The helicopter climbed higher, the roar of the rotors drowning out all other sounds. James glanced at Annika, then at Nathan, and finally at the horizon, where the sun was just beginning to rise, casting a warm, golden light over the mountains.

For the first time in a long while, James felt a faint glimmer of hope, a spark of light piercing through the darkness. They had fought, and they had survived. And no matter what came next, no matter how many battles they still had to face, they would face them together.

"Let's go home," James murmured softly.

Annika and Nathan nodded, their expressions filled with a fierce, unbreakable resolve.

"Yes," Annika whispered. "Let's go home."

The helicopter turned, banking smoothly as it soared through the dawn sky, carrying the Patriots away from the battlefield and toward whatever awaited them next.

And as the first rays of sunlight broke through the clouds, the shadows of the Carpathian Mountains fell away, leaving only the bright, shining promise of a new day.

Chapter 23

The grand courtroom of the International Tribunal for Crimes Against Humanity was packed with people from all over the world, journalists, diplomats, legal experts, and families of those who had suffered under the dark shadow of Klaus Reichter's vast criminal network. The air buzzed with anticipation, a tense energy palpable in the quiet murmur of voices and the occasional shuffle of papers.

The Patriots stood together in the back row, their presence a silent testament to the hard-fought battles that had led them here. James, Annika, Nathan, Kane, Jackson, and Jennifer, all of them were there, their expressions guarded as they watched the proceedings unfold. This wasn't just the culmination of their mission against Klaus Reichter; it was the moment the world would see the true extent of the corruption, manipulation, and suffering that he and his associates had wrought.

James shifted slightly, his gaze sweeping over the courtroom. It was a grand, imposing chamber, with high ceilings and marble columns that gleamed under the bright lights. The wooden benches were filled with people leaning forward, hanging onto every word spoken. At the front of the room, behind a high podium, sat the presiding judge, his face stern and impassive as he studied the defendant.

Klaus Reichter stood in the center of it all, looking remarkably calm for a man whose empire had crumbled beneath him. He wore a neatly pressed suit, his gray hair combed back, and his eyes, cold, calculating, swept over the room with a faint, detached curiosity.

He had been transported from the high-security prison where he had been held for the past several months, awaiting trial as the legal teams from every country affected by his schemes and crimes compiled the mountains of evidence against him. This was no ordinary trial, it was a spectacle, a reckoning long overdue for a man who had manipulated governments, funded terrorist organizations, and lined the pockets of corrupt politicians for decades.

"Order in the court!" the bailiff announced, his voice booming through the chamber.

The room fell silent, the low hum of whispers and murmurs ceasing instantly. The judge, a tall, thin man with silver hair and sharp eyes, adjusted his glasses and looked down at Reichter.

"Klaus Reichter," the judge intoned, his voice carrying a weight that echoed throughout the chamber. "You have been found guilty on all counts, including conspiracy to commit terrorism, money laundering, bribery of public officials, and crimes against humanity. Your actions have directly contributed to the destabilization of governments, the suffering of countless innocent people, and the loss of thousands of lives. This court will now determine your sentence."

There was a collective intake of breath from the onlookers as they waited for Reichter's response. He stood straight and tall, his hands clasped in front of him, his expression betraying no hint of fear or regret.

"Do you have anything to say before sentencing is carried out?" the judge asked, his gaze boring into Reichter.

Reichter's lips curved into a faint smile, his eyes sweeping the courtroom once more before settling on the judge. "Say?" he murmured softly, his voice smooth and controlled. "What more is there to say? You've all made up your minds already. This is nothing more than a show, a public execution dressed up as justice. But justice... justice is not what you think it is."

The judge's gaze hardened. "You speak of justice as if you understand it, Mr. Reichter. But your actions have shown nothing but a complete disregard for human life and the principles of justice. The court has heard the testimonies, reviewed the evidence, and reached its decision. This is no show, no spectacle. This is the world holding you accountable for your crimes."

Reichter's smile didn't waver. "Accountable," he repeated softly. "And what of those who stood by and let it happen? What of the politicians, the officials, the business leaders who were only too happy to take my money, to look the other way while I did what needed to be done? Are they to be held accountable too?"

James felt a surge of anger rise within him, his fists clenching at his sides. Reichter was trying to turn the tables, to paint himself as a scapegoat, a man who had been dragged down by the same corrupt system he had exploited for years. It was a twisted, desperate attempt to justify his actions, to deflect blame.

And the worst part was, there was a kernel of truth in his words.

But that didn't change what Reichter was. It didn't change the suffering and death he had caused.

"Every individual involved in your network will face justice, Mr. Reichter," the judge said firmly. "Those who accepted your bribes, who aided and abetted your crimes, are being pursued and prosecuted in their respective jurisdictions. Your network is being dismantled piece by piece."

The judge glanced at a stack of documents on the bench before him and then looked back at Reichter, his expression unyielding. "You will spend the rest of your life in solitary confinement, cut off from the outside world. You will have no contact with your associates, no means of influencing events from behind bars. This is the court's decision, and it is final."

There was a murmur of approval from the onlookers, a ripple of satisfaction at the judge's words. But Reichter simply nodded, as if he had expected this all along. He looked past the judge, his gaze settling on James and the rest of the Patriots.

"You think this is over?" he asked softly, his voice carrying just enough to be heard by the Patriots. "You think locking me away will make any difference? There are others, Donovan. Men and women who share my vision. You've cut off one head of the hydra, but the others will rise. My network is more resilient than you can imagine."

James took a deep breath, his gaze steady as he stared back at Reichter. "We'll be ready for them, just like we were ready for you."

"And we'll find them," Annika added, her voice calm but firm. "Every last one of them. We'll expose them, and we'll bring them down."

Reichter's smile widened, a hint of something almost like admiration flickering in his gaze. "I suppose we'll see, won't we?" he murmured. "But remember this, all of you, you've only delayed the inevitable. The world is changing, and people like you... people who cling to old ideals of justice and honor... you're a dying breed."

"Enough!" the judge snapped, his gavel coming down with a resounding crack. He turned to the guards stationed around the room. "Escort the prisoner to his transport. This trial is concluded."

The guards moved forward, their grips firm as they took hold of Reichter's arms and began to lead him out of the courtroom. The Patriots watched silently, their gazes following Reichter as he was marched down the aisle, his head held high.

As Reichter reached the doors, he paused, glancing back over his shoulder one last time. His eyes found James, and he nodded slowly, as if acknowledging something unspoken between them.

"Goodbye, Patriots," Reichter murmured. "I wonder... how many more of us will you have to face before you realize you can't win?"

Then he turned and was gone, the doors swinging shut behind him with a heavy, final thud.

The silence in the courtroom seemed to stretch on forever, the weight of everything they had accomplished, everything they had lost, settling over them like a thick shroud.

James turned to his team, his gaze sweeping over each of their faces. There was a mixture of relief and exhaustion in their eyes, but also something else, something deeper.

Resolve.

They had brought Klaus Reichter to justice. They had exposed the corruption and lies that had allowed his network to thrive. But as Reichter had said, there were others out there, others who believed in his vision, others who would step up to take his place.

And the Patriots would be there to meet them, to fight them, to bring them down.

"Let's go," James said softly. "We've got work to do."

The Patriots nodded, their expressions hardening as they turned and made their way out of the courtroom. They had won this battle, but the war was far from over.

But no matter how many more enemies they faced, no matter how many more battles they fought, they knew one thing for certain: They would face it together.

Milton Keynes UK
Ingram Content Group UK Ltd.
UKHW021900231024
450133UK00016B/1090